INSIDE THE DEVIL'S NEST

JOHN DURGIN

D & T
PUBLISHING

PRAISE FOR INSIDE THE DEVIL'S NEST

"A journey through the worst nightmare of any father, INSIDE THE DEVIL'S NEST seduces with its mysteries and atmosphere, then eviscerates with its ghastly horrors. John writes as if channeling the whispers of a cult, and he terrifies with the malice of a soul-starved god..."

   -Felix Blackwell, author of Stolen Tongues

"John Durgin's sophomore novel plays notes from King's The Shining, but adds a fresh harmony and dynamic new rhythms. INSIDE THE DEVIL'S NEST is a tale of family and loss, mob bosses and cult leaders, threaded throughout with genuine chills and near-unbearable tension."

   -Brennan LaFaro, Author of Noose and Slattery Falls

"I haven't been this riveted while reading a piece of fiction in a long time. INSIDE THE DEVIL'S NEST is visceral and unflinching and emotion-filled, one of the best novels I've read this year."

   -Jeremy Hepler, Bram Stoker-nominated author of Sunray Alice.

To my mom and dad,
Thanks for getting me into reading at such a young age, opening my mind
to the adventures that awaited...

AUTHOR'S NOTE

I always loved how Stephen King brought so many horrific stories to his home state of Maine. When I read *IT* in middle school, I knew right then and there that I wanted to be a writer. Furthermore, I dreamed of bringing horror to New Hampshire and the small towns I grew up near, just like King did with Maine. Every time I read one of his books and he mentioned a town I had visited, I thought it was so cool. My first book, *The Cursed Among Us*, took place in my hometown of Newport, NH. Most of the locations listed in the book were written exactly the way they were when I grew up. With *Inside The Devil's Nest*, I visit the smaller town (yes, it *is* possible to get smaller than Newport) of Goshen, located next to Newport. Anyone from the area will quickly find that I changed some things around to fit my story, but the landscape is 100% New Hampshire. My first job growing up was at a campground on Coon Brook RD called North Star Campground. There is another campground in Newport called Crow's Nest, which inspired the name Bird's Nest Campground in the book. I basically combined the two camp-grounds to fit my story, so don't hold me accountable if I start some turf wars with the local campgrounds... I can't wait to visit other towns in the area for future books, and who knows… Maybe every-thing's connected.

   —JD

   09/22/2022

"I'm not in the habit of blaming Satan for every phenomenon."
—Father Ryan | *The Amityville Horror*

"You know, a long time ago being crazy meant something.
Nowadays everybody's crazy."— Charles Manson

PROLOGUE: THE GREAT BAPTISM

To a simple mind, the scene unfolding would have brought on fears of chaos and destruction. But to Alister Burns, it was the most beautiful sight he'd ever seen. In front of his tall, lanky figure sat a large pond, the water giving off an unnatural green glow with the moon shining down upon it. A smile spread across his bearded face while he looked around the perimeter of the water at his followers. Their expressions differed from his own—a mix of fear and excitement in their eyes, unsure of what to expect. Alister assured them their lives would not be lost in vain. As a matter of fact, their lives wouldn't be *lost* at all. They would live on, for centuries, the water giving them the power to exist with the God Below. What they were about to do was for the greater good. Not for the pond, but for what lay *beneath* the pond. It had taken a lot of convincing, but after years of showing them the way, they were finally ready for the next step.

Looking to his left, Alister noticed one of his disciples, Rebecca, holding her cup close to her mouth. Her hands were trembling. He walked over to her and gripped her shoulder.

"It will all be okay, Rebecca. This is what must be done. This is what they want, and it's going to be the most glorious night our group has ever experienced." He spoke in such a calm, reassuring way that she immediately felt at ease.

His long, black hair blew in the evening breeze as he stared into her soul. The green of his eyes matched that of the water, their calming effect forcing itself upon her consciousness.

"I know, Father Burns. I'm ready for what comes next. It's merely the anticipation of the Great Baptism that's doing this to me. I... *we'd* do anything for you. For Him," she replied, struggling to maintain eye contact with him.

His smile grew behind his bushy, black beard.

"Do you remember the purpose of this Baptism, Rebecca?"

She nodded.

"Good... Then you understand, this is how we profess our faith. How we ask for forgiveness for letting the boy slip away. He was to be the biggest sacrifice, before he... *escaped*."

"Yes, Father Burns. I just hope He forgives us, and accepts us as his own," she said.

"The wait will soon be over, my dear. I look forward to seeing you on the other side."

Alister gently petted her shoulder and continued on his way, taking in all twenty members of the group. They stood exactly three feet apart from one another, completely smothering the land's edge where it dropped off into the green abyss. Men, women, children. It didn't matter their age, all of them had accepted their fate. Their blank eyes focused on the center of the water, waiting on him for instructions. Miles of forest surrounded the pond, protecting their compound from the outside world.

After completing his lap, saying calming words to each member, Alister decided it was time to move forward with the plan. Slowly, he walked out along the dock which ended twenty feet across the water. He raised his hands high above his head; all the members knelt at the edge of the water with their cups in hands.

"My people, this is the moment we've all been waiting for. Where we become one with our God, and sacrifice ourselves, leaving this rotten world behind for a place that accepts us for who we are. *What* we are. For this is just the next step in our evolution. After the Great Baptism, we will rise again. When the time is right." He watched them cry and tremble. Not out of fear, but out of excitement.

"Now, raise your cups, and drink. The time is now, and we ask of you dear Vodyanoy, please take us in your water as one of your own. We are here to serve you..."

One by one, the members drank the contents of their cups, and within minutes their eyes began rolling into the back of their heads, their bodies going rigid and stiff as if having an intense seizure, looking straight up at the sky. Alister smiled—it was finally happening. He raised his own cup, preparing to drink.

"Now, enter the waters, my family, I will see you below." With that, he tossed back the liquid, burning the back of his throat as it slid down into his stomach. With his body beginning to lock up, he stepped off the edge of the dock, dropping below the surface of the warm water with a splash. They all followed, walking into the pond like robots that hadn't been oiled properly in a century. Each step was painful, their muscles seizing up so much they could rip with simple movements. A moment of madness followed, some of the members continuing to walk out until they were completely below the surface, never attempting to come up for another breath. Their bodies were drawn to the center of the pond like metal scraps to a magnet. A few of the other members, however, did not experience the full effect of the concoction Father Burns had provided. They flailed around like children being tossed in the water for the first time, unable to get out. By the time they were alert enough, the water was far too deep for their drugged bodies to navigate through. A child's head bobbed up for air before going back under. A few feet away, Rebecca came up for breath, screaming for anyone who cared to listen. Her hand struck another member trying to resurface next to her. In a moment of desperation, she pushed down on their shoulders—man, woman, or child, she had no idea—submerging the helpless body and using it as a human flotation device.

"Help me! I'm not ready!" Rebecca yelled out.

The body underneath her went lifeless as it slowly sank deeper below. Rebecca looked around frantically for anything else to hold on to. There was nothing to grab. She felt her chest constrict, realizing this was it. As her head sank below, she saw other bodies plummeting toward the pond's floor. Through the haze of green, she spotted Father Burns floating halfway down with his eyes closed. It seemed impossible; his body was frozen in place as if he was hovering. Behind Alister—in the darkness of the depths beneath him—a set of burning eyes like red-hot coals observed the madness.

Rebecca looked back to Alister, floating peacefully.

His face snapped in her direction and his eyes shot open. Pure white orbs rested in his sockets. His mouth opened wide, and while she couldn't hear anything underwater, it was clear what he was doing. He was *laughing*. Struggling to take her last few breaths, all she could think about—cling to—was that Alister was right. The time would come when the world would be theirs. As that last thought crossed her mind, the green blur in front of her faded to black.

1

"SON OF A BITCH," Anthony Graham muttered as he slammed on his brakes.

His head jerked forward, sending his Ray-Ban aviators tumbling to the floor, the car coming to a sudden stop. He was lucky his face hadn't smacked off the steering wheel with the way his day had been going. He sat in the bumper-to-bumper traffic that New York City loved to greet people with during the evening commute. The melodies of horns honking and angry citizens swearing at one another filled the thick, city air. Anthony looked at the clock on his dash and realized he was going to be late for dinner. After a full day at the office, he'd sprinted out the doors ready to beat the traffic home.

The security alarm app on his phone jingled, alerting him someone had entered one of his properties. *Entered* without his consent. Anthony remained so focused on his phone he didn't realize some of the honking background music was directed at him. The traffic had moved in front, yet he sat in place with a line of vehicles stuck behind him.

"Yeah, yeah, easy tough guy," he said as he stepped on the gas.

Flipping to the recent calls on his cell, he found Holly, and hit dial. After the second ring, his wife picked up sounding out of breath.

"Anthony? Is everything okay? I expected you home by now. Dinner's ready."

"Why are you so out of breath? You running from Barbara's poodle again?" he asked jokingly.

"Real funny, ass. I was on the treadmill trying to get a few quick miles in before we ate. You know how I feel after lasagna."

"Well, I thought I'd be home by now too, and now that I know we're having lasagna, I'm even more pissed off about why I'm calling. I have to turn around and go back to one of my properties. I just got notified the alarm's going off. I need to make sure it gets resolved before the cops show up."

"Seriously? Can't you have Hank go down and check on it so you can get home? I mean, I can always reheat it, but you know how good it is fresh."

"Hank's probably the reason the damn thing's going off in the first place. It's tough to find good help these days. The kid has drive, but good lord, if I have to teach him how to set the alarms after giving a showing again, I might lose my shit on him."

"What property is it? Close at least?" she asked.

Anthony double checked which location it was and sighed.

"Unfortunately, no. It's the new property down in West Harlem by Hamilton Heights. Should be a lovely drive this time of day." Sarcasm dripped from his words.

"That's going to take you half the night during rush hour! I'm sorry, I'll have a stiff drink waiting for you," she said.

Anthony forced a smile. "Wow, you are in an extra good mood tonight. You make me a stiff drink and I'll be sure to give *you* something stiff in return later on."

"You pig!" she said laughing. "As long as you make sure the kids are asleep first, we'll see what we can do about that."

"Okay, don't you go passing out on me before I get home. I'm going to drive like one of these nutty cab drivers and make sure I cut out as much time as possible. See you soon."

"Be safe, Anthony, you know that area sketches me out. I love you."

"Love you too. And don't worry about me. I got my property binder with me, this thing could knock out Conor McGregor with one swing," he joked.

"Who?"

"Never mind, I'll see you later," he said, and hung up the phone.

Anthony owned one of the most successful real estate agencies in all the northeast. It had taken years to build up the business—nights away from the family, fast food dinners—but they now lived a life of luxury, and they sure weren't complaining. At first, he'd taken a risk, bought a few buildings, knowing they were a good price, hoping he could flip them. Not only did he do just that, but he also got connected with some of the top agencies in the area who were impressed with the new guy in town turning such a profit right out of the gate. Within a few years, Anthony was on the rise in the real estate world. Eventually, he felt comfortable enough to branch off on his own and founded his own company. Fast-forward a few years, and he'd spread through the entire northeast region.

The loud blare of a horn snapped him out of his thoughts, leading him to glance in his rearview mirror. As if he needed to look to know it was an asshole cab driver trying to use his middle finger as a turn signal.

"Oh, eat shit, you impatient prick!" Anthony yelled.

As he looked out over the Hudson River, Anthony turned on his blinker to get off the exit. He knew Hank didn't have any showings in the area tonight, so it was more than likely either a squatter or an alarm malfunction.

————————

Nightfall greeted Anthony as he turned down a side street heading to the commercial building where the alarm had been triggered. Traffic picked up the pace as he got farther away from the main highway, allowing him to make decent time. *Thank God for small favors*, he thought. He parked his Mercedes on the street and exhaled. Looking down at the app, he noticed the alarm had already been turned off. Confused, he hopped out of his car and walked at a brisk pace in the direction of the building, noticing a dim glow coming from one of the windows as he got closer. No vehicles occupied the parking lot in front of the building, only adding to his curiosity. The streets were oddly quiet for this time of day. Anthony intentionally parked a bit down the street so he could quietly approach without being seen. As he got closer, he debated going back to his car and just taking off, let Hank deal with any squatters in the morning. But he'd already come this far, there was no sense in putting more on the kid's plate while he was still trying to learn the ropes of the job.

Slowly, Anthony closed in on the front entrance. He took out the set of keys to unlock the door, but then an idea came to him. If someone had broken in—which by all indications, they had—it made more sense to walk around the back of the property and come in where nobody would expect. He crouched, walking along the side of the towering brick building. As he neared the back, he heard a muffled yelling coming from inside. *What the hell is going on?* He leaned against the dumpster sitting in the alleyway, trying to come up with a plan. It was becoming clear his best option was to call the cops and get them involved. That just meant more time and paperwork once they arrived, but this was more serious than he wanted it to be. He went to pull out his cell, feeling around in his pants pocket —only to find the pocket empty.

"God damn it," he said, realizing he'd left it in his car.

A putrid smell wafting out of the dumpster stung his nostrils. Anthony pushed himself off the rusting metal box and froze, a realization hitting him. What if he needed to defend himself? He had nothing. Sure, he'd joked with Holly he would use his binder, but the fact was he'd never anticipated needing to protect himself. Before he entered, he needed to find something to help. He lifted the lid of the dumpster, hoping to find something heavy he could swing if things got violent. Instead, all he found was the desire to vomit. He forced the bile back down his throat, no longer having the appetite for Holly's famous lasagna. The scent of blood and human shit drifted out of the opening. Something compelled Anthony to look inside—an urge he subsequently wished he'd ignored. With the sky now dark and no streetlights in the alleyway to aid him, he couldn't make out much, but he knew something was wrong. He prepared to shut the lid and go back to his car when something caught his eye. Under all the food wrappers and trash bags, the front half of a shoe poked out. His heart was pounding in his chest as he reached down to remove one of the bags lying on top of the sneaker. The trash bag rolled down, exposing part of a leg. Anthony jumped back and leaned to the side, vomiting on the cement.

"Oh God, Jesus fucking Christ..." he said while wiping the filth away from his mouth.

Why was there a body in the dumpster? Why had the alarm to the building been tripped? Anthony decided to hell with it, he wasn't trying to play a hero today. He would call 911 as soon as he got back to his car. Then he remembered the scream inside. Was someone else in danger in the building? If he went back to his car and left the place, there was a good chance whoever was here would be long gone by the time cops showed up. The video surveillance system had yet to be installed on the property, so he couldn't even go back and look at the footage later.

It was too much of a risk. He was not about to get involved in this nightmare. He started to head back to his car when voices came from around the front of the building. If he exited the alleyway, they would see him. Ignoring his gut telling him to get as far away as possible, Anthony snuck around the back. He reached the back door, which already sat slightly ajar. Quietly, he opened it wide enough to sneak in, listening for the voices. It was completely dark in the wide-open room; the light Anthony had seen from the outside had been coming from the front of the building. Voices resonated up ahead but were too far away to make out what was being said. Part of Anthony was thankful for the lights being off, making it easier to remain undetected. But the darkness also freaked him out. The voices were amplified due to the empty, spacious rooms.

Footsteps approached, getting louder.

Anthony trembled, nerves jolting through him like a shot of electricity. He searched for a place to hide, spotting the bathroom door across the room and quickly ran to it. Slipping inside the small room, he shut the door almost completely, leaving it open just enough to look out through the crack and see who approached. He couldn't help but feel like he was exposed, even though there was only a sliver of light to look through.

A silhouette approached in the dark. Anthony held his breath, trying to steady his nerves. A long metal rod belonging to a towel rack they had yet to hang on the wall sat next to him, so he grabbed hold of it, prepared to swing as soon as the pursuer opened the door. As the man got closer, Anthony noticed he had a black ski mask on, with all black clothes. He held a gun in his hand, and he was walking right toward Anthony. *Shit, shit, shit.* He raised the metal rod, ready to swing at the man's face, knowing full well it was no match for a pistol.

The man was now only ten feet away…

Five feet…

And then, he walked past the bathroom, heading out the back door of the building. Anthony leaned over, putting his hands on his knees, taking deep breaths. Sweat worked its way down his forehead, sliding past his brow and resting on his upper lip. He licked away salty perspiration and closed his eyes, fighting back tears. Why had he come in? Anthony would rather the culprit got away than find him snooping around and shoot him in the head. Then what? Sure, he had great life insurance. Holly and the kids would be taken care of, but the thought of his kids growing up without a dad, his wife a widow, or *worse*, remarrying someone else, gnawed at his brain. He continued taking deep breaths, feeling his amplified heart rate steady. *Think damnit, think!* Going out the backdoor was too much of a risk; there was no telling if the man was still out there.

And he didn't dare go deeper into the building, unsure of how many intruders had come in. The only thing he could think to do was stay in the room and hope nobody had to take a piss. God, he wished he'd just grabbed the damn cell phone when he parked. Something so inconsequential now seemed like the biggest mistake of his life.

The back door swung open with force, and the masked man came storming in again, bothered by something.

"Hey boss? We got a problem! Someone discovered our little friend in the dumpster out back. The lid's open, and the pussy apparently couldn't handle what they saw because they yakked all over the fucking ground."

That voice! Against all odds it sounded familiar.

Commotion out in the main lobby cut into the silence, and more footsteps approached.

"What did I tell you? Keep it down," another man said as he came into view. "We aren't supposed to be here right now, and if you keep fucking yelling like that, we'll have more than one person to worry about. Now… any signs of them?"

Anthony's stomach dropped. The man now standing in the room was none other than Vincent Costello, better known as the man in charge of the most powerful crime family in the city. Anthony knew if the crime boss spotted him, he was a dead man. He wished he never got involved with them, but he didn't really have a choice. A few years back, while doing a showing for a high-end property in the city, Vincent and a few of his men had decided to show up to the open house. At that point, Anthony had never spoken to Vincent before, but he knew who he was from seeing him in the news many times. He was much taller in person than Anthony would have expected. The smell of expensive cologne wafted through the air as he walked toward him. Black hair with graying temples looked like it had been glued onto to his head with thick gel.

After all the other interested buyers had left, Vincent and his men remained. Unfortunately for Anthony, they wanted far more than a new office. They had a proposal for him, something that would make his business thrive, even during the down housing market. It was simple: Anthony and his company would allow access to some of their vacant locations when Costello demanded, and in return, Anthony would get a cut of their business ventures on those nights. Anthony had asked as many questions as he felt comfortable asking, but when he saw one of Vincent's goons flashing the firearm under his jacket, he decided the less he knew the better. Judging by the information he *did* get, it sounded as simple as illegal card games and some late nights with escorts. He asked Vincent why he needed an agreement like this to do those activities when he could do it wherever he wanted. Vincent told him he needed to stay out of the FBI's crosshairs for a bit. He figured if he had spots like this planned out ahead of time, they wouldn't know where to look for the illegal activity. He also let Anthony know that if the Feds ever got tipped off, there would only be one person to look at as the rat. Anthony didn't need to ask who.

He knew it was either agree to the deal, or Costello would make his life miserable. So, they agreed with a handshake on the spot. It was something he'd never told Holly about. Not because he was trying to hide it from her, but he didn't want her to live in fear that their family was in danger. The extra money over the last few years had allowed them to get enough saved up to put both kids through college when the time arrived and helped his already growing business take off like it was strapped to a rocket.

One demand Anthony had insisted on—convincing Costello it was a necessity to make sure none of their events got busted—was that he needed to be informed ahead of time when and where they planned to be. He would "accidentally" leave the alarm off so they could get in without issue. Which is what made tonight so confusing, and why he hadn't suspected it to be them until it was too late. He wasn't stupid. As nice as Vincent had always been to his face, he was now an accessory to murder. There was a slim chance they would let him out of here alive if they found him. He'd heard of Costello killing for less. That thought forced him back further into the darkness, away from the door.

"Keep looking, it's possible they fled when they saw the body. I told you not to put the smelly fuck in the dumpster, at least not until we finished up here. Grab the kid and bring him in here, we need to figure out what to do with him," Vincent said through gritted teeth.

What kid? Anthony thought.

It only took a few seconds for his question to be answered, and it made him sick to his stomach. Vincent's men dragged Hank's limp body into the room and held him up to eye-level with their boss. His face looked as if they had taken a baseball bat to his cheekbone, his left eye swollen shut. Moans escaped from Anthony's protégé while he struggled to stay conscious.

"Drop him on the floor," Vincent demanded.

Hank's body hit the tile with a thump. The poor kid was barely out of college, why would they be doing this to him?

"You see, kid, here's the thing. I feel bad, real bad about what has to be done next. On account of it being these fucking nitwits' fault. But... what am I supposed to do with you, huh?"

Hank rolled onto his back, sobbing. Anthony wasn't close enough to see Hank's expression, but the fear in those cries was unmistakable. Hank might have struggled to remember some of the very basics of the job, but he was smart enough to know what his fate was. He didn't say anything, just looked up at the men in front of him.

"I'm in a bit of a pickle here. Your boss and I agreed to a deal, one which we've followed. Today, we slipped up a bit. It happens. We didn't have time to make sure he knew we'd need to use one of his buildings, so we improvised. That body you happened to see us shoving in the dumpster out back, he had that coming to him—" Vincent was cut short by Hank's sobs getting louder as he attempted to say something.

"What's that, kid? I can't hear you with your mouth full of shit. Sit him up," he said, nodding to one of his men.

"I... said I won't tell anyone, I swear. Please let me go," Hank slurred.

"As much as I'd love to believe you... I can't. I'm sorry kid. You may not say a single word, but then when your mommy or daddy sees your busted face, well… let's just say I can't afford anyone to be digging into my business. We only have one solution, and I think you know what that is." Vincent grinned.

"No, no… Let me work for you, let me have a reason to keep this secret. I swear, I'll tell people I got mugged," Hank cried.

"You know, for someone about to get one between the eyes, you are quick-witted, I give ya that. I see why Tony liked you. It's too bad you have to die, kid."

Anthony knew if he didn't get involved that Hank was about to get murdered. Maybe he could talk them out of killing him. There was a reason he was so successful at what he did. Holly always joked he could sell a cheeseburger to a cow. It felt like too much of a risk though. If he couldn't talk them out of it, then both he and Hank wouldn't live to see the end of the day. He squeezed the metal rod tighter, preparing to charge out and save him. He just needed to wait for the right moment.

"Speaking of your boss, did he ever tell you about our arrangement?" Vincent asked.

Hank lifted his head slowly, the confusion obvious, even under the bruises. "No… what? Why would Anthony get involved with you… people?"

"Good, good. See, that I *do* believe. That means he and his family can live, and hopefully our little arrangement can continue. Assuming we dispose of you and our little dumpster friend outside without anyone seeing."

Without another word, Vincent pulled out his gun and held it point blank in Hank's face. Hank screamed, struggling frantically against the man holding him in place. For a brief second, Anthony could have sworn the kid made eye contact with him, a look of shock at the sight of his boss hiding in the bathroom.

"Hold him still, dammit! This needs to be as clean as possible," Vincent yelled.

Another man grabbed Hank's other arm, locking him in place.

Hank began to cry so hard, the sounds coming from him didn't sound human. Anthony had never heard real fear like this.

"Please...Please...Pl—"

Vincent raised the gun, and before Hank had a chance to move again, he pulled the trigger. Hank's head snapped back as the deafening bang of the gunshot echoed through the building. Anthony jumped back, covering his mouth to hold in the screams. If they heard him, they gave no indication. Anthony slowly crouched down, hugging his knees and cried. That could very easily have been him out there with his brains painting the floor. It made Anthony sick to recall that he had just taught Hank to use the alarm app only a few days ago.

"Get him outta here and be sure to make it look like a mugging. The kid had a good idea. Then clean this shit up and let's get the hell out of here before anyone else comes. You fools see what needs to be done when you fuck up? That's innocent blood on your hands right there. The poor bastard probably just stopped sucking on his mom's titty, and now he's dead." Vincent shook his head in disgust.

The boss walked out of the back door and into the night; one of his men followed him. That left two men to clean up Hank's mess. The man wearing the mask lifted it off his face, looking down at Hank's lifeless body.

"Shit. I didn't sign up for fucking mop duty tonight. Get started while I go look for cleaning supplies," he said. The other man, who must have been of lower rank, walked closer to Hank and crouched.

It took a second to click, but Anthony realized the cleaning products were with him in the bathroom. *Shit!* He backed fully into the darkness and hid behind the closed door, praying they would look somewhere else first so he could make a run for it. His grip on the metal rod tightened some more, waiting. Now that he was against the wall, all he could see in the room were shapes and shadows. The door slowly opened, blocking Anthony from view.

The lights flicked on.

Anthony prepared, knowing it was only a matter of seconds before he was spotted. The man entered with his back to Anthony, looking under the sink for cleaning products. It was now or never. As he snuck up from behind, the man stood up, seeing Anthony's reflection in the mirror above the sink.

"What the fuck—" he said and whipped around.

He was too late. Anthony swung the rod with all his strength, clubbing the man in the face. The unsuspecting thug's head snapped to the side, a loose tooth flying out of his mouth and hitting the tile wall. He dropped to his knees, instinctively reaching for his mouth. Anthony swung down again, cracking the metal into his temple. The second blow dropped him, his head smacking off the toilet bowl on the way down with a loud crack. The body remained motionless. There was no time to see if he had just killed the man, because the sounds from the bathroom got the other guy's attention.

"Quiet down in there, you trying to get us—" He stopped as he entered and saw his partner on the ground. Shooting a glance to the side, he spotted Anthony swinging the metal rod toward his face and dodged back in time to avoid most of the impact.

Anthony missed the thug's head, the rod striking down on his collarbone instead. The second thug screamed in pain and clutched the area that had been struck. With his other arm, he fumbled around, trying to get his gun out before Anthony attacked again.

"You stupid fuck. You're a dead man, you know that?" he snarled.

"I was dead no matter what," Anthony said, then charged at him.

He slammed the guy into the wall, forcing the gun out of his hand. Anthony swung a fist, popping the man's jaw. Before he could get a second punch off, the guy kneed him square in the nuts, dropping him to the floor.

"Oh, you dumb motherfucker. Vincent is going to make you and your family suffer after this!" the man said. He punched Anthony in the face.

Anthony flew back, landing at an awkward angle. He looked over and saw the man bending over to pick up his gun and forced himself to crawl through the pain in his stomach. Pushing himself up, he kicked the gun away, stepping on the man's fingers in the process.

"Aghh, you fuck!"

He grabbed the man's head with both hands, slamming it back into the tile wall. The tile cracked, sending dust particles into the air. Anthony did it again, this time pushing his thumbs into the man's eyes in the process. He could feel the eyeballs squishing beneath his force. The man screamed again, but Anthony used all the power he could muster and smashed the back of his head into the wall one more time, cutting the scream short. He let go of the body, which promptly fell limp to the floor. Before he could even get his breath back, he heard voices coming back toward the exit door. There was no time to stand around. He sprinted out of the bathroom, getting one last glimpse of Hank's dead body on the way by and ran toward the front door. He grabbed the deadbolt to unlock it, hearing the backdoor swinging open and slamming against the brick wall outside.

"What the fuck's going on in here?" the third man yelled out.

Anthony glanced over his shoulder as the thug peered into the bathroom, spotting his two friends on the floor. He shifted his attention to the front door and saw Anthony messing with the lock. He aimed his gun and fired off a shot, the bullet clinking off the metal by Anthony's head. Whether it was his imagination or not, Anthony thought he felt the bullet whizz by his ear.

The lock unlatched and he swung the door open. He reached the steps, preparing to jump down them two at a time when he heard the gun go off again. This time, it didn't miss. The bullet forced its way into the back of his tricep. He screamed in pain. Instinct took over and he clutched his arm while ducking low and sprinting down the steps. Up ahead, he saw his car still parked, sitting alone on the side street. He raced toward it, pulling his keys out of his pocket as he went. Vehicles driving by honked in frustration at a crazed lunatic running across traffic. None stopped to see what was wrong. The pain shooting through his arm was excruciating, a burning sensation working its way from the inside of his arm outward and pulsing out with each step he took. With the keys in his hand, he pushed the automatic start button, watching his Mercedes come to life. He flung his door open and jumped inside, putting the car into drive. Before the door was completely shut, he sped off, his wheels screeching on the tar of the quiet neighborhood. He looked over at his building as he drove by, just in time to see the third man charging out and aiming his gun. Anthony winced, expecting another bullet to come in his direction, shattering the window and entering his skull. Instead, the man stood there, aiming the gun without firing. Anthony watched in his side mirror to see if the man followed, and instead saw Vincent now standing on the steps, pushing the man's hand down to prevent him from shooting. He didn't take his eyes off the mirror until they were out of sight.

2

ANTHONY DROVE LIKE A MAN POSSESSED, weaving in and out of traffic while blaring his horn. For once, the cabdrivers were looking at him like *he* was the crazy one. Without thinking, he switched hands on the wheel so he could reach over and grab his cellphone. The throbbing intensity of the bullet wound shot through his arm. Tears escaped his eyes as he bit down on his lip to try and manage the pain. He dialed Holly and the call automatically transferred over to the vehicle's Bluetooth. It rang three times, each ring felt like an eternity, before she finally picked up.

"Holly, listen to me. Get the kids dressed, pack a few bags as quickly as you can and put them in the van, and be ready for me."

"What? What's wrong, Anthony? Are you okay?"

"I'll explain everything later. Right now, I just need you to do as I say. Okay?"

"I… I guess so. Do you need me to grab the money in the safe?" she asked.

"Yes, that's a good idea. Pack just the essentials. I want us out of the driveway as quickly as I pull in."

"Babe, you're scaring me," Holly said.

"You have to trust me on this."

"Okay, I'll see you when you get here."

"Holly? Pack the gun too. Try not to let the kids see it." A sharp pain shot through his arm again and he let out a growl.

"What happened to you? Is this related to the alarm going off?" she asked.

"Holly! Just do what I fucking said! I will tell you later... and do not pack electronics." He hung up the phone.

He felt awful for snapping at her, but she didn't get the seriousness of it all and he didn't have time to explain it. He had no idea what they would do or where they would go. Calling the cops was off limits—Vincent had half of the corrupt bastards on his payroll. They needed to hide out, to get away from Vincent and his men. He looked over at the passenger seat and spotted his property binder. Yes, that's it. *I need to find a place where they won't look*, he thought. The problem was, because of the deal he had with Vincent, they had exchanged a list of all his properties, and would likely check each of them until they found Anthony and his family.

Then it hit him. Some of the locations Anthony had bought out of state were not in the binder nor on his website. His mind quickly raced through all the properties he bought up in New England. It would be a hike, but if it saved their lives, it would be worth it. *The campground*, he thought.

Two years ago, he'd purchased an old campground in New Hampshire called The Bird's Nest. At the time, he thought it would be an easy property to flip, purchasing it at a significantly discounted price. To his surprise, he hadn't received as much as a single phone call. He still checked in with the groundskeeper from time to time, making sure it was presentable if he had any interested parties reach out to get a tour of the place. Locals had warned him not to buy it when he went up to visit, calling it the Devil's Nest. He'd asked why, but when they started going into all the old stories and folklore of the area, he got bored with it and tuned them out. Apparently, there had been a lot of strange occurrences in the past, some murders in surrounding towns, and the locals avoided the area like the plague. He didn't care about that though; he wasn't trying to please them or have them come over for a cookout. To Anthony, it was a beautiful twenty-acre property in a quiet New England town. The perfect spot for people to get away from it all. In other words, an easy pitch to sell to the first investor who showed any sign of interest. What he didn't expect was for everyone else to buy into the hoopla of the small-town gossip. If it was as bad as the locals said it was, why the hell were they still around to talk about it? It all felt like a planned pitch to keep some city big wig from buying the land and attracting outsiders. *Stupid fucking hicks.* However, at that moment, he was happy it hadn't sold yet.

It was decided. They would go to New Hampshire and hide in the campground until things hopefully blew over. His business would have to wait. And now they didn't even have Hank to handle the work while they were gone. Poor Hank. Anthony couldn't help but feel responsible for his death. And selfish. But he had a wife and two kids; he couldn't afford to put his life on the line for some bachelor kid who didn't even have a family.

Vincent would stop at nothing until he found them. Vincent knew Anthony wouldn't go to the cops, because that would just put a bullseye on his back. Even if he somehow avoided the dirty cops that worked for the Costello family, Vincent wouldn't spend more than a night in jail once his high-end lawyer sunk his teeth into the case. Anthony felt as if his plan was just setting the timer on a bomb and waiting for it to count down until the eventual explosion. But at least it gave him time. Time to come up with a better plan without peering out of his windows, looking out for some hitman coming for his family.

The city lights illuminated the urban landscape, people going about their business like everything was fine. Skyscrapers towered over the road as if they were looking down, judging him for his mistakes. Anthony punched in the address to the campground. It would take them approximately six hours to drive there. He just hoped he got to his house before the men with guns showed up.

———————————

HOLLY TOSSED THE PHONE ON THE BED AND RAN TO THE CLOSET. SHE threw two suitcases onto the floor, followed by random shirts and dresses. The tone of Anthony's voice wasn't one she'd heard during their entire marriage. He sounded *scared*. Over the years he had displayed many emotions such as love, happiness, and anger. The *anger*. Something that almost ended their marriage on numerous occasions. But one thing he'd never shown was fear. After many blow up fights, they agreed to go to therapy to get help. Both still loved one another very much, but the busy day-to-day lives they lived got in the way of actually enjoying each other's company. Anthony had always shown signs of a short temper even early on in their dating life, but nothing that overly alarmed Holly. The longer their relationship went on, however, the more he'd cracked. He never put his hands on her, she knew he wouldn't do such a thing. But the angry, snapping remarks he responded with to even the most basic statements from her or the kids were worrisome. Not only had they started going to therapy—which seemed to help to an extent—but he also set up appointments with his doctor to see what he could do to help with the anger issues. One thing she would always love about Anthony was how self-aware he was of it all. In the moment there would be screaming and shouting, insults they would both later regret, but when all was said and done, he almost always came to her saying he knew there were bigger issues. She didn't completely blame him. For one, his dad was one of the angriest men she had ever heard of. Fortunately, she never had to meet him, as he passed away. Anthony would tell her stories of his childhood, how the smallest thing would set his dad off, and that short temper led to his parents divorcing when he was in middle school. Growing up in a split household situation had been tough on him, but he knew it was for the best with how much his parents fought. Anthony often told Holly that he never wanted to be in that same situation, that he would do everything to make sure they stayed together.

There was also the fact that she wasn't the easiest to deal with, and she knew it. Her sarcasm had often got her into trouble growing up, and it only escalated as she got older. Anthony had thought it was cute early in their relationship, but it turned into one of his biggest issues with her through the years, especially after having kids. His short temper mixed with her blatant sarcasm was a recipe for disaster. The silver lining of it all was that they both understood their issues. And they both wanted to fix it no matter how hard it got. He was such a great dad to the kids too, something Holly was extremely grateful for. He provided for their family, worked long hours so she didn't have to (which helped avoid paying for childcare), attended every sporting event for the kids, and made sure they had whatever they needed to succeed in life. It always came back to that anger though. Whenever he snapped at one of the kids, all bets were off. Their biggest blowups almost always started because of him saying something mean or shouting at the children, and she would have none of that, whether he could help it or not.

Holly looked down at the suitcase and decided she'd packed enough of her own stuff. She jumped up and hurried to Anthony's dresser, grabbing as many items of clothing as she could and dropping them into his empty suitcase. They could worry about folding them later. Once she packed all the clothes she could cram in, she went back to the closet. Sitting in the back corner was the safe. She typed the code as fast as she could, throwing the door open and examining the contents. The gun, all their excess cash, and their passports sat in the padded interior. Holly peeked out the door to make sure the kids weren't around before grabbing the gun and bullets out of the safe. She stuffed them under her clothes in the suitcase so they would be hidden from plain sight, then zipped up the bag. She wiped sweat off her forehead with the back of her hand, thinking of the next logical step. It was time to tell the kids they were leaving. Spencer would be fine; he was only eight years old and the thought of leaving in the middle of the night would be an adventure to him. It was Allie she worried about. Their daughter was sixteen, In full-blown hormonal hell. A sophomore in high school who was stressed enough as it was planning her upcoming prom. She would ask questions Holly didn't have the answers to. Like, why are we packing up and leaving in the middle of the night? Where are we going? Things Holly should know but didn't. Allie also possessed her mom's sarcasm, which was not ideal in this situation.

Holly hurried down the hall, dragging both suitcases behind her. The sound of wheels speeding across the hardwood floor rumbled through the hallway. She first approached Spencer's room, giving a soft knock on the door. Even at eight years old, the kid wanted his privacy, to the point where he made a "no truspasing" sign and taped it to the outside of his door, spelling be damned. It was too cute to correct, and his sister would likely do that for them when she was in one of her moods. Holly cracked the door open and studied Spencer on his bed, his big, blue eyes watching YouTube videos on his tablet. He wore his massive noise cancelling head-phones over his shaggy brown hair that he refused to get cut, not hearing her enter. All she wanted to do was stand in the doorway and watch her son, soak in every last second of him being so young and innocent. She didn't get the chance, as he looked up and tossed his tablet to the side when he spotted her.

"Jeez mom, don't you know how to knock?"

"Hon, I knocked, you just couldn't hear me with those things on your head," she said, smiling. Her smile quickly hardened when she remembered why she was at his door in the first place. "Spence, we are going on a little road trip. Let's pack some clothes and stuff you want to bring. As soon as Dad's home, we're taking right off, okay?"

"Awesome! Does that mean I don't have to go to school tomorrow? Where are we going?"

"I think we can let you skip school tomorrow. And I can't tell you where we are going, it's a surprise," she said with a wink.

"Okay! I'll hurry."

"Just pack what fits in your travel bag that's under your bed, no need to pack any more than that. And Spence?"

"What?"

"No electronics, okay?"

He glanced down at his tablet, internally debating if it was worth it to leave what he considered his life behind.

"Okay, this is so cool!" he said and jumped off his bed, yanking out the bag from underneath it.

Holly continued down the hall, taking a deep breath as she approached her daughter's room. She set the suitcases down outside the door and knocked. This time she knocked a bit louder and leaned in close to the door.

"Allie? Hon, are you awake?"

"Mom, I'm sixteen, not eight. Of course, I'm still awake."

Closing her eyes and preparing for the wrath of a teenage girl, Holly opened the door. Allie had her laptop open in front of her, lying on her stomach and typing away, likely messaging her boyfriend. Normal teenage stuff that Holly was about to rip right out from underneath her.

"Hey… I'm trying to keep your brother calm about this, but we need to pack, now. Dad called and I don't know the details yet, but he sounds scared, like he's in trouble. He told me to pack stuff quickly and be ready when he gets home."

"What? Why the hell would we leave our home? Where are we going?"

"I just told you I don't know! Please, I don't have time to argue with you right now, we need to get out of here and be ready when your dad pulls in." Holly waited for her daughter to blow up on her. Shockingly, it didn't come. Allie sensed the urgency in her mom's voice.

"Okay… are we in danger, Mom?"

"I… I don't know that, Allie. Not until I talk more with your father. Now pack and meet me downstairs in ten minutes and leave the laptop." Holly picked up the suitcases before her daughter could respond. As she walked down the stairs, she heard Allie running around her room grabbing stuff frantically. She was a good kid, but right now it was a coin-flip which version of her you got after a basic request. Holly had been in her shoes as a teen, so she usually remained patient with her. Anthony, however, couldn't handle the sarcastic, know-it-all attitude of a teen dealing with mood swings. Ever since Allie had been planning for prom, her attitude had really taken a turn for the worst, the stress apparently too much to handle. Holly got the feeling that prom was going to be the least of their concerns.

3

ANTHONY'S HEART sat in his throat the entire ride. On multiple occasions, he almost crashed into the guardrail while staring too long into the rearview mirror for signs of anyone tailing him. There were a few times he could have sworn two bright dots burning his eyes were the headlights of Vincent's men coming to chop him to pieces and throw him in the Hudson. Every time someone turned behind him or got off an exit, he felt a sense of relief—until another set of lights replaced them.

He drove down the road toward their house, hoping Holly had the kids ready to go when he pulled in. *Hoping* he got there before anyone else. As he rounded the corner approaching their driveway, he exhaled a sigh of relief at the sight of his family standing in the driveway, the streetlight across the road shining down on them like a beacon.

The brakes screeched slightly as Anthony pulled into their driveway. He was out of the car instantly, locking the doors—as if that mattered.

"Dad, what the hell's going on?" Allie asked.

"There will be plenty of time to explain later," he replied. "Right now, I need you to stay quiet and just do as I say. Get in the van, we need to go."

"I already got the bags in the van; I did everything you asked on the phone. Anthony... are we in trouble?" Holly asked.

"Jesus, Holly. I just said I'll talk once we get out of here, okay? Just get in and be quiet," he snapped.

They all scurried into the van in silence, afraid to upset him anymore than he already was. Holly saw the wound on his arm and bruises on his face but didn't dare say anything yet. Once the doors were shut, Anthony backed out of the driveway and sped off down the street, watching the mirrors the entire way.

"LISTEN, THERE ARE THINGS YOU NEED TO KNOW, HOLLY. HANK'S dead... there's no way to sugarcoat it. I watched him get shot..." Anthony whispered. Both kids were asleep in the back, so now seemed as good a time as any to spill the truth.

"What? Oh my God, Anthony. We have to call the cops!" Tears pooled up in her eyes.

"We can't do that. I wish it were that simple, I really do. I'm sorry I snapped at you guys, it's just... we needed to leave. They'll likely come for me next."

"Who will come for you? What are you not telling me, Tony?"

After leaving the house, they'd travelled a few hours in silence, everyone feeling they were walking on eggshells around Anthony and afraid to question anything. He wanted to wait to talk, clear his mind, and think more about his plan. When they stopped at a rest area, Anthony was relieved to discover the bullet wasn't lodged in his arm like he'd initially thought. It had exited the other side. It still hurt like hell, but for now a bandage from his med kit would have to do.

"It was never supposed to get to this... A few years ago, Vincent Costello and his men barged into an open house. They waited for everyone to leave, and then cornered me and basically forced me to agree to their proposition—"

"*The* Vincent Costello? The mob guy? What the hell would you get involved with him for?" Holly asked.

"For Christ's sake, Holly. Let me finish before the kids wake up. I promise I'll tell you all you need to know. Yes, him. I didn't tell you because I didn't want you to worry. It felt mostly innocent—until tonight. They wanted to use some of my available listings for underground card games and meetings, to stay out of the Fed's eyes for a bit. They offered to pay me to allow this. In turn I just had to give them access to whichever location they planned to use and make sure I wasn't around when they needed it."

Holly just stared at him. She couldn't comprehend how her innocent husband had become involved with a crime family behind her back, and now they were on the run with their lives in danger. Just hours ago, her biggest concern had been which episode of *Dateline* to watch on the DVR. She felt betrayed. All the therapy in the world couldn't have prepared their marriage for this, and she was having trouble holding it all in while he talked.

"What a *great* fucking idea, Anthony!" she snarled. Then she bit her lip, holding back further sarcastic tirades. "Why did you do it?"

"I didn't have a choice! You think it's as simple as saying, 'thanks but no thanks, now be on your way so I can try to sell this house?' You don't tell Vincent *fucking* Costello no, Holly."

She shook her head. There had to have been a way to avoid the situation they now found themselves in. But it was too late for that now. He still hadn't told her where they were going yet.

"Okay, so please, tell me how that led to Hank getting killed, and why we are on the run when it's just stupid card games?" she asked.

"The alarm went off... I went to check it out because I had no reason to think it was Vincent, he hadn't reached out to me ahead of time. He's never gone against our agreement since this whole thing started. So, it didn't even cross my mind. Well, apparently Hank figured out how to use the alarm app for our properties, because he also decided to go check it out." Anthony ran his hand through his hair. Holly could see how upset he was getting, reliving the story.

"When I got there, I heard screaming inside and because I left my phone in the car, I decided to check it out. Hank caught them dumping a body, so they decided to make sure he didn't tell anyone about it. I... I hid in the bathroom and watched them kill the poor kid. He was just doing his damn job and they shot him in the head like it was nothing, Holly."

Holly couldn't believe what she was hearing, it sounded like something out of a movie, and here they were living it in real life.

"I'm so sorry you had to see that; it must have been awful. Thank God you made it out alive," she said. After a moment of silence, she asked, "Where are you taking us?"

"That's the problem. We don't have many options right now. We can't tell the cops because half of them work for him. We can't stay home or at any hotels because he will find us. It got me thinking, at least for now, of a place we could lay low and try to come up with a better plan. Do you remember that old campground I bought in New Hampshire? The one that's supposedly cursed or some shit?"

"Yeah... that dump you can't sell. What about it?" she asked.

"Well, it's not on my property listing right now. I pulled it down because I hadn't even gotten a phone call showing interest. I felt if I left it up on the site, it would give me a bad look and stand out like a sore thumb."

"So... it's not on your listings... meaning he doesn't know about it?"

Anthony smiled. "They won't think to check there, at least not for a while. It's our only choice."

Holly put her head in her hands.

"I'm trying to process my boring husband all of a sudden becoming a wanted man by the biggest crime family in New York."

"Boring?" Though exhausted, he managed to inject mock outrage into his voice.

Holly smiled. Her smile soon faded, however, and that nearly broke Anthony's heart.

"Promise me we'll get through this," she said.

Anthony swallowed.

"I promise." He cleared his throat, lest the emotion overwhelm him. "When we get to the campground, it should be early morning. There's a large house there that we can sleep in. Let's just hope it buys us some time. The groundskeeper I kept on the property won't be expecting us, so that should be a fun chat."

— — — — — — — — —

After a few pitstops for bathroom breaks and detours to avoid popular highway routes in favor of some back roads, they finally arrived in New Hampshire as dawn approached. The roads were deserted in this area of the state; Anthony hadn't seen another car for at least twenty minutes. After getting his emotions in check, he looked over at Holly, wanting to apologize for everything. The kids had been through enough, watching their parents argue and yell over so many petty things the last few years. They had been able to keep control of the outbursts after therapy for the most part—at least in front of Allie and Spencer. But on occasion, it slipped through the cracks. Those failures seemed small compared to what they were now up against.

He placed his hand on Holly's leg, prompting her to look over at him. He mouthed the words "I'm sorry," and she gave a forced smile to let him know it was okay.

The narrow road twisted in every direction until it disappeared into the mouth of a forest. Trees sprouted from each side of the road, hiding the track from the rest of the world. The vehicle's clock said it was just past seven in the morning, but one would think nightfall was settling in under the thick canopies.

"Tony, I know we are coming out here to be secluded, but this road—this *place*, gives me the creeps. It feels like a path to Hell. And you keep looking behind us like we are being followed. Are they close?" Holly asked.

"Jesus, I don't have a radar in my head, Holly. How would I know that?"

"Here we go again with the fighting..." Allie mumbled from the backseat, looking out the window.

"Who is following us, Daddy?" Spencer spoke up for the first time since leaving the house—unusual for the garrulous kid.

Anthony and Holly shared concerned looks with one another, unsure what to tell their son. While it was important for them not to lie to their kids, they also didn't want to scare him. Allie was a different story; she could handle the harsh realities of the world. Spencer, however, was still an innocent little boy. The biggest concerns he should be worrying about at this age were something hiding in the closet, or a spider crawling on him, not some assassins coming to kill their family.

"Oh, nothing buddy. We thought someone was following us, but we were wrong," Holly said and patted him on the leg.

"Okay. Are we almost there? I really have to pee," Spencer said. Holly was relieved that her answer was good enough for him. For now.

"Yep, it's just around the corner, okay?" Anthony said with a smile on his face. "Daddy will put the pedal to the metal to get you there faster."

"Yeah! Put the pedal to the metal, Daddy!"

Allie rolled her eyes at the age-old tradition, one she used to take part in when they went on rides before she grew too old to consider it fun anymore. She continued looking out her window toward the woods with her headphones blaring music. Anthony glanced at the clock on the dashboard and hoped that when they arrived at the campground, they would be able to get some rest after driving all night. He wasn't looking forward to dealing with the groundskeeper. But from what Anthony recalled, the man was very nice. They would be showing up unannounced, which he would have preferred to avoid, but when you have people trying to kill you it's easy to let common courtesy slide. Hopefully he didn't find the old redneck doing anything strange when they showed up.

With his nerves now calmed, Anthony picked up speed, looking at his son in the rearview as the boy smiled at the vehicle's acceleration through the narrow road. Up ahead, Anthony saw the dirt road they needed to turn down. He slowed, turning on his blinker as he saw the sign "Coon Brook RD".

"*Coon* Brook Road? Where the hell are you taking us, Tony? Sounds like some intro to a *Deliverance* sequel," Holly said.

Anthony ignored her, knowing any response would lead to another argument that they'd vowed to avoid. They drove for a few miles down the dirt road, only trees and wetland surrounding them. Anthony had never envisioned willingly traveling to such a secluded place, but this felt like the perfect spot to hide. In the distance, a large blue sign stood out from the reoccurring backdrop of endless forest. As they got closer, he saw the name on the sign had been mostly chipped away from years of sun and neglect. He pulled the vehicle up to the gate—which was closed with a padlock—and put the van in park.

"I'll be right back, just need to open this gate," Anthony said and hopped out. The sign read "BIRD'S NEST CAMPGROUND". Someone had spray-painted over the word "Bird's" and written "DEVIL'S" instead.

"Fucking Devil's Nest," he muttered to himself, and pulled out his keys to the property. He found the one that fit into the padlock and heard it click open. After he pushed the gate wide enough to drive through, he got back in the van.

"Well, I won't argue that this place is hidden. Does anybody live within a fifty-mile radius? It feels like a ghost town," Holly said.

Again, Anthony ignored his wife's sarcastic tone and pulled ahead. He'd been working so hard to control his anger issues since they started therapy. His doctor had him on anxiety medicine, thinking that might help. It had, to a certain extent. He didn't want to be this way; he knew when he snapped that it was usually uncalled for. It was the worst when he did it toward Spencer though. The poor kid was still trying to figure out how to be a child, yet he would often say or do something harmless that would coincide with Anthony being agitated with work or Holly, and he would take it out on his son. One time he made Spencer cry after snapping. The boy was trying to get his attention and was just excited. Anthony had just finished arguing with Holly and followed that up by getting a call from a contractor that needed to go well over the budget on a remodel of one of his properties. Spencer kept seeking his attention, leading to Anthony yelling at him, asking what the hell he wanted. He turned to see his son crying, holding a card he made for his dad. The card said, "everything will be okay, I love you Daddy." Anthony promised himself he would do everything in his power to never act like that toward his kids again.

A large white house with a spacious farmer's porch came into view at the bottom of the steep declining driveway. An old, Ford truck sat parked in front of the house. The area looked far bigger than Anthony recalled from his visit to sign the papers a few years back. He parked the van next to the truck, took a deep breath, and looked over to Holly.

"Okay, this is it. Let's get our things and I'll go knock to let this guy know we're staying for a bit."

"Does this *guy* have a name? I'm not sure how I feel staying with someone I don't even know," Holly grumbled.

"For the love of God, would you rather the alternative? I'll be right back."

As Anthony approached the steps to the front door, he never got the chance to knock. The screen door shot open, the silhouette of a man holding a shotgun stood in the doorway, aiming the barrel directly at him. The morning sun shining through a window in the house hid most of the man's features in shadow, but the gun itself was as clear as day.

"Don't fucking move, mister..."

4

"Woah, woah. Easy does it. Please, put the gun down, I have my family with me, sir," Anthony said calmly.

The figure walked out of the door, revealing a man in his late-fifties with a prosthetic leg; his face appeared worn and tired behind his grey scruff. He'd lost some weight since the last time Anthony had seen him, but he got the feeling it wasn't from healthy exercise. The man looked like one wrong move would snap him mentally, sending him on a rampage. *Can I go twenty-four hours without getting a fucking gun pointed at me?* Anthony thought.

"Do you not recognize me, Cole? I own the campground. You and I have talked on the phone a few times over the last couple years, and we met when I came to sign the papers for the place."

Cole's face held its hard expression, like he was still trying to decide if he did in fact know the man standing in front of him. He glanced over Anthony's shoulder to the vehicle, spotting Holly and the kids sitting inside, watching in fear. That's when his expression lightened, and he lowered the gun.

"I'm so sorry... This place has the tendency to make you live on the edge. I'm usually good at remembering appearances, Mr.

Graham. I wasn't expecting ya though." There was a hint of embarrassment in Cole's voice.

"No worries, I should have called you. We didn't really have a chance to do that though. Can we come in? I have something I need to talk to you about," Anthony said.

Cole scratched his chin, looking around the woods like he expected something else to appear.

"You own the place, who would I be to say no to that?" He forced a smile.

"Thank you, I really appreciate it, Cole. I'd like to talk with you in private, my son is too young to hear the stuff I need to tell you," Anthony said.

Nodding, Cole came off the steps and walked toward the van, flashing another smile.

"Sorry about the scare, kids. Easy to get spooked out here alone in the woods when you're not expecting company. Why don't you guys get out and stretch your legs? There's a nice backyard where you can enjoy the views of the place behind the house."

The kids both looked at Holly, unsure if they should follow the strange man. She hesitated a moment but gave a nod of agreement, and they all got out.

"Hello there, the name's Cole. Cole Springer. And you are?"

"Holly, I'm Anthony's wife," she said coldly.

He looked to the kids next. "And who do we have here?"

Neither kid dared to talk. Spencer hid behind Holly, and Allie looked at the man with disgust. Holly realized that they weren't going to answer, so she did it for them.

"This little man here is Spencer. The grouchy teen is Allie."

"Mom! I'm not a grouch," Allie said defensively.

"Hey, I just aimed a gun at your dad, I'd say I got a little grouch in me too. Nice to meet you guys under the circumstances." He paused, waiting to make sure things had smoothed over. "Follow me out back, you'll love the view," Cole said, leading the way to the path around the home.

"This home here, it used to be the office to the campground before it went out of business, but I have renovated it a bit to feel more like a home. Still left the office intact of course, in case your dad can actually ever sell the place." Cole winked toward Spencer, making the boy laugh.

"Back when the campground was open, they used to have big cookouts back here, throwing some of the biggest parties these woods have ever seen. Please, enjoy the scenery and I'll bring out some lemonade for the kids. Would you like anything to drink, ma'am?"

"I'll take a water, please."

"Water it is. Please, make yourself at home back here. It *is* yours, after all." Cole walked to the back door and headed inside the house.

Anthony came around the corner to join his family and approached Holly. He made sure the kids were distracted before saying anything.

"I can't tell him everything, but I do feel I need to prepare the guy for what could be coming," he whispered to her.

"I know this is our place, but it feels wrong to just show up and scare the poor man, doesn't it?"

"Yeah, I know. I'll figure it out, just keep them busy, okay?"

She nodded as Cole came out with a tray of drinks and set them on the large patio table.

"Here you guys are, hope you enjoy. My son seems to like my lemonade, so I suppose I do something right, eh?" he said with a chuckle.

"You have a son? How old?" Holly asked.

"Teagan's thirteen, going on thirty. Kid thinks he's a grown man already. He's out in the fields taking care of some stuff for me at the moment, keeping the place maintained."

"Oh, very nice. I can't get these two to pick up their dirty under-wear, let alone mow the lawn," Anthony said.

"Dad! Stop being so embarrassing," Allie snapped.

"Yeah, yeah." He nodded at Cole. "Shall we?"

"After you, sir." Cole gestured toward the front of the house.

They walked around to the van, Anthony opening the hatchback to grab the bags. He noticed Cole looking at the luggage confused and figured he better say something.

"So… I said I wanted to talk about something. I'm trying to get the kids away for a bit, maybe a week or two. I just lost someone close to me, I haven't told them yet, but I wanted to get away somewhere secluded before breaking the news. You don't mind if we stay here for a bit, do you?"

"Hey, like I said: it's your place. You could kick me out on the streets if you really wanted to. I appreciate you even letting me stay here until the place is sold to begin with. Not many realtors would be so kind," Cole said.

"I actually like our arrangement, to be honest. You know how much it would cost for me to hire a company to come out here regularly and maintain this property? Might look like some apocalyptic wasteland by the time I get an offer for the damn place if it wasn't for you," Anthony said.

"Well, you guys are no bother to me. It's nice to have guests for once since it's been just me and Teagan alone for so long…"

"What happened to his mother, if you don't mind me asking?" Anthony asked, immediately regretting the question.

"She passed. It's been just me and the boy since he was two. Coming back here was a way to have him close to where I met her." Cole grabbed one of the bags from the trunk to help Anthony carry them in.

"Sorry to hear that, didn't mean to ask something so personal… About that sign out front, maybe we can get that painted over? I can't imagine any buyers seeing "Devil's Nest" spray-painted on the sign wanting to pursue it any further. Damn urban legends. People believe some wild shit, huh?"

"Yeah, I'd like to believe it was all fake campfire stories, but some of what you hear is likely true. We can get that sign painted over though, been meaning to do it but the local kids all seem to think it's funny to paint back over anytime I fix it."

They walked up the stairs and Cole opened the front door, holding it for Anthony as he walked in with travel bags in each hand. The smell of the downstairs area reminded Anthony of his grandparents' house growing up. A stale, musty scent, absent of a good cleaning for who knew how long, filled the air. He made a mental note that he would need to hire a cleaning service to give the place a good scrubbing before they did their next open house. *Who the hell are you kidding? Nobody is going to buy this place, and your career is down the shitter now that one of your employees got murdered thanks to you.*

"Excuse the mess. If I knew someone was coming I woulda made a point to tidy the place up, Mr. Graham," Cole said as if reading Anthony's mind.

"Not a worry, and please, call me Anthony."

The downstairs consisted of an office area with a desk, an old computer that looked like it hadn't been used in years still making itself at home on the desk. A set of stairs sat a few feet in, leading up to the bedrooms. They walked upstairs, coming to a narrow hallway.

"The place has four bedrooms, so unless you guys planned on camping on-site in a tent, there's plenty of space in here, as long as your kids don't mind sharing a room. Or I can have Teagan sleep in my room with me, whatever's easiest for you guys," Cole said.

Anthony laughed before saying, "My wife sleeping in a tent? Man, she hasn't left the city willingly since she was a little kid. That would be quite the sight. And my kids can share a room. They may not like it, but no need to make your boy move out of his room. Thank you though."

"With that being said then, here's the first open room, the larger of the two if you recall. I assume you and your wife will take this one, the kids can share the smaller one down the hall." He gestured further down toward another door.

"It's settled. We'll try not to be in your hair too much. Hell, I'll even try to kick in with some of the maintenance if it helps while we're here. I really need to clear my head and being out in nature will do a world of good," Anthony said.

"About this place though... I'll give you the tour later today if you'd like, but some areas I'd just steer clear of if I was you." Cole sounded like he was trying to hold himself back from saying more. "I'll make a point to show you as we go."

"Okay, sounds like a plan. I think Holly and I will probably rest up once we get the kids situated. It's been a long, exhausting drive. I look forward to getting to know you and Teagan more." Anthony threw the bags down on the empty bed. Cole nodded and walked back down the creaky, old stairs while Anthony looked around the room. The mattress didn't look ideal—not close to the two-thousand-dollar bed they had sitting in their home—but it would have to do. He'd rather the lack of sleep come from bed firmness as opposed to sleeping with one eye open looking for a gun pointed at his face. This would work. He just needed time to think of a clear plan, so his family wouldn't have to live in hiding and would be safe from Vincent and his crew. Maybe he could find a way to contact Vincent without giving up his location, try to smooth things over and show his loyalty. Holly wanted him to call the cops, C.I.A, F.B.I., whoever the hell could protect them. While it might give them temporary protection, Anthony knew it would only be a matter of time before that shell cracked and they were given up.

There was also the concern of Hank's death. It wouldn't be a good look to have an employee go missing and then disappear off the face of the earth. If he knew Vincent like he thought he did, the kingpin would cover those tracks as well, getting some of his dirty cop friends to mess with evidence and make it look like a random act of violence. Anthony wondered how long he would be able to last before telling Cole the truth behind why they were here. He got the vibe Cole was also not telling the full story about *his* history with Bird's Nest, he just couldn't put a finger on what it was. Every time the groundskeeper talked about the place, he started showing hints of concern before quickly catching himself and changing his tone. Could the old hick really believe some of the stories about this place?

Something he'd never told Holly after buying the campground was the pushback he got from the locals when he came to Goshen to check the place out. The clerk at the lone convenience store in town told him he should avoid the place, that the previous owner was a creep who up and vanished one day along with all his followers. The clerk used the term "cult" while referring to them, saying when the campground went out of business, this man swooped in and bought the land, turning it into some type of compound.

That was the other thing he didn't tell Holly—why the campground went out of business in the first place. It was a thriving area to go camping back in the eighties and nineties, a place packed with tourists from the time flowers bloomed in late spring, all the way through late fall when the autumn leaves peaked. In the late nineties, a school event in the neighboring town of Newport turned into a massacre. Countless deaths and injuries around Halloween of 1999 scared off tourists from coming to the surrounding towns. Then the same town had another batch of murders the following year, putting the struggling campground in so much debt they couldn't recover. The owner lost it to the bank, leading to whoever this "cult" guy was buying it. Once they disappeared, the banks waited the legal minimum amount of time before gaining back control of it and putting it on the market. Anthony couldn't turn down the amazing deal, it was something he'd been on the lookout for to expand his listings into different areas and grow his business.

So, when he came to check it out and the locals all tried to frighten him and send him on his way, he politely gave them the imaginary middle-finger. If anything, he envisioned the spooky history of the area lending mystique to the campground, so that it would become a huge attraction around Halloween time. Up until now, he'd been proven wrong. Nobody wanted to step within ten miles of the place, treating it like the next Chernobyl.

He walked over to the window, gazing out over the backyard at his family. They sat at the table, drinking their lemonade, talking with Cole about something. They were all laughing—a good sign under the circumstances. It remained important to Anthony that Spencer stay out of the loop about their situation. The boy dealt with early stages of anxiety. They'd taken him to see doctors, looking for anything that could help that didn't involve swallowing a pill every day. Holly insisted that a child so small should not depend on medication to survive in life. It was one of the topics they fought about all the time. Anthony saw the struggles his son went through, much like himself, and wanted to help the boy. Instead of getting him on something that could help normalize his life, they continued to try and find workarounds for it. The situation was heartbreaking and yet another crack in the unstable marriage. Anthony's anger would often be triggered by the issues, and he struggled not to take it out on his family in the heat of the moment. It was a cycle for he and Holly, a pattern that felt like it was now stuck in the bad phase and only getting worse. And then there was Allie. Anthony loved her to death, but it was getting more and more difficult not to resent his own daughter. She carried the typical teenage angst but packed on an extra punch with her mother's famed sarcasm. Every time she responded to one of his demands with a backhanded comment, all Anthony could picture was Holly sitting there with a smile on her face thinking "that's my girl."

He went through every day battling these inner thoughts, trying to push past them and get back to a point where they were a happy family. Right now, that seemed about as achievable as climbing Mount Everest barefoot through shards of broken glass, but he would continue trying. He had no choice. Once they got back to their normal life, *if* they got back to it, he was ready to give it one final shot. The meds he took helped the anxiety, but the anger had never fully left. Anthony found himself always on the verge of snapping, and when he had what Holly referred to as a "good day", it was mostly because he was able to bite his tongue enough times to string together a few good hours. He had issues, and he knew it. The biggest issue though, was that he didn't see a way to overcome it. But he had to try. For his wife. For his kids.

Holly looked up at the window, noticing him staring down at them and gave a smile. She motioned for him to come down and join, so he let out a sigh and closed the curtain. She could always appear so cheerful and happy around others when inside she was likely falling apart. He gave the room one last look and walked downstairs to join them.

5

HOLLY WAS KEEPING everything under control for the sake of her kids, but deep inside she was ready to explode. Mob men trying to hunt them down and kill them, some strange man pointing a gun at her husband's head, this creepy ass town where something felt *off*. Spencer still appeared to believe this was a vacation, in awe of the forest around him. He'd never been out of the city, so to him she could only imagine this looked like some alien planet. Allie was too distracted with her own issues to put much thought into what was going on. Holly kept a close eye on her to try and see any signs of stress. The seriousness she showed in her room the previous night was gone, replaced with annoyance and impatience. All she cared about was that she couldn't see her friends or boyfriend, that she couldn't be online or on her phone chatting with them all hours of the day. Anthony had made a point to say no electronics to Holly; he didn't want to give Vincent any way to track them down. Allie fought to bring her old iPhone to use it for music, arguing that it wasn't even connected to a phone plan and couldn't work for anything besides music. That was the lone exception Holly allowed. She knew Anthony wouldn't be thrilled with it, but Holly could convince him they had to give a little to make her happy. Anthony had possibly seen one too many movies, but she thought he had a good point in limiting all possible scenarios that could put them in danger.

Cole spent the last hour telling them about his tour in Iraq, how he lost his leg and moved to New Hampshire when he got back to the states. He didn't give too much information on why he was at the campground, but she assumed it was because someone in his condition had limited work options.

The more Cole talked, the better she felt about him. He exhibited a level of calmness that nobody in her family did, and that helped her feel more at ease. The kids really latched on to him quick, too, something that neither of them typically did with strangers. Cole finished a story he was telling the kids at the far end of the lawn and walked back toward the table where Holly and Anthony sat in silence.

"I don't suppose you want to get that tour of the place, do you? We got the 4-wheelers we can ride around, and we could show your kids what you own here," Cole said.

"Man, that sounds good, but I'm zonked. I don't know about Holly, but I think it's time I took that nap I mentioned earlier," Anthony said.

"Yes, let's take a raincheck on that, Cole. We drove through the night, and I'd be afraid to pass out somewhere in the woods," Holly said laughing. Cole didn't find the woods comment funny, his expression hardened, making her feel uneasy.

"A lot of dangerous things out in those woods. I wouldn't recommend getting lost out there…"

Holly and Anthony both looked at each other, and while their marriage was slowly rotting away, they still retained the ability to read each other. The way Cole kept hinting at things but not delving into the details was becoming annoying, no matter how nice he was.

"Come on, Mom! I really wanna check this place out!" Spencer demanded.

"I—"

Before she could finish, they heard a faint motor, getting louder as it approached out of sight. Holly's stomach twisted in knots wondering who could be coming for them. Her body tensed up, and the silence between them only amplified the revving of the distant engine. She looked to Anthony, seeing the same concern in his eyes while he stared off in the distance to see where the noise was coming from. She got up, preparing to grab Spencer and make a run into the house to get to safety, when Cole stood and smiled.

"Finally! You guys can meet Teagan, he'll be shocked to come back to a house full of guests," Cole said.

Holly slumped, letting the tension escape her body. She had come so close to slipping up and ruining their dirty little secret. If Cole noticed, he showed no indication. A kid on a 4-wheeler came into view through the woods, speeding toward the house. Holly looked over to her family and noticed for the first time since they had left New York, Allie had a genuine smile on her face. Having another teen stuck in the woods with them would at least help get her through the boring, electronics-free trip. The boy got closer, his features now distinguishable, and Holly knew right away he would be trouble for Allie. He was a great looking young man; his flowing brown hair blew back in the breeze as he raced along the trail. The boy carried himself in a way that made him appear much older than he really was.

The 4-wheeler threw up dust clouds behind it, giving off an aura around him as he braked and turned the engine off. He looked at everyone out back and smiled, giving a friendly wave. Allie returned the signal, a bit too enthusiastically if Holly was judging, but she tried to not let it bother her. She still wasn't ready to trust this place, but she was afraid to bring it to Anthony's attention, worried he would get too stressed.

"Everyone, I'd like you to meet Teagan, my wonderful, mischievous son. Teagan, this is the Graham family, they own the place and will be crashing here for a little bit."

"Hi everyone! Pleased to meet you all. This place is wonderful, and I think you'll really enjoy it," Teagan said, focusing most of his attention on Allie.

Holly understood the boy was good looking and charming, but her daughter had to understand he was a few years younger than her. And she had a boyfriend, who mere hours ago she had been upset about missing prom with. However, Holly understood; she had been that age once, and her interest from one boy to the next changed with the snap of a finger—prom or no prom. Teagan's smile was electric, even to Holly, and she was pushing her mid-forties. Who was she to judge her daughter for being drawn to it?

"Nice to meet you as well, Teagan," Anthony said, reaching out to shake the kid's hand.

Teagan approached Holly next, shaking her hand gently and moved down the line to the kids. Spencer looked thrilled to see an older boy around; someone he could play with that didn't treat him like a little brother all the time. When Teagan got to Allie, he smiled, and Holly saw her face flush red with embarrassment. That was all the confirmation she needed to know her motherly intuitions were correct.

"Hi, I'm Allie. That 4-wheeler looks fun! Maybe you can show me how to use it while we're here?"

"Sure thing. As long as your parents are cool with it?" He looked over to Anthony and Holly.

"Let's get to know you a little bit first before we agree to let her on that deathtrap," Holly said, more jokingly than serious. She knew the more she tried to pull her daughter away from the boy, the more Allie would be drawn to him, so she had to be careful.

"Mom! I swear they live to embarrass me," Allie snapped.

"Me too!" Spencer said, in an attempt to sound older like his sister.

"Shut up, Spence. You can do no wrong in their eyes."

"Kids, kids. Enough bickering in front of our hosts. Why don't you guys get to know Teagan a bit? Your mother and I need to go rest. Not all of us got to sleep on the car ride," Anthony said.

Holly wanted to question leaving them with complete strangers while they napped but bit her tongue. She would let Anthony know in private how she truly felt about it. She doubted very much that she would sleep knowing they were out here unsupervised.

"Awesome! Can you show us around?" Spencer asked Teagan.

Teagan's eyes went to Anthony, then to his dad, unsure of what to say.

"I'm fine with it if you are, Cole?" Anthony asked.

There was a moment of uncertainty in his face, Holly saw it and knew she should call him out on it. But he spoke up and once again she had to bury the thought in the graveyard of her mind.

"Sure. I don't see why not. Just be careful out there. Teagan is used to this area, you aren't. I think you should walk instead of riding the 4-wheelers for now, got it?" Cole asked.

"Got it, Dad. I'll do a loop around the trails with them and get them back before dinner."

"Perfect, don't be going out in the woods either. No need to get lost their first day here. And stay away from the pond, got it?" Cole asked.

Teagan nodded and led the way. The kids started walking down the trail, Holly watched as their bodies shrank into the horizon. She hadn't seen either of them this happy in a while, maybe it was a good idea after all. She just couldn't shake the feeling this place was giving her. She wasn't sure what it was. Cole was really nice; his son was as well. The land looked beautiful. So, what was it? Ever since they turned onto the dirt road, the area had been spooking her out. Holly hoped that sleep would help and followed Anthony inside to check out their room.

6

SPENCER TRAILED behind the two older kids, trying to keep up with their teenage strides. As soon as they were out of sight from the grownups, his sister turned off her fake smile with him, acting as if every action he did was the most annoying thing in the world. It was so obvious she was attempting to impress Teagan, trying to act way cooler than she really was. It wasn't fair. The first time he had the chance to hang out with an older boy to play with and she'd found a way to ruin it like she always did. All he wanted was for her to be nice to him, to treat him like a person and not some bug that she wanted to squash with the bottom of her shoe. He knew his parents fought all the time, and that it brought a lot of meanness out of his sister toward him. She used to tell him that before he came along, they never fought, and when it was just three of them, life was far more enjoyable. She'd deny saying that if her parents asked of course, but it didn't matter because he would never tell them that anyway, worried it would lead to another argument between them.

It was so hard to pretend he was sleeping in the car on the way here, listening to what his parents were talking about. For smart people, they often assumed he didn't realize what was going on when it was clear as a sunny day right in front of him. Everything they said on the drive to New Hampshire was now etched into his brain. He knew someone killed his dad's friend, and he knew that same person was coming to try and kill his dad. When his mom came in his room the night before to tell him they were going somewhere fun, he saw the truth in her eyes even though he wanted to remain excited, and then heard it when she stopped by Allie's room to tell her to pack.

And then there was the fact that his dad had blood all over his shirt and a bruise on his face when he raced into the driveway. Spencer knew better than to ask him what happened, but he had been dealing with that uncomfortable tightness in his chest that often came along when he felt nervous about stuff. His parents called it anxiety, but he didn't really know what that meant. All he knew was it scared him even more when that feeling came along and made it hard to breathe, like he was choking on his own breath. The older man, Cole, at least made him feel better. He was very nice, and Spencer could tell he was looking out for them. He wasn't doing it in a rude way, but some of the questions he asked made it seem like he wanted to make sure the kids were safe without blaming their parents for anything. One thing he said that stuck with Spencer, was that if they saw anything strange around to let him know. He said he wasn't trying to scare them, but there were many stories of the place going around and he just wanted to make sure if anything happened that he knew about it. Again, he had no desire to bring the conversation to his parent's attention, fueling another fight, and he knew Allie wouldn't say anything because she was too busy putting all her attention on the shiny new toy, Teagan.

He couldn't hear what they were saying, so he ran to catch up. The deeper into the trail they got, the spookier it all was to Spencer. He could see why Cole didn't want them going in the woods, the trail was almost like a maze by itself, a bunch of scary trees towering over them like they were watching the kids' every move. He was also getting the feeling he did when he thought there was a monster under his bed or in his closet, except the entire forest was his dark closet, and the monsters were surrounding him.

"Hey guys, wait up!" he yelled.

Allie turned around, rolling her eyes. "Spence, if you can't keep up, so be it. Once a bear took a bite of you it would spit you out anyway as soon as it realized you taste like the inside of a clogged toilet," she said, laughing—until she looked to Teagan and saw he felt bad.

"Don't worry little man, bears don't tend to come around these parts. No animals do really. Outside of the random bird here and there, maybe some squirrels and chipmunks. But the deeper out here we get, the less of them we see. It's strange." Teagan patted Spencer on the head.

If that was supposed to make him feel better, it only added to the creepiness of these woods. Until Teagan said that, Spencer hadn't noticed how silent the wilderness really was out here. Not that he was an expert on the matter considering the only wild animals he ever saw were pigeons and rats in the city.

They continued walking, the conversation between Teagan and Allie hogging most of the trek and forcing Spencer to remain silent —something that was very difficult for him to do with so many questions swirling around in his head. As much as the place scared him, it also fascinated him in equal measure. The only trees he'd ever seen were in Central Park. His dad always assumed because he made good money and bought them whatever they wanted that everyone was happy. Spencer would trade in half of his toys and video games if it meant his parents being happier and going on fun, family trips around the world to see different places. It wasn't fair that they had so much money, yet he had been confined to the same city his entire life.

The forest gradually filled out the longer they walked. All Spencer could see in every direction were more and more trees on each side of the trail. They rounded a corner, the house long out of view behind them, and approached an open space up ahead.

"This up here's the first camp site. My dad told me it's where he camped the first time he came here. I've tried to keep all the weeds out and cut back the branches from it so it's good to go for your dad when he sells the place," Teagan said.

"There isn't any running water at the sites?" Allie asked. "We haven't really been camping before, but I assumed that would be customary?" Spencer noticed her face turning red again, thinking she must have asked a stupid question.

"Actually, you *would* think that's the case. I can't say I've been to many campgrounds myself, but I think most do have at least a water spigot at them. This place feels very old-school, like the previous owner wanted to keep it off the grid to give people the sense they were sleeping in the wild," Teagan said, shrugging.

They walked past the first site deeper into the woods, seeing many other campsites along the way. Each of them had been well maintained, proving Teagan and his dad really had done a great job taking care of the place for them.

"So, how'd your dad know the previous owner, anyway? My dad said he was the groundskeeper for the campground before it went out of business?" Allie asked.

Teagan looked away from her. "I guess so... my dad doesn't tell me much about that time. He said we came back here to look out for the place. I didn't really think anything of it when I was as small as Spencer, but the older I get, the more questions I have. And he does everything he can to change the subject when I do ask."

"Like he's hiding something?" Spencer asked.

Allie gave him a nasty glare. She said nothing, but she didn't need to.

"I would like to hope not, bud. He isn't the type to usually do that sort of thing. I've kinda learned to avoid asking about the war, what went on here before I was born, and my mom. As much as I want to know things, I can tell it upsets him, so I try to avoid bringing that stuff up if I can."

"What happened to your mom?" Spencer asked.

"Jesus, Spence! Stop asking him all these personal questions, we just met him," Allie said with another angry look.

Teagan smirked before saying, "It's really okay. He's just a kid. My dad tells me stories about my mom all the time, but as far as what happened to her, well he really doesn't say much. Part of why he wanted to come back here was to be close to where he met her. He says she was the most beautiful woman he ever set his eyes on… that she saved him from depression and made his life worth living." Teagan's eyes shone.

"That's so beautiful… I wish we could've met her. She sounds amazing," Allie said.

"Yeah… then he says she got really sick, and it changed her. That's where the stories stop. But that's okay, I just want to hear the good memories anyway." Teagan looked down at his feet.

"What was her name?" Allie asked.

"Her name was Rebecca."

———————————

They had been walking for a while longer when Teagan stopped at the edge of the trail.

"Okay, we should probably head back so we get you there in time for dinner like I promised."

Allie wanted to keep going, she couldn't help but be fascinated by Teagan. Yes, he was younger than her. But the way he looked at her, the way he presented himself with such confidence… It made her okay with being away from her friends for a few days. She was about to turn around and head back toward the house when Spencer got excited by something he saw through the woods.

"Wow! Is that a pond? Can we swim in it?" he asked excitedly.

Allie looked through the trees and could just make out a body of water down behind a small hill. She had no idea how Spencer saw it, so hidden from plain sight. From where she stood, the water looked gross, almost like antifreeze it was so green.

"No, buddy. You don't want to go near that water, okay? It's contaminated or something, we don't get close to it. My dad insisted from the day we got here that I don't go down there.

Besides, does it really look like something you'd swim in?" Teagan asked with a smile.

"You should see how gross his bath-water gets," Allie joked.

"Just avoid that area, man. Pretty much every other spot is fine to walk through," Teagan reaffirmed.

"Okay... It just looks so *cool*," Spencer said, still in awe as he walked a little closer to the edge of the path.

Allie approached him, ready to head back to the house and eat. She put her hand on his shoulder and pulled him back in the direction they had come.

"Let's go. I'm starving..." she said.

As they all started to head back, Allie stopped and glanced down one more time toward the strange pond. Spencer and Teagan didn't notice that she'd stopped following.

The water was bright green, giving off a slight glow. A dock sat in the center, proving that at one point people must have swum in it. Before she turned to leave, something in the water caught her eye. For a brief second, she thought she saw dark shadows under the surface, moving around slowly. *What is that?* she thought. It was unlikely that fish would be able to survive in there. But as green as it was, it strangely looked very clean. The longer she stared at it, the more it drew her in. A buzzing voice spoke in her head, telling her to come. Touch the water, it would feel amazing. So smooth, so *soft*.

"Hey! You coming or what?" Teagan yelled from the trail.

Allie jumped, the voice snapping her out of her daze. She felt her face go red again.

"Yeah, sorry... I thought I saw something is all," she said and hurried to catch up to them.

Teagan gave a look of concern, staring over her shoulder toward the water, and then smiled and kept walking.

7

ANTHONY FELL INTO A DEEP SLUMBER, something that came easy after not getting an ounce of sleep the previous night. It didn't take long for strange dreams to follow, but he knew he was dreaming. His subconscious told him so. That didn't help the uneasiness he felt pumping through his veins.

In the dream it was nightfall, and he was sitting in the woods next to a pond. He recalled seeing this body of water when he bought the place, hidden down farther in the woods, only now it was giving off a green glow a few inches above the surface. He had no idea why he was here; since he bought the place, he hadn't been back to this spot. The spaces between the trees surrounding the pond were pure black, an infinite nothingness where the world ended. Anthony stood up, confused, and walked toward the dock while he looked around for any sign of life. The area was blanketed in the darkness of night, all except for the water. He could have sworn the brightness of the water was pulsating, like it had its own heartbeat. *What the fuck is this place?* He walked closer to the water, which started to move. Dark shadows shifted below the surface, getting darker as they rose closer to the top. Anthony couldn't help himself, he continued walking, stepping onto the dock and trudging to the very end.

All of a sudden, the stillness of the pond changed, water crashing against the dock like the waves of a powerful ocean. Then the water began to bubble, increasing in temperature to the point that it started giving off a dense layer of steam. He wanted to run, but the dream was insistent that he stand and watch whatever was about to happen.

The bubbles stopped, the night returning to silence.

And then, one by one, figures slowly rose out of the water. Their bodies were moon white, their skin covered in thick, green algae. Men, women, and children all rose out of the water with glowing white eyes—perfect orbs with no pupils in the center. Their faces were sunken in, but some of the skin still appeared bloated in areas due to water soaking them like human sponges. He noticed they all had white robes on, but the colors had stained green from the algae and muck. Every single one of them floated in the water submerged from the chest down.

They stared at him in silence, and even though he knew it was a nightmare, his throat tightened up, squeezed by an invisible set of hands. It was the most terrifying thing he'd ever seen in his life. He was afraid to move, worried that if he did, they would no longer remain still, and he didn't think he could handle seeing the rest of their bodies coming out of the water and reaching for him. Anthony began hyperventilating and took deep breaths to calm his nerves. *It's just a dream. It's just a dream.* In unison, all the figures lifted an arm and pointed toward him—no—pointed *behind* him. And then, the unsettling feeling of heavy breathing on the back of his neck sent gooseflesh into a frenzy. Slowly, he turned around, and came face to face with a tall, lean figure. The man was one of them, but one look at him and Anthony knew right away he was their leader. He had long black hair that clung to his head in wet muddy clumps. His thick beard dripped green pond water onto the dock as he stared down at Anthony. His skin was a light green. Unlike the others, his eyes weren't white, they glowed green to match the water, and for a brief second Anthony thought maybe the pulsing water matched the pulse of his eyes, like they were connected to one another. The man towered over Anthony, scrutinizing him. Even if Anthony had wanted to run, there was nowhere to go now, the man was blocking the narrow dock, and he sure as hell was not going to jump in the water with the rest of them—dream or not. All he wanted in that moment was for Holly to wake him up.

"Bring us the girl..." the man said, his voice immediately soothing Anthony.

Those eyes, he couldn't help staring into them.

"What girl?" Anthony asked, already knowing the answer.

"Your daughter. Bring her to us, and in doing so we will protect her, and your family," he said with a smile.

"Who are you? How will you protect us?"

"My name is Alister Burns... this is my family," he said, while pointing out toward the pond at the floating figures. *"And this is our home. Bring her to us, and she can live on forever."* Alister's smile now expanded to an unsettling gape. But Anthony didn't care about that. Staring into those eyes made him feel like he'd do anything asked of him.

"How do I know you will keep her safe?" Anthony asked, knowing he was going to do it regardless of the answer.

"You have my word..."

"I don't know... I love my family." Anthony felt as though he was merely cycling through the stuff it thought he *had* to say before eventually giving in—his heart wasn't in it.

The grin still on his face, Alister slowly shook his head. *"All the more reason to do as I say, my friend."* He then slowly walked toward Anthony, snapping him out of his hypnotic trance. Alister's face started to shift, his skin turning translucent. Underneath the surface, veins pulsed, matching the water, matching his green eyes. Anthony was suddenly paralyzed with fear. He realized Alister was coming toward him, preparing to do something. He forced himself to back up, trying to keep the distance between them, afraid to let the tall man get close enough to touch him. And then, his feet reached the end of the dock, he turned to see his next step would in fact drop him into the water with... *them.* The bodies looked frozen in time; their white globe-like eyes all locked on him.

The dock creaked, snapping his attention back. Alister was much closer now, his face stretching, his mouth opening abnormally wide like his jaw was made of putty. A soft moaning escaped the tall man as he reached his hand out toward Anthony and continued striding closer.

"Come HERE, let me show you the way Anthony..."

"NO! Leave me alone!"

The hand was boney and white, the skin caked with green algae where a webbing that looked like loose skin connected each finger, the nails an even darker shade of green.

It was inches from his face.

He closed his eyes and screamed.

—————————

"Anthony! Wake up! You're having a horrible nightmare," Holly said as she shook her husband awake.

He opened his eyes, which darted around the room looking for something that wasn't there.

"What... Holy shit! It was so real..."

"It's okay, take some deep breaths. Were you dreaming about them?"

At first, Holly could see the confusion in his face, taking a moment to register with him who she was talking about.

"No... I don't wanna talk about it, okay?" Anthony said, slightly agitated.

"Well, when you want to talk about it, I—"

"Jesus! I said let it go, seeing one therapist is bad enough, I don't need you pretending to be one too!"

Holly flinched. Hearing him talk like that reminded her how imperfect their relationship truly was. All she wanted to do was make him feel better, yet he treated her like she was nagging away at him. She got up from the bed and walked toward the door. She was about to walk out when Anthony spoke again.

"I'm... I'm sorry. I'm stressed beyond belief. All this shit is really starting to get to me. And to top it all off, I forgot my anxiety meds at the fucking house," he said.

Holly shook her head, holding in what she truly wanted to say. She was trying so hard to avoid confrontation right now; they had enough trouble to worry about.

"It's okay..." she said and walked out the door.

8

AFTER DINNER, they all sat outside talking amongst one another, laughing, and telling stories. Cole knew they weren't telling him something, but he didn't want to pry too much in front of the kids. And hell, who was he to judge? He hadn't said a damn word about why he returned to the place after being gone for so long. Once the kids were in bed, he planned to tell them everything about the place, but he also intended to get more information from them about why they were really here.

When he'd been in the war, one of the many skills he'd mastered was interrogation. How to read if someone was telling the truth or not. How to read the emotions someone was feeling just by looking into their eyes. Cole knew the Graham family feared something, and he liked to be prepared for any scenarios. He may have lost his leg in the war, but his knack for needing to know all the logistics never went away. Cole stood, walked around the patio table, and grabbed the dirty dishes. It was a cool summer night, the only light illuminating from the flickering torches he'd set up around the walkway from the house to the table. The dinner brought flashbacks of his time living at the campground.

"Let me help you with those dishes," Holly said, bringing him back to reality.

"Oh, thank you. I usually just stick them in the sink and load the dishwasher in the morning. No need to ruin a great dinner by doing more work after," he said with a smile.

"Thank you so much for the lovely meal. You sure grill like a pro," she said.

"About the only thing I can cook is meat and vegetables. Please don't ask me to bake a cake."

Holly laughed. "No birthdays to celebrate anytime soon, so you're safe on that front."

They walked in the backdoor with their hands full while Anthony sat out at the table talking with the kids. Cole noticed he seemed off since his nap, almost as if he were more tired now than he had been before he slept. Anthony told Cole he slept like a baby and felt great, but Cole didn't believe him.

Cole tried to loosen him up with a few drinks—which he quit himself years ago—but he still only got short answers and half of Anthony's attention while they ate. The rest of his attention was focused on something over Cole's shoulder toward the woods, leaving an uneasy feeling in the pit of Cole's stomach.

"Can you tell us where the closest pharmacy is? Anthony needed to grab some medicine that he forgot at the house," Holly asked, rinsing the plates in the sink.

"Well, your best bet is to head back over the town line into Newport and hit up one there. The gas station here in Goshen might have some painkillers on hand, but I wouldn't trust them. Not many people come through these parts since the campground shut down. I'd put money on anything they have being well past expiration."

"Thank you, I'll let him know so he can head into town tomorrow then."

Holly turned off the sink and started to walk toward the back door to rejoin her family.

"He looking for something to help the pain on that arm of his?

Looked like a nasty wound covered up there, what on earth happened to him?" Cole asked, knowing it was time to start digging for information. His suspicions were quickly confirmed when she appeared flustered at the thought of having to answer.

"He... well he got a deep cut on his arm and tried to bandage it himself. But no, he takes a medication to help with stress," she said, changing the subject.

"I see. Anyways, I'll bring out some drinks if you want one."

"*I* need to go to bed is what I need. I didn't sleep like Anthony did earlier. Thanks for offering though. I'm just going to say goodnight to everyone." She walked back outside.

Cole grabbed a beer for Anthony and a water for himself and followed her out. He had a feeling they had a lot to talk about tonight.

———————————

Anthony sat staring at the fire Cole started after dinner. Holly and the kids had all gone to bed; it was now just the two of them. After a few beers, he started to feel more like himself, the stress of the previous night with Vincent's crew, mixed with the God-awful nightmare he had earlier, numbed for now.

"So, I've kept you on here all these years, but I never really got to know you well, Cole. Let's hear your story. I know you got injured during the war, but why come *here*? This town has nothing," Anthony said.

"Suppose you're right. And I suppose there's a lot I need to tell ya. You sure you don't need another beer before I start?" Cole asked, trying to lighten the mood.

"Man, I got two here ready to go after this one. I needed to blow off some steam, so thanks for having these on hand. You said you quit drinking though, why do you stock up on beer? Doesn't that tempt you at all?"

"I'm well past the point where temptation calls to me anymore. I have all I need in Teagan. As far as having it on hand, once in a while we get some straggler kids that want to get off on some kind of thrill and sneak out here camping without permission. A group tried it last weekend and I chased them off; they left the booze behind."

"Wow, look at me. Reminds me of my R.A. days in college. Take the beer from underage kids and save it for later," Anthony said with a smile.

"So… I guess starting at the beginning's as good a place as any. Hope you don't think I'm crazy once I tell my story."

"After the shit I've been through the last two days, I'm not so sure anything would seem crazy…"

"I told you guys about my time in the Army. All of that's true. What is also true is I came here to this rinky-dink town to get away and start fresh. Getting a high-end job isn't exactly something I can do with one leg. I get enough off disability to survive, but only when I live somewhere that has a low cost of living. Anyways, I moved here, minding my own business, and working random dead-end jobs for a few months. Then I met Alister Burns—"

Cole stopped, seeing the name bring a reaction he didn't expect out of Anthony.

"I'm sorry, Alister Burns? Why do I know that name?"

"I don't know, but he was a bad, *bad* man. When I met him, he offered to bring me back here to introduce me to his family. Said he could help heal the pain I was dealing with every step of every day. Have you noticed how much pain I'm in, Anthony?"

"Actually, no. You seem fine for someone that went through what you did."

"Exactly. So, please understand before this story gets batshit crazy, everything I'm about to tell you is the God's honest truth, I swear on my life. Anyways, I reluctantly followed him here. Like I said, I worked dead-end jobs and made enough money off disability, so I didn't care about my job. He introduced me to everyone, at least twenty others that lived here. It's where I met my Rebecca.

"The first night I was here, we all walked down to the pond— that pond I tell you all not to go near, and for good reason— and he told me he could make the pain go away in my knee, ear, hell, my entire *body*. I thought he was a quack, but I had nothing to lose, so I went along with it for shits and giggles. We get down to the pond, and I see the odd color of it which immediately threw up red flags, but his eyes had a way of making you do what he wanted. Then some other fella—who'd been giving me the strange eye all night—walks out on the dock and carries some peculiar cup with him. Next thing I know, Alister's talking to the water like some freak, asking them to help heal me, and in return this man with the cup says he'll *sacrifice* himself to them.

"I couldn't believe what I was seeing or hearing, I just stood there dumbfounded watching it all happen. Alister starts talking in some foreign language, all the others surrounding the pond chanting along. It gave me the creeps." Cole paused to see if Anthony was following along.

"So why the hell did you hang around? I would've jetted the fuck out of there in a second."

"Well, I'm getting to that. The man out on the dock, he looked scared at first, but then he starts smiling at me. I felt goosebumps down my back when he did. And then—it all happened in slow motion—he drank from the cup and started convulsing, tweaking out, with his eyes rolling into the back of his head. Then he drew a knife... I tried to run out and stop him, but my damn leg wouldn't let me. I fell to the ground on account of wine and a fake leg not mixing too well together. When I looked up, he'd slit his own fucking throat and fallen into the water..." Cole stopped for a minute, the pain in his eyes obvious.

"In that moment, I thought I could kill Alister. I'd fought in the war to stop people like him from brainwashing crazy followers to sacrifice themselves for their religion. I rushed toward Alister, but as soon as his eyes locked on mine, the urge to strangle the bastard drained from my body. Don't get me wrong, I was still pissed off inside, but I knew I wasn't going to do anything to him. What happened next is really hard to talk about... to this day it is the scariest thing I ever saw, and that's saying a lot after being blown up by a car bomb."

Anthony found himself fascinated by the story, not wanting Cole to stop. He needed to know what happened next. His dream from earlier had come crashing back—and what Alister had asked of him. The thought of *sacrificing* his own daughter made him sick. How could he have agreed to do it in the dream? He had no intention of telling Cole about it, that was for damn sure.

"So, I stood on the dock, face to face with Alister. He saw the rage in my eyes, but he knew I saw the calmness in *his*. The cocky son of a bitch didn't even flinch when I came at him. Then the water starts moving, like a miniature ocean, splashing against the dock as if it had a current with massive waves slamming against the beams. I asked him what was happening, but he just smiled that smile. After that, dark shadows appeared under the green surface. I wasn't sure what they were at first. I tried to run off the dock to get away when a set of hands shot up from the water and grabbed hold of my leg, tripping me. More hands came out of the water, all of them forcing me down on the dock while Alister spoke in the language of their God, putting his palm over my face. I could feel something being sucked out of my body but didn't know at the time it was the pain he was sucking out. Like a damn vacuum. But whatever he did, it took all my energy away and I blacked out. When I woke up, I was strapped to a bed, the pain I'd been living with since the war was completely gone."

Anthony sat with his mouth open, in disbelief. "Wow... So, you're telling me he sacrificed this other man and that it *fixed* you just like that?" he asked, snapping his fingers.

"Yes... I know it sounds crazy, but to this day I can walk without agony sucking the life out of me with every step. And I gained back hearing in my left ear, something I'd lost during the explosion. I'm telling you all this, so you understand why I stayed after. I didn't feel great about it, watching him sacrifice people year after year, but I saw that it worked. And one look into his eyes made it impossible to say no to him."

You don't have to say that twice, Anthony thought, recalling the dream again.

"Even if I wanted to leave, I was head over heels for Rebecca at that point. Not only would I do anything Alister asked of me, but she had me wrapped around her finger. I'm sure you could put the pieces together, but Teagan is her son. *Our* son," Cole said, staring into the crackling of the fire pit in front of them. A moment of silence followed, allowing the crickets to pick back up with their nightly song.

"On Teagan's second birthday, Rebecca came running out of the house crying. It was the dead of winter... I was freezing my ass off about to walk back down to my campsite when she came to me. She said they planned to sacrifice Teagan. Now, I went along with everything he asked up until that point, but he'd *never* sacrificed a kid before. And this was my kid. My blood was boiling, I could feel the fire building inside myself. I told her we needed to come up with a plan—in private—to get out of here..." A log collapsed in the fire, making Anthony jump slightly.

"I'll spare you most of the details from here—you get the point. But what I will say, is that when I went to our spot later that night, she wasn't there. Only blood-soaked snow covered the ground. I panicked, running to the house knowing full well that they did something to her. What I never expected, was for her to *help* them. I know for a fact that earlier that day she was on my side. Alister must have done something to her in between and made her remember who she was truly there for. She was ready to let them take Teagan when I found her in the house. I had to fight for my life, but I got the boy and I out of there alive."

"What about Rebecca? You said she was dead, but it sounds like you left before anything happened?" Anthony asked, his curiosity now outweighing his courtesy.

Cole scratched his beard scruff, staring into the fire, his eyes welling up.

"Yeah... Well, whether she's dead or not... she's dead to *me*. I returned years later, once Teagan was older, to bring them to justice. Whether that meant getting the police involved, going rogue myself, I didn't know. I didn't really have a plan, which isn't like me. But I wanted Alister to pay for what he tried to do to my boy, and what he *did* do to my Rebecca. Only, when I showed up... nobody was here. They vanished. Didn't you wonder why I was clinging to this place like a crazy ex when you came to buy it? I made a pact with myself to hang around for any sign of them, whether it be in person or down at the pond. But it feels like even if they did stay here and sacrifice themselves in that water—something Alister always talked about doing eventually—they aren't going out of their way to let me know it. Nothing happens when I set foot near the pond..."

"Man, that is some crazy shit right there. I'm sorry you went through all that. I can't even imagine," Anthony responded.

"Now you know why I practically begged you to let me stay on the property and maintain it until you sold it. In my heart I always believed they would come back here, one way or another..."

"Once the bank took over the land, it would have gone to shit had I not had someone on to keep it groomed. You were a blessing. Now that you mention it, it *was* odd for you to be around when the place had been shut down for a few years. And hell, I wish I didn't just laugh at the stories I'd heard about the place. I might be stuck with this place forever now." Anthony shook his head.

"They aren't exactly the easiest stories to believe. I don't fault you for having common sense and thinking it's all bullshit. So, now you know my story. Let's hear *yours*. Why are you *really* here, Mr. Graham?"

Anthony sighed and cracked open a new beer. He was going to need it.

9

BILLY THREW his high beams on as he pulled onto Coon Brook Road. He looked over in the passenger seat at Nikki, wishing she would give him a little shotgun love while he drove in the dark. They were still only a few months into dating, and he had no idea how he'd gotten a girl as hot and cool as Nikki. Maybe she was just going through her bad boy phase, dating the biggest slimeball she could in hopes of pissing off her parents. Maybe she had weird taste in guys —his crooked teeth and awkward posture somehow a turn on for her. Whatever the reasons, Billy didn't care. He and Nikki were a few years removed from high school, the victims of getting stuck in the hometown blues. She never would have dated him in high school considering how popular she was. Billy was at the complete opposite end of the popularity scale. Nobody picked on him, however, knowing if they did, he would kick their ass and send them to the hospital.

He glanced over at her again, taking his eyes off the narrow dirt road that only the dual beams of his headlights kept from being completely shrouded in darkness. She wore a revealing tank top with her breasts firmly pushed up, exposing ample cleavage to his wanting eyes. She knew what she was doing, and she was doing it to perfection. He found it hard to concentrate on the road while imagining all the things he planned on doing with her tonight. They lived a few towns over in Claremont but had found it was starting to bore them to death. If Billy's dad cared enough about him to joke around, he would have said the two fucked like a couple of rabbits, finding any hidden spot or dark alley to get each other off. It was a thrill to them, but something that was starting to lose its excitement while sticking to their normal spots. So, when Nikki suggested they drive to Goshen and sneak into the old Bird's Nest campground for the night, he couldn't pack his bags fast enough. Her friends had tried the same the week prior and it ended abruptly when the crazy man living there scared them off.

They'd heard all the stories, how the place was haunted, how it used to be owned by an evil cult that disappeared before the bank eventually seized control of the place and sold it. But that's what made it such an exciting adventure.

"How about a little pre-game action before we set up the tent?" Billy asked, faking an innocent tone.

Nikki looked over and smiled, then stared down at his lap. "Looks like you already pitched a tent, Mr. Billy."

She said it so seductively, Billy wasn't sure he could wait until they set up before they had sex. Up until he met Nikki, his life had been headed in the wrong direction. He'd gone from weed to dabbling with more hardcore drugs; started drinking hard liquor instead of beer. It was a wonder he could hold down a job, not that he held one of importance. He also knew that girls like Nikki eventually got bored of the bad boy lust, and that it was only a matter of time before she left him for a more serious relationship. She'd straightened him up a bit, but not enough to ruin his image. Part of him did want to straighten up even more, to get a real job, or hell, even go back to school and make something of himself. His mom had left him with his dad when he was just a toddler. As much as she loved him, she loved heroin more. He was too young at the time to comprehend it; all he knew was that his dad said she was a useless whore who couldn't raise a child anyway. But when he got older, he found out that her love for the drug had ended her life at the ripe age of thirty-five. His dad took out the fact that he had to be a single parent on Billy every day growing up. It's why Billy moved out the minute he turned eighteen, telling himself he wouldn't be a lowlife like both his parents. Funny how things turn out because a lowlife was exactly what he'd become. *The apple doesn't fall far from the tree,* he thought.

He drove past the campground sign and continued up the road, driving slowly to not awaken anyone that might happen to be around.

"Hey, where are you going, Billy? You missed the entrance," Nikki said.

"We need to sneak in through the woods, find a place to park on the side of the road up here. You said the guy with one leg still lives here; don't need to be waking his old ass up. Last thing I need is him seeing my white ass on top of you before we finish," he said with a grin.

As they rounded a corner, Billy spotted the perfect place to park his truck, a flat area that he assumed had previously been used as a pull-off for campers while they waited to check in at the office off to the right. He slowed the truck down and turned off the main road into the old lot. Trees hung over the opening, creating the ideal spot to hide the vehicle without being detected. Billy killed the engine and quietly opened his door. He noticed Nikki wasn't moving, just staring out the window into the darkness.

"What's wrong? Don't tell me you're having second thoughts?" he asked.

"No... It's just... This is fucking creepy, Billy. I wasn't thinking we'd have to walk through the woods to get there. It's not exactly a turn on to hike through a haunted forest in the dark," she said hesitantly.

"This place is shut down, what are you worried about? I'll be doing things far worse to you than anything out there," he joked.

"It's not that. Don't the stories scare you at all? Like, for that many people to be afraid of this place, some of it *has* to be true, right?"

"Which is why this was your idea in the first place. To get our rocks off in a cursed forest. Isn't that the damn point?" he asked, now starting to get frustrated.

"I know... Sorry for being such a wimp. Give me a sip of that bottle you got hidden over there before we go at least," she said.

Billy handed her the bottle of bourbon he always kept tucked in his driver's side cubby. She pulled the cap off and took a long swig of the liquor, her eyes squeezing shut to try and calm the burning sensation sliding down into her stomach. She shook her head and let out a deep breath, handing him back the bottle.

"That's a damn good idea," he said, then took a giant gulp himself. Unlike Nikki, he didn't even flinch, years of drinking numbing him to the burn.

They got out of the truck and were struck with the sound of complete silence. Billy knew they would be changing that in short order; he intended to make her scream his name so that all the birds and rodents out in these woods could hear it. The plan was to set up far enough away from the main office so the old man wouldn't wake, then take off before dawn. He grabbed the tent and backpack out of the bed of the truck, then with his free hand he took out his phone and turned on the flashlight.

He nodded toward the woods and looked at Nikki.

"Okay, you ready? Let's get dangerous."

———————

Nikki followed Billy into the dark woods, the dead branches crunching under their feet as they walked. She wouldn't admit it to him, but she really was starting to have second thoughts on her brilliant idea. The truth was, she didn't see them lasting much longer together. Things had begun getting boring. The main reason she started sleeping with Billy in the first place was to make her ex-boyfriend, Steve, jealous. He cheated on her, and when she found out his excuse was that she was waiting to have sex for the first time, she decided to seek out losing her virginity. He called her a prude, saying she thought she was too good for him and that it was *her* fault he cheated. Steve was one of the most sought-after men in town, but she wouldn't allow anyone to talk to her like that. Nobody would cheat on her and get away with it.

When she started seeing Billy, she never intended to take it as far as they did. She got drunk one night, and when she came across him in the school parking lot smoking weed with a few friends, she walked up to them and asked to join. Nikki was heartbroken, just wanting to ease the heartache and get fucked up. After Billy's friends left, it was just the two of them. They talked late into the night, talked until things got a bit more intense. Maybe it was the weed, maybe it was her drive to show Steve he messed up. The night ended with them having sex in the bed of his truck, a spot that became fairly regular over the proceeding months. To her delight, when Steve found out, he lost his mind, getting his friends together to try and beat the shit out of Billy. When Billy took them all out single-handedly, something changed in Nikki. Something she never expected. She found herself *falling* for Billy. The spark was real for the first month or so. The longer they dated, the more she realized Billy really wasn't her type at all. And the thought of even introducing him to her parents was out of the question. Coming to Bird's Nest was a last-ditch effort for her to try and rekindle the spark before she determined if she wanted to end things with him.

As they got deeper into the woods, her drive for passion was shifting to a drive to get the hell out of the woods. Sharp branches poked and scraped at her exposed skin while she walked through the darkness. Billy's phone only provided a few feet of light in front of them, and with her trailing behind him, she got even less of the illumination to use. She squeezed onto the back of his shirt, like a baby holding its blankie. The closeness of Billy only made her feel slightly better. The forest was dead silent, not a single cricket chirping, no wind to rustle the leaves. It only added to the eeriness as they walked deeper into the suffocating black hole of the forest.

"Billy, are we almost there?" she asked.

"How the hell should I know? It's not like I go scouting places to bone my lady beforehand," he said.

She decided to stay quiet and let herself trust that if anything happened, he would protect her. He *did* take down Steve and all his loser friends by himself, what could be worse out here? Up ahead, Nikki noticed the woods thinning out approaching what appeared to be a campsite. *Thank fucking God*, she thought. They picked up the pace at the sight of open land. When they arrived, Nikki turned to look back at the woods they had just come from, watching for any sign of life. Even though they didn't hear anything, she could *sense* something there. The woods felt much colder, like they were hiking in a giant freezer, and as soon as they hit open land, she couldn't help but notice the temperature increased by at least twenty degrees. She told herself that when they left, she wouldn't go anywhere near those woods again.

"Okay, I'll set up the tent here. Quick and easy access… just like I want with your shorts tonight," he said with a large grin.

Nikki couldn't help but smile. On the other side of the scary woods, the thought of fucking his brains out thrilled her once more. She realized how ridiculous she was being. One minute she was turned on, and the next she wanted to scream and run home. In the end, it would all add to the excitement. Billy handed her his phone to hold the light while he set up the pop-up tent. He moved with precision, as though he'd done this many times before. Maybe he was just overly excited, or maybe he had done this with many other girls. She tried to push that thought away and bring her focus back to his toned triceps as he pushed the stakes into the ground to hold the tent firmly in place. Within five minutes, the tent was ready to go… and so was she.

Billy threw down the sleeping bag he'd shoved into his backpack, followed by a pillow. Once he zipped the door shut, he picked her up with ease and brought her down to the floor of the tent, kissing the side of her neck. Nikki closed her eyes and inhaled deeply, enjoying every single kiss. *Maybe this will last after all*, she thought.

She threw her head back, allowing him access to her neck. Nikki opened her eyes, and from her upside-down view, she spotted multiple silhouettes standing outside the tent, like they were frozen in place and observing. She screamed, pushing Billy off and turned back over to a crouched position.

"What the fuck, Nik—" Billy started, then shifted his attention to what she was staring at. The tall figures were still there, motionless.

"Billy, you need to do something..." Nikki trailed off, panic seizing her.

"Hey assholes! If you want a peep show, why don't you try to come in here and see what happens!" Billy yelled, sounding much more confident than he looked.

He jumped up, unzipping the tent, and burst out into the darkness, leaving Nikki alone. She felt helpless, now unable to see or touch the one person she felt would keep her safe. Billy's shadow moved along the side of the tent, hardly visible, with only the moon providing any sort of light outside. He walked around to the side where they'd spotted the figures. Billy laughed. Nikki realized the shadows were now gone. Only Billy's shadow remained.

"Babe, it's just trees back here, the moonlight must be playing tricks on us," Billy said quietly.

"No, Billy. They're gone. Whoever it was isn't there anymore!"

"Quiet down, Nikki. I'm telling you, the trees here are casting off the strange shapes. The moon must have shifted." He walked back around the front of the tent.

She didn't believe him, her eyes locked in place on the far wall facing the forest. With her attention focused on the tent, she momentarily forgot about her boyfriend. The door unzipping made her jump, leading Billy to laugh even harder.

"Oh man, this is going to be so fun... Isn't this just what we wanted? To be scared shitless and live on the edge a bit?" he asked.

Nikki let out a nervous laugh, then hesitantly nodded.

Billy was about to re-enter the tent when he looked off to the side at something Nikki couldn't see. She watched another smile slowly spread on his face.

"Say... I have an idea. Come with me, Nik," he said, holding out his hand to her.

Unsure what he had in mind, she reached out and grabbed his hand anyway. Any place would be better than here. They slipped their shoes back on and Nikki followed him along a trail, deeper into the campground.

"What exactly is your idea, genius?" she asked.

"Well, rumor has it there is a swimming hole at the rear of the property. What do you say about getting frisky in the water before we head back to the tent?"

The idea seemed ridiculous. They had spent less than half an hour in this shithole and she'd already been spooked more times than she had from all the horror movies she had watched combined. There was absolutely no way it was just in her head. After walking for a few minutes, the trail came to an end. Taller grass welcomed them, still on the windless night. Billy stopped and searched for the pond. Nikki glanced down at her feet and realized that while they were now standing in tall grass, the remains of an overgrown trail headed in the direction they were facing. Her eyes followed it until she saw through the batch of trees in front of them. Through the darkness, the water's surface shined with the moon beaming down on it. Billy followed her gaze and pulled her closer.

"Good eye, babe! Let's go check it out," he said, marching down the slope through the trees before she could argue.

When they got through the trees, the pond came into view more clearly, and Nikki found herself staring at the water, wanting to touch it. All the fears she had leading up to this moment vanished. It looked so... *soothing*. The moon shining down produced a slight, green glow, giving the pond a magical appearance. She spotted a dock going out into the water and squealed with joy, charging past Billy.

"Don't seem too scared now, do ya?" he asked while trying to catch up with her.

Nikki ran out onto the dock and held up her hands toward the sky, spinning like a Disney princess.

"It's beautiful, Billy, isn't it?"

"No... *you're* beautiful," he countered.

She lowered one of her hands, gesturing him to come join her. As he walked toward the dock, she pulled her shirt up over her head and threw it to the wooden floor. Billy picked up his pace, not wanting to waste another second. The air was brisk, but a small fog clung to the surface of the water, indicating the temperature was enticing. As he approached, he began taking his clothes off and dropping them to the side. When he reached Nikki, he had nothing on.

"I want you so bad right now," she said.

"Then come and get me!" Billy yelled, charging past her, and jumping into the water.

A warm splash shot up and hit Nikki's exposed chest, and for a moment she was tempted to jump in after him. It felt like bathwater.

"Come on, Billy! Every time I start getting comfortable out here you decide to make it that much creepier. I don't want to go out there, I can't even *see* what's in that water," she pouted.

Nikki sat on the dock, then lay down and stared up at the stars. The thrill she was feeling was exactly what she wanted when the idea to come here popped into her head. There was no way she would jump in after Billy though. She planned to wait right here until he realized he was an idiot for hopping in the water when he could already be inside her.

"Oh, man. You have to come out here. This water's so nice. Let's go for a swim first. I'm telling you, you won't regret it!"

She looked in his direction, barely able to make out his head floating above the water.

"I don't think so... if you want to do this, it doesn't happen until you're back up here," she responded.

The fresh air felt so good. Nikki closed her eyes and inhaled deeply, taking in the peace and quiet. The sounds of Billy swimming continued with soft, consistent strokes of the water. *Maybe this will work out after all*, she thought again, enjoying the spontaneous night to its fullest. Through her closed eyes, she sensed it getting brighter around her, like staring at the sun with only her eyelids to block out the UV rays. Confused, she opened them and looked back at the water. The brightness was intensifying, the green color so vibrant.

"Billy, what's happening?" she asked.

Billy didn't answer.

That's when she realized she didn't see him in the water, and that the sound of his strokes had ceased.

"This isn't funny, Billy! Come out of the water, or I'm leaving!"

The joke was over. She wanted to get back to the tent, or maybe even the truck. The pleasant sensation she initially felt looking at the water was now overtaken by fear. Billy was nowhere to be seen. For what felt like an eternity, Nikki continued staring at the last spot she'd seen him swimming. A dark blur slowly became visible under the surface, leading her to believe his awful joke was coming to an end as he needed to come up for air. The figure drew closer.

A sudden splashing sound shot out of the water behind her, confusing her, as the figure in the water had yet to break the surface. Then came screams.

"Ahhh, help me out of here! Nikki!" Billy yelled.

She forced herself to take her eyes off the dark figure below the surface and looked in the direction Billy was yelling, watching him struggle to come up for air. If Billy was to her left... who was coming up from the depths of the pond in front of her? Nikki pried her attention off her struggling boyfriend and looked back towards the shadow lurking below. What she saw had her choking on fear. There was not just one shadow approaching the surface, there were now at least a dozen scattered around the water. Nikki screamed and began crawling backwards in a crab walk, keeping her eyes locked on the pond. Billy let out a bloodcurdling howl, bringing her attention back to him while she continued backpedaling.

She still couldn't see what was causing him to scream, but it was obvious he was in pain. He fought to keep his head above the water, frantically taking in gasps of air.

Something was pulling him under.

"Billy! Swim to the dock, get out of there!" she yelled.

He looked at her with desperation eating away at his eyes while large gulps of pond water forced their way down into his throat. When she thought the scene couldn't get any worse, a hand shot out of the water behind his head. No normal hand, but one that looked as if it had been painted white. Green strings of algae wrapped around its forearm, like an exterior vein, pulsating. She watched as the hand grabbed ahold of Billy's face, its finger locking into his screaming mouth like a deformed fishhook pulling at his cheek. Billy's eyes bulged, and Nikki heard a ripping sound as his cheek was torn apart.

"UGH! 'Elp me..."

Nikki continued crawling backwards, crying, shaking. Another hand came up next to Billy while the first continued to pull at his face. The second hand gripped the top of his head and squeezed, forcing a high-pitched screech from Billy. One of the fingers located his eye, shoving its way into the orbital cavity. Nikki heard the squishing sound from the dock, like a kid forcing play-doh into a wet cup. She picked up her pace until her back slammed into something. Whatever it was didn't budge. Slowly, she raised her head, looking up at a towering man standing over her. He was one of them, water dripping off his deformed body onto her terrified face. She screamed at the top of her lungs as he bent over, the smell of his long black beard revolting. The man grabbed ahold of her head with both hands and yanked her up off the dock. She flailed, trying to break free. He forced her to look at his damaged face. Something moved under his green skin, squirming around underneath like a parasitic worm trying to burrow its way out. And then his eyes shot open—until that moment she didn't even realize they'd been closed, the darkness hiding his features. His eyes were bright green, glowing and throbbing in rhythm with the water. He tightened his grip on her head and began dragging her to the end of the dock. Nikki curled her toes, trying to dig them into the wooden boards. She slapped at his arm, hoping to loosen his grip, but her power dwindled the tighter he squeezed. She looked over to Billy, praying he'd somehow found a way to break free, to run and get help before it was too late. But all she saw was one last glimpse of his shredded face—that just moments ago she had been kissing—his eyes lifeless. And then his body was pulled under completely, never to rise again.

"Let me go! You fucking freak!" Nikki yelled.

The silent man snapped her head back by the hair, once again forcing her to meet his gaze. He took one of his ghost white hands and moved it toward her face. His nails were long and jagged, dark green and covered in sludge, like they'd just been digging at the bottom of a swamp. He took the index fingernail and in one swift motion slid it across her throat, sending blood shooting out into the water below. She tried to scream again but nothing came out. Slowly, the monster raised her off the ground, leaning over her sliced jugular. Nikki was fading in and out of consciousness, but she felt him drinking from her neck. He stood and lifted her up higher, bringing her face to face. Blood ran through his beard; his long black hair lay matted across his forehead. The thing squirming below his skin was now going crazy, as if the blood had given it the energy.

"*Thank you for sacrificing yourself to us... We have gone far too long,*" he said in a raspy but somehow soothing voice.

Nikki could do nothing; her body was rubber with the blood pumping out of her throat. As the man threw her into the pond, she thought she saw a figure at the edge of the woods, watching everything happen. She wanted to yell for help, but she plunged below, only a green haze visible in the murky water.

Sinking below the surface, she no longer cared. She was at peace, sacrificing herself for them. At that moment, she *knew* Alister Burns. She *knew* Vodyanoy. Knew that his words were the truest she had ever heard.

10

ALLIE AWOKE from a deep sleep to a frigid air hanging over her exposed skin. It was freezing, much colder than it should be. When she opened her eyes, she realized why—she was in the woods. It didn't make any sense. After dinner, she'd gone inside with Teagan and Spencer, playing some boardgames and having a fun time. Eventually she got too tired and said goodnight to everyone. She faintly recalled Spencer coming into the room a little while later, making a ton of noise and not caring who he woke up as per usual. But she'd been so tired that she didn't even have it in her to snap at him. She just grunted and rolled over in bed. Lately, she rarely had a dream to coincide with sleep. So, to find herself in the woods, covered in dirt, was disturbing to say the least.

She stood, glancing down at her legs. *Disgusting*, she thought. In the dark of night, she could see them caked in what looked like dried mud. Allie searched around for any sign of something familiar. Everything was so foreign, from the trees to the sky, it was if she explored some undiscovered land. Shaking away the grogginess, Allie walked slowly through the woods, watching each step to make sure her bare feet didn't step on anything sharp. She was equal parts scared and confused, trying to recall what would have led to this.

Could Cole have stuck something in her drink at dinner? Had he planned to take her out to the woods and kill her? The thought of it made her sick to her stomach. She needed to keep an eye on him the rest of their trip, however long that would be. That was if she could even figure out how to get back to the house from here.

All she wanted was to go back to New York and live her normal life. Although she had plenty of her own issues back home—some that she didn't have the heart to tell her parents about—it was still appealing compared to what they were dealing with now. Her parents thought they were hiding the fact that their marriage was collapsing like a poorly constructed Jenga tower, but Allie knew. One look at the way they communicated with each other was all she needed to know for sure. They *hated* each other. She also knew that they were getting help, talking to a therapist to try and save what little hope they had left.

It wasn't the fact that they were going through all of it that upset Allie the most. What frustrated her beyond belief was they treated her the same as they did Spencer who was barely older than a toddler. She was an adult, at least close enough, and talking to her about what was going on would have made her respect them far more. Instead, she almost hoped they *would* split. At least then she wouldn't have to hide in her room all the time and pretend to be happy. For her parents to think that she was just some teen with hormonal mood swings instead of facing the elephant in the room, understanding it was their fractured household that was causing her to have an emotional strain in her life, really showed how deep into their own shit they were.

Allie knew Spencer wasn't old enough to get it, but the poor kid definitely knew something was up. She saw it in his eyes when there was even a hint of a blow-up argument coming. She saw it every time their dad came home from work in one of his moods that led to his short temper being put on full display. Until the uneasy feeling she got from Cole, she considered that maybe this trip would be a good thing for all of them. It was why she didn't put up a fight with her mom when she told her to pack. Prom wasn't as important to her as they thought. What was most important to her was her family. If there was any chance for them to make it, this was it.

Her thoughts went back to Cole, replaying the night in her head, examining any time he could have slipped something in her drink. One thing she knew for sure: *something* had happened to her—you don't just wake up foggy in the middle of the woods. The last thing she needed was to blame Cole only to have her parents think she was staging some dramatic event to get them to leave and go home. They still thought prom was the biggest thing in the world to her, mainly because she played along with it and treated it as such. She didn't have the heart to tell them that Troy broke up with her weeks before the big day and still agreed to go with her so both sets of parents wouldn't be pissed at all the money they had spent on attire and renting a limo. She didn't have the heart to tell them what caused the breakup.

A noise to her left brought her alert and out of her thoughts. It was faint, but sounded like someone whispering.

She paused to listen.

The darkness mantled the forest, but the sound wasn't imaginary. She followed it, ducking under branches while feeling out in front of her to avoid walking into anything.

"Hello? Is someone there?" she yelled.

The whispers stopped.

For the second time since they had arrived here, Allie felt the sensation of being watched. Somewhere, someone was observing her. She knew it with every fiber in her body. She no longer cared who it was. She started into a full sprint, the bottom of her feet be damned. As she ran, the voices started back up, but this time they were coming from every direction, like the trees themselves were telling her a secret. The path—and in her mind, safety—lay just up ahead. She looked back over her shoulder and saw a still figure, standing in the distance, watching her. Allie was so focused on whoever it was that she forgot she was still running. Her foot landed in a large divot, rolling her ankle and sending her tumbling.

She dropped to the ground, screaming in pain. That was when she noticed what was really on her legs. The moon now had enough of an opening in the canopy to shine down on her. It wasn't mud caked on her legs. It was *blood.*

She screamed again, this time in fear. A rustling sound came from the direction she'd seen the figure, and she whipped her head back toward it. It was a lady, now much closer. Her blond hair was up in a tight bun, water dripping down the side of her face in dark green trails. The dress she wore was torn and discolored, like it had been soaking in dirty swamp-water for years. Her eyes were glazed over and white, the pupils all but vanished. Allie gagged at the smell of her, a combination of old sewage water and fish. She attempted to jump up and run but pain shot back through her ankle, reminding her that wouldn't be possible. Attempting to army crawl away from the sickly-looking woman, Allie thought if she could just get back to the trail—out of the woods—that she would escape. But it was as if the woods were holding her there.

"Stop resisting, darling... It's as inevitable as life and death. You will *be one of us. Father Burns will show you the way..."* the lady said, with a smile that drained the pigment from Allie's skin. In the moonlight, Allie saw that her teeth were stained green with strings of algae caught in the gums.

"Who... who are you?" Allie asked, trying to force down the sobs.

The lady stood in place, silent. Allie thought she might be losing her mind, that this place was making her see things and do things that no sane person would. The whispers returned, but they were not coming from the woman. They were coming from all around, and as Allie peered into the darkness, she saw the outlines of more figures lurking in the woods. It sent chills down her spine, and she wanted to scream again, but it was stuck in her throat. She had enough trouble forcing herself to continue crawling toward the trail.

"Don't worry about them, they won't hurt you. It's been so long since Vodyanoy has been given a sacrifice of his choosing. Join us..."

"Leave me alone! I'm going to tell my parents right now and we're leaving this awful place—"

A sadistic laugh bellowed out of the lady. *"Darling, there is nothing that can be done. Your time to join us is fast approaching. The more you fight it, the worse it will be on you."*

She'd heard enough. Allie jumped to her feet, the pain in her ankle like needles poking at her nerves. Gritting her teeth, she hobbled through the agony, through the sharp, poking branches, and made it to the path. When she felt the dirt under her feet, she risked looking back to the woods. The figures—including the lady—were gone. She glanced down at her legs, staring dumbfounded where the blood had painted her skin moments ago. It was gone. *What the hell?* This place was doing something to her, forcing her to see stuff that wasn't real. Was it whatever drugs had been slipped to her? Could it be the stress of their family being on the run from a group of killers? Whatever the reason, the evil lady and her shadow friends had disappeared along with the blood she *knew* had been there seconds ago. The one thing that remained were the whispers. She heard them the entire way back to the house.

This time she didn't look back.

11

HOLLY SAT AT THE TABLE, sipping a cup of coffee that Cole had made for her while the morning sun pierced the kitchen window. She'd slept as best she could the previous night but found herself constantly waking to strange noises and bad dreams. The caffeine still hadn't kicked in, leaving her in a mood that she was trying not to take out on others. Anthony remained in bed, sleeping like a baby. She envied that about him: no matter how bad things got, he still slept like he'd chugged a bottle of Nyquil. Spencer sat across from her, eating a plate of pancakes. She watched his innocence, wishing again that they could all live through the eyes of an eight-year-old and avoid thinking about being murdered. He scarfed down the food like a starving dog finding a piece of meat hidden in a trashcan, his manners taking the day off while he devoured his breakfast.

Allie sat next to Spencer. Holly spotted her strange behavior the moment she came downstairs. She kept staring at Cole, watching him while he cooked more food for them in the kitchen. Allie had never looked at Cole like that before. Holly knew those eyes and knew that stare was one of distrust. Why would Allie be worried about him? He'd been nothing but nice to them since the initial gun incident. For the first time since Anthony called her telling her to pack their bags, Holly felt safe. She wanted to kick her daughter under the table and tell her to stop being rude, but Allie was smart. Holly had no doubt her daughter could outsmart an old redneck and hide her concerns when Cole had his attention on her. She would make a point to ask her what this was all about in private later. Right now, she just wanted to enjoy a stress-free breakfast.

"How are the pancakes, Spence?" she asked with a smile.

"So good! Mr. Cole cooks the best ones I've ever had, Mom. I didn't know pirates could cook so good," he said.

"Pirate?" Allie asked, frowning at her brother.

"Yeah, duh. All pirates have one leg, didn't you know that?" Spencer asked.

"Spence! That is so rude," Holly snapped.

"Oh, I've been called far worse than that in my day," Cole said as he walked in with plates full of food.

Holly's face burned with embarrassment. Not only had her son insulted his disability, but he heard the whole thing. Cole looked at her with an expression that said, "It's okay."

"Arrr, buddy. Maybe after breakfast we can go out back and dig up me hidden treasure?"

"You're really a pirate?" Spencer asked with his mouth open wide in amazement.

"Moron…" Allie mumbled under her breath.

"That's enough of that, Allie. Show some manners, will you?" Holly asked.

"I'm not the one calling a guy with one leg a pirate, but sure, Mom. Whatever you say."

Cole chuckled and sat at the table next to Teagan, who, like Spencer, sat shoveling food into his mouth as though it was his first meal since a long, winter hibernation. For a few moments they ate in silence, and Holly felt the need to end the awkwardness that her kids had created.

"So, Cole… What sort of things do you and Teagan like to do around here for fun? I'm sure Anthony's taken every chance he can to let you know I haven't spent too much time out of the city; this lifestyle is all new to me."

"Well, not much *to* do, if I'm being honest. But that's what I wanted when we came back here. And your husband keeps us plenty busy with all that needs to be done to keep the place looking nice. When we do have some down time, we often relax on the porch and read books, go for rides on the 4-wheelers through the trails, stuff like that. Probably sounds boring compared to the hustle and bustle you folks are used to, huh?" Cole responded.

"It actually sounds like just what we need. I think it's about time these kids get off electronics for a bit. Between YouTube and Facebook, you would think the two needed them to survive," Holly said, shaking her head.

"Facebook is for old people, Mom…" Allie said in disgust.

"I don't know nothing about no Facebook, and I'm old. So don't go too hard on your mom," Cole said.

Holly went to respond but noticed Allie acting uncomfortable again when Cole spoke. Allie feared Cole, and Holly wanted to know why. He'd been so nice, and came across so innocent in the ignorant, small-town sort of way. Before she could say anything, Anthony came lumbering down the stairs with his hair in a frenzy, looking as if he'd attended a raging party last night.

"Morning everyone, sorry I slept in. I had a few too many brewskis." He rubbed his temples and sat down at the table next to Holly, sighing deeply.

"Care for a cup of coffee? Fresh off the pot," Cole asked, getting up before Anthony answered.

"Oh, God yes. I'll take it black, please. Thank you," Anthony said, putting his face into his palms. "I have to say, ever since we've been here, I've had the strangest damn dreams."

Cole came back to the table and poured a full cup of steaming coffee for Anthony. Holly didn't really believe in all the hype of haunted places and cursed lands, but if any place could make her a firm believer, this seemed to be it. She'd put off the feelings she'd been having since they had arrived: uneasiness, paranoia even.

There was also the fact that her husband was being hunted down by the fucking Mob, of course, but that didn't quite sum up the unnerving feeling Bird's Nest gave her.

Every time she remembered why they came here, she felt another blast of resentment for Anthony. He had put their family in danger. Not only that, but he *hid* it from her and continued living his life as if everything was normal. She truly believed he hadn't thought it would come to something like this. But when had getting involved with those sorts of people ever ended any differently? As she watched him nursing a hangover, a wave of disgust hit her. Things were already on thin ice; this might be the final tipping point, assuming they got out of this alive.

And then she looked at each of her kids, both still very much loving their dad to death. It was a constant struggle to remind herself this wouldn't be easy, and it was bigger than her. The easy way out was divorce. Hell, that's why half the country did it these days. She needed to keep trying for them.

"Thank you so much," Anthony said, gulping down the hot coffee. He looked around the table and focused on Teagan, who still hadn't said a word all morning. "What's up with you kid? You look worse than I do," he said jokingly.

Teagan lifted his head from his plate, dark circles residing under his eyes. As bad as her husband's appearance was, Holly would have to agree that the boy looked rough. He looked around like he was unsure how to respond.

"Sorry, I don't normally stay up as late as we did last night. I'm a bit tired today is all."

"I hear that, kid," Anthony said, raising his mug in a mock cheers. "So, I told you I would help around here while we stayed. What's on the agenda for today, Cole?"

"Well, I'm glad you asked. I have to split some wood down at a few of the sites where a couple trees fell from a bad thunderstorm we had a few days ago. You handy with a chainsaw or ax?"

Holly laughed, the idea of Anthony, who'd spent most of his

working life behind a desk, using a chainsaw was funny as hell. Anthony's eyes bored into hers.

"Much to my wife's surprise, I actually *have* used an ax with my dad growing up. She loves to think I can't handle anything bigger than a pen, but I'd be glad to help you today." Anthony glared at Holly.

"Don't we have some more important things to take care of?" Holly asked him. She didn't want to get specific but knew that would be enough for him to get the hint.

"There isn't anything we can do at the moment but help around here, Holly. I know you have this constant need to get things done, a list of objectives in your head that are more important than what everyone else needs to do, but we came here to get away from all that," Anthony snapped.

"Yeah, *that's* what we're getting away from..."

She knew she needed to settle down and avoid saying too much, but Anthony made it difficult to do that. Allie pushed her chair back from the table and got up. She scoffed at her parent's inability to sit together for more than ten minutes without fighting and stormed up the stairs.

"I'm sorry, I just didn't sleep well again last night. I was thinking of going into town today to grab your meds—that you forgot. Is there anything else we need?" Holly asked.

"I'm okay without the meds for now. I think it's best if we all just stay together, okay?" Anthony asked.

"Do you think that's a smart idea? Isn't it bad to throw off the schedule of taking them every day?" Holly responded.

"I'll be *fine*," he said firmly. It was a tone Holly knew all too well —let it be.

Anthony got up from the table, grabbed a piece of toast, and walked toward the back door. With his coffee in the other hand, he pushed the door open and walked outside; the door slammed shut behind him. Holly looked at Teagan and Spencer, both of whom continued eating, oblivious to what just happened. Cole had his back to her, working in the kitchen again. The whole scene was embarrassing. Therapy seemed to be helping with the day-to-day stresses they dealt with. But no help in the world could have prepared them for the pressure they found themselves under now. She liked to think even the healthiest marriages would struggle to maintain calm in this situation. *Though what normal families get put in this spot to begin with?* She wondered.

The therapist told them the kids very likely knew more than they were showing—that many kids tend to either pretend they don't notice or intentionally learn to ignore it like it's nothing. She thought about this as she watched her son eat his breakfast like he was ignorant to everything. Holly felt sick to her stomach, the realization hitting her that as much as they tried to hide it from the kids, it was bleeding out into the world like a flood blasting through a dam. The poor kid had to be so stressed on the inside, it was no wonder he suffered from such crippling anxiety.

"Hey Teagan, why don't you go show Spencer where all the frogs hide down in the stream," Cole said.

Spencer's eyes lit up with excitement; he looked at Holly for approval.

"Go on, it's okay. Just do whatever Teagan says, got it?" she asked.

He nodded and jumped up from the table. Teagan took a big gulp of his orange juice and set the cup down on the table. He smiled and stood.

"Wait till you see the size of these things, buddy," Teagan said, rubbing the top of Spencer's head.

"Have fun, Spence," Holly said, but he was already out the door and out of sight.

"Thanks for that, we just have a lot on our plate right now, it's been tough to keep it together," she said.

"Listen, your husband told me your story last night, you're doing better than most considering the situation."

She didn't know what to say. They agreed not to tell him anything, yet Anthony went behind her back and told him everything, making her look like an idiot. At least she *assumed* he told Cole everything—who knew with Anthony?

"Don't worry, I get why you guys hid it from me at first. I'd have done the same. Protecting those little ones is most important. And I just want you to know, I'm here to help you guys. I may not be what I once was, but if anyone comes around these parts looking for a shootout, they'll be in for a rude awakening, I promise you that."

"I… Thank you so much, Cole. I don't know what to say."

"Say nothing. Keep doing what you are doing. Be the rock those kids need. It's obvious that you're the backbone of the family. They need you to stay strong. Both of you for that matter. I'll talk with Anthony today and try to help as best I can."

Holly started crying; it came so unexpectedly, like a tidal wave slamming into her, that she didn't even have time to get up and walk away before it happened. Cole put his hand on her shoulder.

"Hey now. It'll all be okay. Please, try and get some rest, I can tell you haven't slept well since you've been here," he said.

She nodded and put her hand on top of his. "Thank you again, you're so kind, Cole."

"Everything is going to be alright, Holly." Cole walked out the back door to catch up with Anthony.

It was a statement that didn't carry much weight with her. The thought of everything being alright seemed damn near impossible right now. One thing Cole said *did* carry weight, however. She needed to be there for her kids. The stress was bringing out the worst in them, and she needed to be the rock that Cole said she was. Holly took a deep breath, wiping away the last tear that was too stubborn to fall, and continued sipping her coffee.

12

VINCENT COSTELLO SAT behind his desk, reading through documents in his dimly lit office. His desk lamp provided enough light to read through all the balance sheets, something he'd hated doing ever since he took over the family—but if a leader wanted something done right, they had to take charge and control everything top to bottom.

He'd arrived more agitated than normal this morning after spending the better part of the past two days searching for Anthony. If the dumb fuck hadn't killed one of his men and severely injured another, he might have let him live. Now, he had no choice but to not only kill him but take care of all the other loose ends this clusterfuck of a situation created. That meant Anthony's family. Vincent hated killing women. He hated killing kids even more. Especially since he lost his own son to cancer a few years back. Every time he saw a family walking around the city with a smiling child, he found himself getting choked up. He'd even vowed never to hurt a child after they lost Vinny Jr. Unfortunately, there was no other choice.

He threw down the papers, unable to concentrate. The office was silent, which he usually preferred when he was doing his morning work. Nobody else had arrived yet, but he hoped when his men showed up, they would bring some good news with them.

Vincent went to The Graham residence shortly after the shootout, eager to catch the family before they made a run for it. The damn mess that had to be cleaned up before they left the vacant building had given Anthony enough time to get out of dodge... for now. To lead the family, many traits were required. One, a necessity in moments like this, was determination. Vincent was not about to let his empire crumble because of some low life twat who deserved to die. Had his men reacted before thinking? Yes. But the fact of the matter was they made the right choice killing the junkie, who had been trying to steal from Vincent.

Vincent growled. He'd thought they would be out of the office building before anyone came, but the kid that worked for Anthony must have already been in the neighborhood because he showed up within a few minutes of the alarm going off. A small mess turned into a bigger shit show when the kid walked in and had to be dealt with. A bigger shit show turned into a colossal train wreck when Anthony followed suit. The last time he had to clean up a mess this big, his lawyer worked around the clock to make sure Vincent didn't serve a single minute inside a cell. Over the last few years, they had done everything right, remaining out of the Fed's eye and going about their business as smooth as a sweatshop pumping out knockoff purses.

Vincent rubbed his eyes, taking a sip of his coffee, then lit a cigarette. His head was pounding—a combination of lack of sleep, deteriorating eyesight, and the stress of keeping things running at peak performance. His wife wanted him to wear his reading glasses at the office, but he insisted that he'd look vulnerable and old if his crew saw him squinting over a pile of money like an old man trying to find his prick while taking a piss. She told him it was better to let them see it now before he had no choice, and it would prevent headaches that eventually led to his bad temper getting the best of him.

After checking Anthony's house, Vincent split up with his crew to drive around searching some of the vacant listings they knew of. It felt like a lost cause; Anthony knew Vincent was aware of the locations and wouldn't likely hide in any of them, but they couldn't afford to leave any stone unturned. Hours passed; they checked a total of eighteen buildings before calling it quits for the night. There were many houses and buildings still to comb through, but Vincent was done with it. He put his top men on the hunt, specifically telling them not to kill Anthony and bring him in alive if they found him. He had no intention of making the family suffer—their deaths would be quick and painless—but he wanted his crew to see what happened when someone killed a member of *his* family. His top guy and next in command, Christopher "Money Bags" DePierro, had a team searching the remaining properties.

The thought of doing bookwork while waiting to hear back from them was a struggle. Vincent inhaled deeply from his cigarette and stubbed it out in his ashtray, rubbing his temples to help ease the lingering headache. He looked up at the clock and saw it was just past 10:00 AM. *Where the fuck are you clowns?* He thought. They should have been back by now with some type of information.

As if on cue, the door burst open. DePierro dragged in an unconscious body with a sack covering the head. At first, Vincent assumed they'd located Anthony, but his hope quickly diminished when he realized the limp body was far too short.

"Who the fuck's this? Unless Anthony shrunk a foot and turned Mexican, you got some explaining to do, Chris," Vincent snapped.

Christopher stood tall, his spiked Jersey blow-out haircut adding an extra few inches to his already towering frame. Vincent insisted many times he get his hair cut, saying nobody would take him seriously as second in command if he looked like he belonged on the cast of *Jersey Shore*. Christopher told him the ladies loved it, and that any chump who dared comment on it would learn to take him seriously the hard way.

"Boss… We searched all the other properties and got nothing, so we decided to circle back to Anthony's house. That's when we found his landscaper peeping in at us while we searched the house."

"What... are you fucking telling me we have *another* loose end? God damn it! I haven't worked this hard to build this family up to the top, only to be dragged down by my own fucking crew!" Vincent yelled, his face turning red.

He slammed his fist down on the table, sending the documents he'd been reading flying through the air. *Take a deep breath, don't show weakness*, he thought. Closing his eyes, Vincent inhaled, his lungs filling with the smell of stale cigarettes and booze—smells that oddly calmed him after growing up in this very room with his dad's crew running the business. He had an idea, one that could possibly turn this newest blunder into a positive situation.

"Set him in that chair in the corner and tie him up. Maybe we can get something useful out of him before we dump him in the Hudson. I swear you imbeciles are trying to drive me to an early grave with these mistakes. This operation has been as smooth as Jasmine's snatch up until a few days ago." He nodded toward the front of the building where the strip club sat. "And now you fucks can't go a few hours without making another mess. Get your heads out of your asses!"

Christopher and one of the other men—Jayme "Birdman" Kennedy—dragged the unconscious body to the chair, forcing him down. Jayme, another tall lackey Vincent used for his grunt work, tied the landscaper in place. Vincent preferred to keep it in the family—the majority of his crew were Italian—something he was proud of. But he took a chance on the Irish kid out of Boston after he proved himself by disposing of a few minor "inconveniences" for Vincent. They had given him the nickname Birdman because he was pale skinned and tall, resembling Larry Bird, if the NBA legend had taken the wrong path in life. Together, he and Christopher usually handled the dirty work for Vincent, but they had been running another errand when shit went down in the vacant building. Had they been there instead of the lower ranked fucks, that generally weren't allowed around Vincent unless he was in a good mood, this whole issue might never have happened in the first place.

"Take the sack off his head," Vincent demanded.

Birdman ripped it off, revealing a dazed Hispanic man, his face bruised so badly that his eyes could have fooled someone into thinking he was having a severe allergic reaction. The whites of his eyes were hidden, not that it mattered. If they had been visible, all Vincent would have seen were bloodied spheres looking back at him, unable to make eye contact.

"How the hell am I supposed to question him if he can't even talk?"

The man started to move, but clearly was in immense pain. His head slowly lifted but quickly dropped back down, lacking the strength to hold it upright for any length of time.

"Hey, shit-stain, wake the fuck up…" Vincent said.

The landscaper moaned, trying to speak, but only spit and blood exited his mouth when he opened it. Vincent didn't have time to wait for the useless bum to wake up on his own, so like everything else, he took it into his own hands and walked over, kneeling to eye-level.

"I bet that hurts, huh? These two tend to get a bit out of hand when I send them off on their own. I'm sorry they did this to you," Vincent said.

The landscaper lifted his chin, confused by the mob boss's kind words. Vincent got a better look at his face and wanted to gag. Christopher and Jayme had really done a number on him; it was a wonder he was still alive. The man attempted to open his eyes, tiny slits providing a sliver for tears to escape.

"I need some information. And I think you are just the person that may be able to give that to me, assuming you can even speak English. Can you do that?" Vincent asked.

A hacking sound came up from the man's throat, and before Vincent realized what he was doing, the landscaper spit a wad of bloody phlegm toward the ground, landing on Vincent's leather shoes. Rage consumed Vincent. He drove his fist into the man's cheek, intentionally avoiding his mouth so he could keep him talking. From deep within the man's chest, a growl forced its way out, not one of anger, but of intense pain.

"Do that again and it will be a knife going into your skull instead of my fist, got it?" Vincent asked. There was no response to the question. "I said, do you fucking got it?"

Flinching, the man nodded in agreement. Vincent reached out slowly, lifting the man's sagging head by the chin. "We're looking for Anthony. We've gone through most of his properties and come up empty handed. If you tell me anything useful, it might keep you alive. Before you say you don't know, I suggest you think long and hard."

At first, the man looked confused. He was likely concussed.

"I just mow the damn lawn... they hardly ever say a word to me outside of... outside of handing me a check each month," he said, struggling to get the words out.

"Grab the pliers," Vincent said, nodding to Birdman. "Now, where were we? What's your name? Or do you prefer I just call you the Mexican?"

A snarl formed on the man's face. "Eduardo..."

"Eduardo. You see, my associate over here is grabbing a pair of needle-nose pliers. Do you know what for?"

Eduardo shook his head.

"My other associate standing next to you, he's going to hold your hand in place. We have ten attempts to get an answer. Each time I feel you don't give me anything useful, those grimy ass fingernails of yours will get ripped off, one by one. Do you under-stand me?"

"No... no, no, please. I don't even know them that well!"

Birdman came back to Vincent's side, holding a pair of pliers with a sadistic smile.

"That was number one," Vincent stated, moving out of the way.

Christopher grabbed ahold of Eduardo's hand, which was tied to the arm of the chair. He gripped the thumb, squeezing it in place. Desperate fear filled the landscaper's swollen eyes as he shook his head.

"You had a chance..."

Birdman approached, jamming one end of the pliers under the

fingernail, ripping the skin from its protective shield. Eduardo screamed, trying to yank his arm free.

"That wasn't the worst of it," Vincent said, then nodded.

With a sudden snap, the fingernail tore completely from the skin, driving Eduardo to cry in misery. Blood poured down his trembling finger. Vincent had done this before; he was all for the theatrics of it. He waited, letting the man cry for a moment, before speaking again.

"Let's try this again, shall we? What. Can. You. *Tell*. Me?"

Eduardo sat mesmerized by his deformed finger, looking down at it while crying. Vincent assumed the man knew he was going to die. The funny thing was, even when someone knew they were taking their last breath, they would still talk to avoid the pain. He had no doubt he would get something useful from this situation.

"I... I know they often would go on day trips to places... but they rarely took vacations, and never left the city," Eduardo blurted out.

Vincent frowned, shaking his head. Once again, Birdman opened the pliers, moving to the index finger. He rammed the pointed metal tip in, again bringing the ripping sound with it, again forcing the painful screams from Eduardo.

"I'm going to need more than that muchacho..."

Birdman yanked back, but this time the fingernail cracked in the center, leaving behind a jagged piece of nail plate. Vincent didn't think the screams could get any louder, but they did. He was enjoying himself more than he should be under the circumstances.

"You missed a piece, Jayme," he said with a smirk.

"Please! Stop it, I can't think of anything if... if you keep torturing me!"

Birdman stuck the pliers around the remaining piece of nail and pulled slower, causing the landscaper's bruised eyes to bulge in shock, revealing a set of bloodshot eyes. With a tug, the rest of the nail broke free, drawing more blood from the wound.

"That was attempt two... What else can you tell me?"

"Oh, God. No more, *please*..." Eduardo mumbled; his tone defeated. After a moment of heavy breathing, his head shot up, some realization had hit him, and Vincent knew he was about to get some information. "Mr. Graham has a shed out back, where he keeps a lot of his outdoor stuff locked up... One day when I was mowing, I—I saw him throw a folder in there..."

Vincent was tempted to move to the next finger, but this felt like it was getting somewhere, and he didn't want to ruin it. "And?" he asked.

"I asked him what it was, you know... just starting a friendly conversation with him. He told me it was for a property he bought up in New Hampshire, one he was having trouble selling... An old campground!" he shouted.

"You see, now *that's* some useful information, Eduardo. I think you just prevented yourself from moving to the next finger," he said with a smile.

"Oh, thank the Lord. Thank you, sir," Eduardo said, unable to hold back the tears.

"Now, now. Don't go thanking me yet. I still need to do this..."

Vincent lifted a gun, aiming at the landscaper's face. Before he could scream, the mob boss pulled the trigger, lodging a bullet in the center of the man's head. Eduardo went lifeless.

"Get me that address... And boys? Don't fuck up again, got it? I got plenty of men who'd love to fill your shoes. And get this fucking body out of here."

Without another word, Christopher and Jayme untied Eduardo's lifeless body from the chair and dragged him to the door. Vincent decided, in that moment, he would accompany them to New Hampshire. Like he always said: if you wanted something done right, you had to do it yourself.

13

THE ANGER BOILED INSIDE ANTHONY. For Holly to cause a scene like that in front of not only the kids but strangers they barely knew, was embarrassing to say the least. No, it was *pathetic*. He lifted the ax high, then drove it down into the log, splitting the wood in two. Wiping the sweat from his face, he looked up at Cole, who was using the chainsaw on the remaining portion of the tree lying in the path. He'd only told him what he wanted him to know. Mostly about the deal he had in place with Vincent, and who would likely be coming for them if they found the campground. Anthony avoided telling him about the dreams he'd had since coming here. Last night, once he passed out after telling Cole their dilemma, the nightmares were even more vivid.

Alister Burns came back, but he was not alone. Alister's followers were with him. The leader insisted that not only could he protect Anthony's family if Allie was brought to them, but he would be able to provide more for Allie than Anthony or Holly ever could. She would live on in eternity, becoming one with them. The more Alister talked, the more his words made sense. Why had Anthony resisted the idea at first? Why would he not protect his family when help was being offered to them? One look into Alister's eyes made him realize he was being selfish and stubborn. At least that was how he felt in the dream. When he woke up, he ran to the bathroom and threw up everything he'd eaten the night before. He blamed it on a hangover, but what really drove his stomach to twist the bile up through his throat like a child forcing up the bottom of a push pop, was that in the nightmare he had been so willing to give them Allie. It had felt so *right*.

There was no way he could really do such a thing. *You're losing your shit, Anthony*. His doctor told him if he didn't take his meds, or somehow messed up the dosage, it could lead to bad dreams and nausea. That had to be it. Add the stress of the Vincent fiasco, and you had the perfect recipe for a meltdown. Sprinkle on a bit of his fracturing relationship with Holly, and you now had a budding psychopath. He laughed. Had he gone so far off the deep end he was seeing ghosts that for so long he didn't believe existed? One thing he knew for sure, was that he would do anything to protect his family. It was very likely Holly would leave him once they got out of this, and he was okay with that. They had done enough damage to the kids; she'd done enough damage to him. He felt the anger returning. He lifted the ax high. *Ungrateful.* Brought the ax down, smashing through the next log. *Fucking.* Once more, he lifted the tool above his head. *Bitch*! Driving it down through the remaining piece of wood, leaving what looked more like a pile of wooden guts than an actual piece of firewood. Anthony breathed heavily, staring down at the mangled pile of pinewood. The chainsaw had stopped.

"You okay?" Cole asked.

Anthony looked up and took a deep breath. *What the fuck is happening to me?*

"Yeah, sorry. This stuff is all getting to me, man. I'm trying to hold it together, but it feels like a ticking time bomb waiting to go off, counting down to the day he finds us."

"I can only imagine the stress you guys are all going through. But taking it out on your wife and kids won't help it get any better," Cole said, catching Anthony off guard.

Who did this prick think he was to say that? Maybe he was

coming from a good place, but to Anthony, it felt more like he was just sticking his nose where it didn't belong. He didn't have to live with Holly every day. He didn't have to listen to the goddamn sarcasm that felt like a knife jabbing into his sanity. Anthony stared at Cole for an uncomfortable minute, debating what to say in response.

"I appreciate your concern, really. But our marital issues are the least of our troubles right now. Besides, I already talk to a therapist, and I'm married to someone who thinks she's another, so I'd really appreciate it if you backed off."

Cole held up one hand in defense, the chainsaw still in the other hand. "I'm sorry to overstep my boundaries here. Just want what's best for you all. I think you're right though. What's most important right now, is you and I talking about a plan for if these bad fellas show up."

"There is no if... They *will* come, it's just a matter of when, Cole. I'm a fucking real estate agent, not some Black Ops soldier planning strategy for an ambush. Hell, I'm lucky I didn't die when I saw them killing Hank." Anthony remembered those few seconds of eye contact with Hank before a bullet blasted into his skull. To think that wasn't the scariest image running through his head right now was ridiculous.

Over and over, he saw the face of Alister Burns, his mouth opening far wider than physically possible, his glowing green eyes paralyzing Anthony, making him do whatever Alister wanted. *They can't have my daughter,* he thought.

"I think it makes sense if we take turns keeping an eye out each night," Cole said. "I know men like this, they won't attack in plain daylight... How hard will it be for them to find this place?"

"There's no record of it on our listing site. I pulled it down once it didn't sell for a few years, hoping if I re-listed it again later, it would look like a new property. But Costello will go through whatever measures necessary to find me. He has connections, people in important places. I have no doubt he's going through all of them right now. And he knows I wouldn't call the cops, that I'm stuck in hiding somewhere." Anthony paused a moment to think if there were any loose ends he was missing. "If I had any chance to survive, I blew it when I accidentally killed one of his men in self-defense. I'm pretty sure that was his nephew, too. He'll plan to make an example of me and my family…"

"Not if I can help it. We need to keep the kids safe. When there's any sign of these men showing up, we'll send them to the basement with Holly. I know you don't give yourself any credit, but you defended yourself against two of his men already, so that's saying something," Cole said.

Anthony laughed half-heartedly. "Yeah, well… If that bullet was just a few feet higher it would have gone through my brain and not grazed my arm. I'm lucky is what I am. What you're saying sounds like a good start. I just… I would do anything to protect them. *Anything*. I fucked up, thinking this little agreement with Vincent would be harmless and get us some extra money. I own that mistake. I'm just glad we have someone with experience like yourself here to help, Cole. Sorry if I've come across like a dick."

"Nonsense. I've done far worse to people under intense pressure, though I've tamed a bit with age and having a kid to look after. I have an idea of how to go about this. Do you know how to use a firearm at all?"

"Me? Man, I haven't shot a gun since playing Duck Hunt as a kid. I'll do whatever it takes, but don't count on me hitting anything my first shot…"

Cole scratched at his scruff with his free hand, looking off in the distance for a moment before speaking. For a guy with so many physical ailments, Anthony thought he handled himself quite well. His story about Alister healing him came back to Anthony.

"Okay. I have an idea, one that'll allow you to stay safe and protect your family at the same time. Let's get the rest of these logs cleared out of the path, and then we can talk more. Another storm's on the way, and I'd like to get this all taken care of before it hits. I need to think this over a bit…"

Anthony didn't argue. He still had some anger buried inside that he wanted to take out on the unfortunate logs in front of him. It felt good releasing some of the rage.

14

Holly finished her cup of coffee and got up from the table after Spencer and Teagan got back from catching frogs. The kids went to their rooms, so she took it upon herself to try and rest. She felt restless, like there was something she should be doing but unsure of what that was. She decided to leave the kids alone and let them cope with the situation their own way instead of knocking on the door and apologizing. That could wait a bit. Resting sounded like a great idea, but she also knew herself well enough to know that any attempt to "relax" would just lead to her analyzing the events in her head. What Holly really needed was to take her mind off the issues. She decided to explore the house a bit, check out what else the property had to offer. When they arrived, all she had a chance to look at were the bedrooms, kitchen, dining area, and the backyard.

She got up and walked downstairs. The first room she entered was the office they walked through when they first entered the house. Old décor cluttered the wall, faded paintings that displayed the beautiful landscapes of the changing seasons in New Hampshire. The room was nothing fancy, but she appreciated the New England charm it brought out. She sat in the chair behind the office desk, stacks of mail and binders obscuring most of the space. A large, old computer monitor sat in the center of the papers, looking as if it hadn't been used in years. Holly booted it up, not sure why she felt like she was intruding in a home they owned. Cole already told them the office was basically left as is after the campground shut down, so it wasn't as if she was about to find some private porn stash that he had saved on the desktop. Still, she couldn't help the feeling she was getting, her body filling with adrenaline. The screen brightened as the antique machine slowly powered up, revealing a home screen with a plain green background. Again, nothing looked out of the ordinary. She didn't even know what she was looking for, but she couldn't help being a little disappointed.

As she started to get out of the seat to look elsewhere in the house, she noticed a few folders on the home screen that stood out. One of them had no name, but the second was titled ALISTER. Holly didn't know what the name meant. She clicked on the folder, which opened to another set of files and photos within. The first file was a Word document. She clicked it, and it opened a list of names. They meant nothing to her, but she read through them quickly anyway. The top name was Alister Burns. A number of other names she didn't recognize followed, and then she saw a name she *did* recognize—Cole Springer. The easy answer was that it must be a list of employees that worked here before. Curiosity got the better of her though, so she moved on to the next file in the folder.

A batch of photos appeared on the screen, once again revealing strangers. One of them showed a group of people looking at the camera like some demented school team photo, except instead of jerseys, they all wore matching white robes. *What the hell is this?* She thought. In the center stood a tall man who demanded her attention. He was clearly the leader of the group; just a quick glance at his face gave Holly the chills. The man smiled for the camera, but she saw through the charm. Something in his eyes drew her attention to them, she was unable to stop staring. Holly shook her head, forcing herself to move down the line of people. As if she needed further proof that something was up with Cole, there he stood in the photo—robe and all—looking happy as could be. A beautiful woman with blond hair propped up in a tight bun stood next to him, holding a newborn baby. Holly hit print, watching as the image slowly slid out onto the tray. She grabbed the picture and inspected it closer, wondering what on earth Cole was involved with. The ink in the printer must have been old, as the picture came out faded and discolored.

Anthony had told her while lying in bed that Cole talked about his past after everyone went to sleep, but Holly had been too tired to care about some groundskeeper's day-to-day living at the campground. Could he have told Anthony about all this? She needed more information, but already too much time had passed since everyone went their separate ways after breakfast. Holly decided to click one last file before calling it quits, hoping it contained more information that could put some pieces together for her. The new file was titled SACRIFICES. She clicked.

Not only did the document list specific names, but it included dates, times, and *reasons*. Reasons as to why each name had been sacrificed. When she realized she was reading a list of dead people's names—people who had been murdered (that's what *she* considered them)—she felt sick to her stomach. These people had all died, and the list was not short, quite the opposite. Holly scrolled and scrolled until she once again saw Cole's name. Against her better judgement, she scanned, looking to see how he was involved. Someone had died, been *sacrificed*, just to take pain away from Cole. How could she trust this man so easily? He came across as down-to-earth, nice, and trustworthy in the limited time she'd spent with him. Hell, he was the one who calmed her down this morning, not her own husband. A tear trickled down her face, something she didn't think she had any left of, and she closed the file. She leaned down to turn off the computer when she heard a floorboard groan behind her.

"What are you doing? Dad said the computer's off limits."

Holly spun around. Teagan stood in the entryway, and his once charming smile had gone cold.

15

SPENCER LOOKED BACK over his shoulder, making sure nobody saw him leave. He needed to get away from the tension suffocating him inside the house. They always tried to hide it in front of him and Allie, but given how bad things were right now, they were destined to slip up. Which is exactly what they did at breakfast. Spencer felt a mix of emotions watching them argue in front of not only he and his sister, but Cole and Teagan as well. Part of him was sad. Another part of him was ashamed. All he wanted was to look cool in front of Teagan. The older boy carried a confidence Spencer admired. The few minutes he got alone with Teagan was the most fun he recalled having in a long time. They caught some big frogs, something he'd never seen in the city before. Teagan cracked some jokes, but Spencer knew he was trying to lighten the mood and make him forget about what just happened. After a little while, they went back to the house and Spencer immediately ran up to his room to find Allie on the bed in one of her typical moods. That only added to his stress.

He knew his dad and Cole had gone off in a different direction on a trail Spencer didn't get to see yet, but that was okay. They wouldn't bother him and tell him to get back inside. Allie was doing what she always did in these situations—listening to music on her headphones and pretending nobody else existed. When Spencer left, she was staring blankly out the window at nothing in particular, probably daydreaming about being with her boyfriend back home, or maybe even Teagan.

Unlike his sister, Spencer didn't have friends. A lot of the older kids at school picked on him, something that got even worse when he had a full-blown panic attack on the playground in front of everyone. The teachers chalked it up to heatstroke, but he knew the feeling all too well. Regardless of what they called it, the fact that he passed out in front of all the other kids after freaking out when his chest began to tighten would be something he could never escape as long as he went to that school.

He looked ahead, realizing he had been lost in his thoughts longer than expected. The trail was already narrowing, the trees thickening around him. Spencer picked up a wide branch and thought it made a cool walking stick. As he continued walking, he dragged the stick behind him in the dirt. The sound from the friction of wood and dirt gave off a low grating noise. He found the sound relaxing, so he continued to drag it behind. In front of him, the wooded area blocking the pond was close. Cole and Spencer said not to go near the water, and he felt it was best to listen to their warnings. When he got to the end of the trail that stopped right before the thicket heading down to the pond, he froze in place, wondering if he should turn and explore an area he hadn't yet seen. Not only did his feet stop, but the dragging stick did as well. That's when Spencer heard another noise, one that the stick had overshadowed until now. He heard *laughing*. It sounded like other kids, but much younger than Allie and Teagan. It was an odd feeling—the sounds were very distinguishable, yet it was impossible to tell where they were coming from. It was like they were coming from every direction. Could there be more kids here to play with? From the sound of it, they were having a great time. Spencer couldn't help himself; his sadness was now being washed away by excitement. The sun escaped from behind a thick cloud, bringing with it a beam of light that obscured his ability to see clearly in front of him. He held up his hand to shield the sunlight, looking through the forest leading down to the pond... and a blur of movement shot behind one of the trees. Something moving so quick there was no clear figure to see. The laughing escalated.

"Hello? Is somebody there?" Spencer asked.

More giggles came from the trees.

Spencer approached the tree-line, allowing the canopy of leaves above to block the sun. He let his eyes adjust, allowing him to see deeper in the woods. His eyes flitted left to right, looking for any sign of the kids. Behind one of the wider trees, a head popped out, revealing a young boy with blond hair. His face was still hidden in shadow, but Spencer knew it was a kid close to his age. *This is so cool!* He thought.

"Hi! What's your name? My name's Spencer," he said.

Instead of answering his question, the boy laughed first, then said *"Hi... come play with us, Spencer. We* love *hide and seek..."*

Hide and seek? He hadn't played that in a few years, not since his dad had been around more and took the time to play with him. These days his dad was far too busy with his business to spend much time at home playing children games with him. The thought of playing brought pure joy to Spencer that he hadn't felt in a very long time. He smiled as he approached the woods, but then hesitated, realizing he was about to enter the forbidden area. From where he stood, he could now see the water down the hill, giving off a dull glow. It was unlike any body of water he'd ever seen.

"Count to ten, then come find us..." The little child's voice trailed off.

Spencer couldn't believe it was really happening. Where did these kids come from? It was possible they lived down the street and wandered into the woods to play their game. Unable to control his excitement, he walked into the trees, getting one step closer to the water below. He found a large tree—the tree that the blond boy previously hid behind—and put his face against the bark, closing his eyes. Slowly, he counted to ten, yelling so they would be able to hear him.

"Ready or not, here I come!"

Careful to avoid tripping over one of the many fallen branches, Spencer kept an eye on where he stepped, also trying to reduce the noise he produced so he wouldn't give away his location. He veered away from the water, walking to the side where some of the bigger trees were rooted. The giggles returned behind him, so he snapped his head back to where he'd come from... only to see nothing.

"*Getttting colddder...*" the voice said quietly.

The laughs returned, this time from a different location. *How many kids are out here?* As he glanced back toward the water, he caught more movement behind one of the trees closer to the opening down the hill. Forgetting all about the rules, he set off in a sprint, ducking under low-hanging branches that appeared to be reaching out for him. He arrived at the tree, positive he would shoot his head around it and find a kid, crouched down and laughing as he waited in anticipation to be found. Instead, he again found nothing but the forest floor on the other side.

"What the heck..." he whispered.

Spencer turned around and noticed he was now only a few feet from the pond, standing in a grassy lawn that to his surprise looked freshly mowed—especially for a spot where nobody was supposed to step foot. Whispers came from his left, back in the trees.

"*Do you want to see us?*" the voice asked.

"Yes! I give up, where are you hiding?"

His foot touched a harder surface, and he glanced down to see he had back peddled to the dock, now standing right next to the water.

"*Walk out on the dock, and we will come say hi,*" the voice said, sounding full of happiness. Something about the voice sounded strange to Spencer, like the happiness was fake, but he paid it no mind, too excited to meet new friends.

Slowly, he walked out onto the old wooden path, looking down at the water as he did. If this even *was* water. The color was so unnatural, it looked like something turtles would swim into and then come out as grown ninjas. That thought made him chuckle, but it was short lived as commotion from behind urged him to turn back and look. Standing at the edge of the dock were two kids, one girl and one boy, both close to his age. Both had straight blond hair. Both wore what appeared to be white robes or sheets. And *both* stared back at him with glowing white eyes. The laughing returned, but their faces remained emotionless, their white eyes burning fear into his brain.

"It's time you join us, Spencer... Out here we can play forever," the girl said.

He no longer found himself excited to play with them. His first thought was to find a way to escape, somehow get by them and run back for help. But out here he was trapped. It was either try to get past them or swim in this poisonous looking water. The joy turned to fear, and it rippled through his entire body when they took a step forward, now at the edge of the dock. Up until now, the water remained still—until a light splashing came from behind him. He didn't want to take his eyes off the kids, but he needed to see what was in the water. When he turned to look, he wished he hadn't, as he saw figures below the surface, mostly a blur beneath the green haze, but knew what they were... they were *people.* Spencer screamed, spinning back to the kids, who were now getting closer.

His chest started to tighten, a feeling he was all too familiar with. Of all times for a panic attack, now could possibly be the worst timing yet. Worse than on the playground in front of all his peers. His knees began to buckle, losing strength. Instinct told him to grab his chest, so he threw both hands to it, as if they would protect his heart from escaping his body. The kids stood in place, not getting closer, but the splashing resumed behind him in the water, intensifying. Spencer's vision went blurry, he was getting lightheaded. Before he had a chance to scream again, his legs gave out, and he collapsed to the dock as everything went dark.

———————

Allie took off her headphones, realizing her brother was no longer in the room with her. Curious, she got up from the bed and walked out into the hallway, only hearing silence. She decided now was as good a time as any to go downstairs, hoping her parents were done with their spat. When she got to the bottom, she went back to the kitchen, expecting to find her mom still sitting there, but the room was empty. She considered going outside, but instead thought she would check the other rooms first. When she rounded the corner and approached the office, she found her mom and Teagan, eerily silent. Her mom sat in the office chair behind the computer, Teagan sat in the corner with his head buried in his hands, like he was crying.

"What's going on? Is everything okay?" she asked.

Her mom looked at her, the color drained from her face.

"Well, that depends on your definition of okay, Allie. It seems our new friends here have been hiding some stuff from us…"

"I *told* you, I have no idea what you're talking about. My dad tells me to stay off the computer, so I listen. You have to understand, this is all new to me as well," Teagan said, choking back tears.

"What is new to you? Why the hell are you guys talking in riddles, just tell me what's going on!" Allie snapped.

"I don't know why, but I decided to start up the computer and see if it still worked. What I found was a whole lot of shit I never expected to find. They—"

The back door opened in the kitchen, and from the office Allie heard her dad and Cole joking around as they walked back into the house. The men were talking about something to do with the gate out front when they came into view and saw the tension in the office. Cole stopped talking and observed the room. Allie saw the expression on his face go from happy to nervous when he spotted Holly sitting behind the desk.

"I'd ask why everyone's looking at me like I got three heads, but I think I might have some explaining to do…" Cole said, shifting his eyes to the side to avoid eye contact.

"You're damn right you do! How could you hide this from us?

Are you some kind of freak?" Holly's rage made it more of a state-ment than an actual question.

"Now listen here. I told Anthony most of my story last night. I may have kept some stuff out trying to protect you all more than anything else. The less you know about some of this, the better," he said defensively.

"Anthony, you *knew* about this? And you didn't fucking tell me?" Holly snapped.

"What in Christ are you talking about, Holly? I tried to tell you last night but you were too tired to listen. Please, lay off me for once, will you?"

"You told me he was the groundskeeper for the campground, not part of the fucking CULT! First you have us on the run from the mob, now you have us bunking up with Charles Manson?" Holly was enraged, now shifting her attention to Cole. "And *you*... To think just this morning I trusted you, thought you were a kind-hearted man who was looking out for us..." She trailed off, the crying now overtaking the anger.

Fury overcame Allie, now certain that Cole was behind drug-ging her. Not only that, but a sudden resentment toward her dad began to fester within as well. Everything he was doing was putting them in more and more danger. She also noticed that when her mom called him out for it, he appeared annoyed more than ashamed.

"Please... I'll tell you everything, Holly. It's not exactly an icebreaker to admit to someone you were part of a cult the first time you meet them. There's some stuff all these years later that I haven't even told my own son, so please don't take offense to it," Cole said.

"Take offense? I'd take *offense* if you said I had one too many wrinkles for my age or told me I was a bad mother. This goes so far beyond that. And to think that you have hidden all this from your poor kid, all these years. When I showed him the picture of his mother you should have seen the look on his face."

Cole looked at his son, who stared down at the floor. His bangs hid his eyes, but he was clearly upset, unable to look at his dad.

"Teagan... I'm so sorry you had to find out this way," Cole said quietly.

"Where's Spencer?" Anthony interrupted.

Nobody spoke for a moment, and as mad as Allie was toward her dad, she felt she had to speak up. It wasn't like Spencer to disappear like this.

"That's why I came downstairs, he wasn't in the room anymore and I assumed he was with Mom..."

The uneasiness intensified when she saw the expression on Cole's face harden. He looked terrified.

"The pond! Listen, I know you have plenty of questions for me, and I promise to answer all of them. But if you want to see your son alive again, we need to find him before he gets there. If he touches that water... It will be too late." Cole hobbled toward the back door again.

"Nothing better happen to my son!" Holly shouted.

Allie cried, everything hitting her all at once. All she wanted was to go back to her biggest problem being how she would explain to her parents that she was going to prom single. She followed them out the door, watching Cole and Teagan run for the 4-wheelers.

"Teagan will hop on back with me! You and Holly grab the red 4-wheeler. Quickly!" Cole shouted.

There was no room for Allie. With all the commotion, her parents forgot about her, leaving her in the dust. She took off in a sprint down the dirt path, her bare feet slamming off rocks as she went, her sore ankle still sending jolts of pain up her leg. She didn't care though; all she could hope for was that her brother would be okay. As she thought back to how badly she treated him the last few years, a cloud of guilt hung over her. If she could just see him again, just talk to him, she would make it right. It wasn't his fault they had a fractured family. Spencer was a sweet kid who had the unfortunate situation of a mean sister and parents who spent more time fighting than making sure he was okay. Up ahead, she saw the trees leading to the water, the 4-wheelers already parked in the tall grass. *Please don't be too late*, she thought.

16

ANTHONY JUMPED OFF THE ATV, not waiting to see if Holly and the others were with him. Spencer was in danger. Everything he did—the whole reason for coming here—was to protect his family. To make sure they were safe from the dangers he had brought upon them. And now, as he ran through the woods down to the pond, he realized he'd put his son in far more danger than he could have ever imagined. He couldn't accept it if something happened to Spencer. It would break him.

Anthony attempted to look through the receding trees out toward the dock, hoping to see the boy, but from his viewpoint it was impossible. *Please, please, please.* He stumbled over a fallen branch, holding onto a tree to keep his balance. Anthony got to the clearing and his heart sank into his stomach. Spencer was on the dock, only a few feet between him and the drop-off into the water, walking slowly in a trance toward the edge, ignoring the commotion behind him as the others burst out of the woods. The boy was alone on the dock, hypnotized by the water. Green foam splashed against the dock's support beams, unnatural waves formed by something beneath the surface.

Anthony realized this is what Alister wanted him to do with his daughter. Bring her here and sacrifice her to them. He wanted to yell to his son, but the words got stuck in his throat as he ran. Holly screamed behind him; what she was saying, Anthony had no idea, all his attention was on Spencer who was now less than a foot from jumping into the water.

"Spence! Don't do it!" Anthony finally forced out.

The boy either didn't hear him or didn't care. He continued his march towards certain death. Anthony reached the dock, his lungs stabbed with razors. He charged at his son, the only thing on his mind grabbing him before he fell in. A glimpse of something under-water—a hand reaching up toward them—briefly caught his atten-tion, but he had to put it in the back of his mind until his son was safe. The scene brought flashbacks of the nightmare he'd had.

"Spencer, stop!" he yelled once more.

This time, the boy paused, turning his head back toward Anthony. Something was wrong, his eyes were out of focus. Anthony didn't realize how fast he was moving. He reached Spencer and yanked the boy's shirt, attempting to throw him down to the dock. As he did, his momentum pulled them to the dock's edge, his balance losing out to gravity. On the way down, he locked on to a set of eyes looking back at him from below the surface. Then they both hit the water with a loud splash, sinking toward the bottom of the pond.

— — — — — — — —

Cole limped along the path, trying to catch Anthony. He watched the boy's father tug on the kid, trying to pull him to safety. In doing so, they fell over the side, down into the water. *Shit!* He picked up speed as best he could, hoping his prosthetic leg didn't come undone along the way. Cole had been through this scenario before. The longer Anthony and Spencer remained in the water, the lower the chance of them being saved. Cole reached the dock. Down in the water, he faintly made out Anthony flailing below, those all too familiar life-forms coming for him like a pack of savage sharks smelling blood. They fed off the blood of the sacrificed, after all, something Cole didn't know initially when joining Burns' Cult.

He looked around for anything that might help him get the boy out of the water without putting himself in danger. A broken branch lay on the dock, out of place, but Cole sure as hell wasn't going to question that at the moment. He picked it up and quickly approached the edge, looking down as Anthony fought his way toward the surface. Cole shoved the stick into the pond, hoping through all the chaos that Anthony saw it penetrate the water.

"Grab it, damn it! Grab the stick, Anthony!" Cole yelled.

A tug on the tree limb, similar to a large fish latching onto bait, almost pulled Cole into the water, but he held firm. Without thinking, Cole knelt at the edge, reaching into the water, feeling for Anthony's hand. Something broke the surface to his left, and Cole glanced over to see one of the deformed hands, bloated and stained green from years of being submerged. The hand fought for control of Anthony with him, like a sickening game of tug-o-war. This wasn't working, Cole needed a better plan. He yanked the branch free from whatever was holding it and struck down on the rotting hand, sending it back below. Anthony's head shot up from the water, his eyes wide in fear.

"Help... Help me get him out!" he said before he was pulled back under. Anthony pushed Spencer up towards the dock; the boy was alive but still in his trance.

Cole didn't notice with his attention on the water, but Holly was screaming. She ran to Spencer's side and helped him up, pulling him back to the safety of land. The boy couldn't walk yet, but Holly dragged him along up onto the grass and set him down. Cole lifted the branch again and struck the dark figure floating behind Anthony in the water, hoping he didn't accidentally hit Anthony on the way down. He wasn't sure what he hit, all he knew is that whatever it was, there was solid contact, followed by Anthony breaking the surface again, choking on water.

Anthony reached up for the edge of the dock, his fingernails clawing the wood, trying to stop himself from being dragged back down. With one final pull, Cole yanked him out of the water, both of them landing hard on the wooden surface. For a moment, they laid on the dock, taking deep breaths without speaking. Cole looked over to Anthony, who was staring straight up at the sky, his face frozen in shock.

Anthony coughed up some of the water, sending splashes of green muck onto the wood. When he turned his head, Cole saw pools of green drool bleeding down from his mouth, his eyes no longer scared but defeated. Anthony dropped his head back down, still trying to regain his breath.

"What... the fuck was that... Cole?" he asked without looking at him.

"I told you... I said stay away from the water. This is why. I also told you last night what happens here. They want to feed, except now there's nobody to barter with Vodyanoy, to... make a deal with them."

The water leveled off, the waves dissipating until everything was calm again, then the bright glow that Cole had come to recognize anytime *they* thought it was time to feed dimmed until it was barely noticeable to the naked eye.

Cole had hoped that by keeping the family away from the water while they were here, he could avoid telling them everything. That strategy had failed spectacularly.

Crying from the shore demanded his attention. Cole looked over and saw Holly kneeling over her son, trying to revive him. The boy had not been in the water too long, but something deeper was wrong with him. Cole hoped Spencer would be okay, praying the hypnosis would wear off. It was Anthony he worried about. He had been under for much longer, choking on the water. In all his years with the Burns family, Cole had never seen someone enter the water and make it back out alive. This was uncharted territory for him.

"Can you stand?" he asked Anthony.

"Fuck... I think so, they clawed my back up pretty bad though."

Anthony stood, grimacing as he reached his hand around to feel for a wound. Cole saw the pain amplify in his eyes when he touched his back.

"Let me see it, turn around," Cole demanded.

Anthony shook his head. "I'm not doing a damn thing until we get off this fucking dock. Let's go." He motioned toward his family, who were preoccupied trying to get Spencer alert.

Cole hesitantly led the way, knowing he was going to receive the wrath of not only Holly but also Anthony and possibly his own son. He hid the pictures of Rebecca on the computer with the intention of one day showing them to Teagan, but he wasn't ready to show his son yet. Cole had a lot of explaining to do, he just hoped it wasn't too late. And he needed to keep an eye on Anthony, monitoring for any signs of change. They may have escaped alive, but Cole now knew for sure… something in the water had awoken.

And it was hungry.

17

EVERYONE SAT at the patio table, awkwardly waiting for someone to speak. Even with the temperature in the 80s, Anthony found himself shivering, the towel wrapped around him doing little good. The water had sat in the sun all day, it should have been as warm as a bath, but his body reacted like he'd fallen in a pool full of ice. Holly sat away from everyone, holding Spencer, rubbing his head while he slowly came out of his daze. He had not said a word since they rescued him, staring off into nothingness.

Cole paced the area, looking straight down, avoiding eye contact with everyone. Anthony couldn't blame him, they all had a reason to be pissed at him, including his own son. The chain of events they had all just survived wasn't just some normal misunderstanding. Cole needed to provide answers quickly, or everyone would turn on him.

"Listen… I want to tell you everything. But I'll start by saying that what just happened caught even me by surprise. Yes, I've told you to avoid the pond, but that was more as a precaution than actually thinking something like that would happen. They have been dormant since Alister and his family disappeared. I came back here to not only hunt Alister down, but make sure the pond didn't feed again," Cole said.

"Who are *they?*" Anthony asked.

Cole scratched his scruff, a tic Anthony now realized was a nervous habit. "I don't have a name for them, but I have a name for who they worship. His name is Vodyanoy. It means 'the one in the water.' Alister referred to him as the 'God below'. That ain't no damn god, that I *do* know." He paused, waiting for questions. When none followed, he continued. "I don't know why Alister knew to come here, or how he communicated with this entity. Many tales around the world have different interpretations of this beast, but one thing they all have in common is how evil this thing is. He can persuade you to sacrifice, offer things in return. And if you make him mad? Well, Alister would be the least of our worries. Seeing as how you didn't tell Holly anything, I might as well fill her in as quickly as possible."

Holly pried her attention away from Spencer for the first time since they rescued him; her eyes could have melted a stick of butter. "Please... indulge me with your damn story, Cole. Give me a reason not to call the cops on you for attempted murder."

"You have every right to hate me, Holly. Please, hear me out. I want what's best for all of you, I swear. I came here after the war, that part was all true. Alister Burns introduced himself to me one day down at the gas station. I was bored and decided to accept his invitation to come check out the compound. That list you saw... I wrote that to remind myself of all the lives lost at his hands. I know my name's on there, and I know I didn't leave after I saw what they were capable of. But I'm telling you, Alister had a way of making you do what he wanted. He was connected with the Vodyanoy. It's not an excuse, it's just a fact."

Anthony knew the feeling. Alister had him ready to give his daughter to them—albeit in a dream. He wanted to say something, but let Cole continue uninterrupted.

"I truly came back here to protect people from them, not harm anyone. That's why—"

Allie stood, unable to stay quiet any longer. "That's why you drugged me? I know it was you now! I woke up in the woods, I saw a lady who tried to force me to the water just like Spencer was about to do…"

This development was news to Anthony, but Cole looked just as confused.

"What? No… I'd never do such a thing. Please, Allie… Tell me everything that happened, who'd you see?" Cole asked.

"She isn't here to answer your questions, not until you finish," Holly snapped.

"Yeah, I suppose I owe you that… Those photos, Teagan… I really wanted to show you some day. It's just… the way things ended with your mom, I didn't have the heart to tell you everything." Cole choked on emotion.

Teagan clenched his jaw, staying quiet.

"I didn't have the heart to tell you because… because she wanted to sacrifice you to them. I saved you the night we left. She was ready to give you to the water. It was the first time he wanted a kid. It made me realize how wrong it all was right then and there. I know I shoulda noticed sooner, but I didn't. Alister's power was diminishing, which meant so was the Vodyanoy. Alister communicated with him, and he desired younger, fresher blood. I wasn't about to watch a baby get tossed in the water, especially my own fucking kid."

"Why'd you talk about her like she was so special then? You made me think Mom was perfect, and that she just got sick at the end…" Teagan snapped back.

"Because, Son. She *was* perfect. But he got in her head and there was no turning back. When I came back to put an end to them, I was hoping to save her, to give her a chance to be the mom I knew she could be to you. But when I got here, everyone was gone. I spent enough time with them to know that one day, Alister planned to sacrifice all of us, a way to make us all one with the God below. It was a ceremony unlike any before. Typically, the sacrificed would slit their throat, to give their blood, and banish themselves from any existence other than serving him. I couldn't be sure that's what happened until I had proof, which until the shit that just happened, I didn't have. Allie said she saw someone. I need to know if anyone else has. They haven't shown themselves to me, I suppose on purpose. But the Great Baptism Alister talked about wasn't one where blood was given. Instead, we were all to drown ourselves in the pond and help Vodyanoy grow stronger by feeding off our souls. You see, the blood fed his faithful, the souls made him stronger."

Anthony sat back, pushing the open wound on his spine into the chair. With all the revelations he'd nearly forgotten that something underwater had ripped his back open, trying to pull him under. The pain was excruciating. He also had a pounding headache, making him want to punch Cole in the mouth with every word he said. He took a deep breath, calming his anger momentarily. There was no way he was going to tell Cole what he saw. Nobody was speaking up.

"When you came to buy the place, Anthony, I tried talking you out of it. I know you took me as some crazy yokel who was just trying to scare you away, but I meant everything I said. When you didn't listen and bought it anyway, I figured the next best thing for me to do was stick close by, and how could I get any closer than to live on the property?"

"Yeah, yeah, I fucked up." Anthony snapped. "Would you have believed any of that shit if the roles were reversed? No, you wouldn't. No sane person would have. So, fucking sue me for trying to expand my business and provide more for my family."

"It's always about your business, Anthony!" Holly said. "You're so damn blind to the rest of the world, your family. You think making more money is all we want, when the truth is we just wanted more of *you*. We have enough already…"

Anthony shot her an angry look; he'd had enough. "Listen to you! I've done everything to provide for this family, EVERYTHING. Am I perfect? No! I didn't see you complaining when you were shopping down on Times Square with all your snooty bitch friends. I didn't see you *complaining* when you showed off the Mercedes to them like you were Queen of New York…"

"Please, we need to focus on the issues at hand here," Cole interrupted.

"I want to leave this place. We're no safer here than we are in our own home, Anthony. If even an ounce of what Cole's saying happens to be true, we might as well be on vacation in Hell itself. I'm not going to fight with you on the subject. You can either come with us, or stay here, but I will not leave the kids," Holly said.

Anthony regretted his outburst, but with the pain in his back, the stress he was feeling in his brain, it was too much to handle. He hadn't even told them what he saw below the water, that would only add to the chaos. *Compromise.* That's what the therapist always said they needed to work on. His gut told him they needed to stay, regardless of the horrors they'd been through, but he knew Holly would have none of that. He needed to buy more time.

"Okay... I'm sorry everyone. I don't know what's coming over me. The stress is no excuse to treat everyone like this, especially my own family. We can leave in the morning. To where? I have no clue, but this place clearly isn't right—"

"Fine. But no more than that! We'll pack tonight and take off first thing tomorrow. I want Spencer sleeping in the room with us. I do *not* want him out of our sight anymore," Holly said.

Everyone sat in silence for a moment, taking it all in. And then, out of nowhere, Spencer spoke. "He wants us... *All* of us."

18

CHRISTOPHER DEPIERRO PARKED the black SUV in the driveway. Before getting out, he observed the surrounding area, making sure there were no other nosey neighbors that needed to be dealt with. He made one quick glance at himself in the mirror, making sure his hair was firmly in place.

"Okay, let's be quick. We can't afford to slip up for the boss again. I've worked way too hard to get where I am to have some lousy real estate scum ruin things for us," he said to Birdman, who sat in the passenger seat finishing off the last of his joint.

"Hold on just a sec, this thing's almost gone. You want a hit?"

"For fuck's sake. Can't you wait until the job's done to do that? How many times I tell you I don't want my Suburban smelling?" Christopher asked.

"Man, you used to be a lot more fun to hang with. We do our best work after smoking," Birdman said, shaking his head and putting the joint out in the soda bottle sitting in his cupholder.

"That was before I was second in command. If Vincent's going to take me seriously, I need to stay off that shit. Let's go." Christopher opened his door quietly.

"Well, maybe all these fuckups wouldn't have happened if you didn't quit smoking... Just saying."

They preferred to do their work at night when it was easier to stay hidden, but time was of the essence right now. The sooner they obtained the address, the sooner they could kill these people and be done with it. Christopher preferred dealing with his regular day-to-day tasks than erasing problems like this, but it was all part of the job. His favorite gig was handling the sports book, where he controlled all the odds and money. Vincent often told Chris how proud he was of the job he'd done with that side of the business. He loved the feeling he got while watching sad, drunken, soon-to-be-divorced husbands seeing one of their bets go sour, knowing they were going to have to turn over boat loads of money to Costello. Either that or get the beating of a lifetime at the hands of Birdman. The truth was, the real reason Christopher quit smoking weed, and drinking for that matter, was that his true vice was gambling. Not only did he run the sports book, but he made—and won—many bets. It was a thrill like no other. The thought of that gave him an idea as they snuck around the back of the house.

"A hundred bucks says I find the folder before you," he said, knowing full well Birdman would bite.

"Okay. Let's up the ante though," Jayme said with smirk. "If I find it first, you have to smoke with me after we kill these bozos, get blitzed out of your mind for old time's sake."

"Sure. And if I find it, you have to give me that signed Paul Pierce jersey you got hanging in your living room."

"Oh, come on, man. You don't even *like* the fucking Celtics, why you need that?"

"Money, money, money my friend. I know I can sell it to one of those lowlifes down at the bar and make bank off the thing. Meanwhile, you just sit there jerking your meat to it and fantasizing about the 2008 Finals."

"I don't jerk off to things that I've already had the pleasure of seeing. That's why I don't think about your mom's tits when I do it anymore..."

"You keep my mom's name out of your mouth, sick fuck," Christopher whispered.

"I'll keep her out of my mouth, I just can't promise she can keep me out of hers," Birdman said while grabbing at his crotch.

Christopher punched him on the shoulder, and both men chuckled. They arrived at the back fence, finding the gate locked. This was something they had come prepared for, of course. Birdman unslung the bag he carried over his shoulder and grabbed a pair of bolt cutters from it, handing them to Christopher.

Christopher didn't want to show his struggle while squeezing the lock, afraid of showing any sign of weakness. In this business, weakness was no good. You had to look in control, always. He turned his back to Birdman, clamping down on the lock and it popped off, falling to the well-manicured lawn. *Too bad they lost their landscaper*, he thought.

Out back, things felt much more secluded, allowing him to let his guard down a little. He still found himself scanning the area for any sign of life. The neighborhood was lined with cookie-cutter homes, just different enough to distinguish themselves from one another but essentially the same American Dream. To have a lawn of this size close to the city must have cost a fortune.

Immediately, Christopher located the shed that Eduardo told them about, sitting in the back corner of the lawn. As they approached, all Christopher could think about was how important it was they got this right. He'd never let Vincent down before, and he wasn't about to do it now. The folder had to be in the shed. The address *had* to be in the folder. It was that simple.

"Okay, keep an eye for anyone while I open this thing," Christopher said while staring at another padlock.

"Screw that, man. We just made a bet. If you open the door, you're going to find it before me," Birdman said.

"Fuck the bet. If we don't get this resolved, who knows what Vincent will do to us. Do you really want to chance that?"

"Please, you're his little pet nephew and Underboss. He'd never do anything to you. I'm the one who'd be fucked. How many Irish men has he ever let in his crew?"

"You would be the first. So, keep watch while I do this, or you might end up not making it to your next St. Patrick's Day parade," Chris said, turning back to the lock.

Without much effort, the bolt cutters sliced through the lock. He yanked the door open, displaying mostly lawn tools spread throughout the inside. The thought of Anthony owning all this stuff when he paid Eduardo to do all the work was hilarious. Just a typical guy trying to pretend to do manly things when he had no intention of actually doing them. Christopher entered the shed, looking around for any sign of the folder. The shelves were cluttered with random tools and cardboard boxes. As he searched, he knocked some of the tools onto the floor, not concerned about their organization. The first box he checked was full of manuals for the lawn equipment, nothing more. He threw the box to the side and grabbed the next. Agitation set in as once again the box had nothing of use, just receipts and warranty information.

"Who the fuck actually keeps this stuff?" he asked himself.

Birdman stuck his head in. "What's that, boss?"

"Nothing, get back out there."

Christopher was losing his patience. He wasn't leaving this house without the damn address. He'd even thought to Google the campground before driving here, hoping to save time. But apparently New Hampshire was loaded with campgrounds and people with nothing better to do than sleep in a fucking tent. Without the name of the place, it would be like searching for a needle in a haystack. There were more boxes on the back shelf, so he made his way over to them and pulled a few down. His eyes brightened when he came to a box with manila folders in it. He opened the first folder and there it was: "Bird's Nest Campground". A smile formed on his freshly shaven face, exposing his pearly white teeth.

"Lookie, lookie. Fucking Goshen, New Hampshire. Is that even a real town?" he called out to Birdman.

"Never heard of it, but I try not to go above the Mass border if I can help it. Too many tourists and rednecks up there for my taste," Birdman said.

"Let's get back to the Suburban, I need to phone the Boss ASAP," Christopher said.

When they got back in the vehicle, Christopher dialed Vincent, putting the call on speaker so Birdman could hear. After one ring he picked up.

"Tell me something good for once..." Vincent's voice echoed through the SUV.

"Boss, we got it. Goshen, New Hampshire. You want us to head right up and take care of this today?" Christopher asked.

"No. I'm coming with you, we move tonight—"

The line went dead, Vincent disconnecting the call abruptly. He had a knack for doing that, nervous perhaps that the call that might be tapped. Christopher looked over to Birdman, who said nothing, only giving a nod. They backed out of the driveway and sped off down the road. Both were so focused on a successful trip that they let their guard down a little *too* much. Across the street, Barbara Hanks, the elderly neighbor of the Graham family, watched as they drove off into the distance, then closed her curtain.

19

ANTHONY SAT in the bathroom with the door shut, wanting privacy. Something was happening to his body he couldn't explain. The sensation of a poison spreading inside, consuming him, increased by the hour. Ever since he fell in the water, things felt off.

His phone chimed shortly after Spencer spoke, but Anthony didn't want anyone to see him look at it, knowing it would just raise more questions and turn his family even more against him. He shifted on the toilet seat cover and pulled his cell out of his pocket. The concern of using a phone, and Vincent finding their location, was real, but he went on regardless, seeing it was a text that had caused the notification buzz.

He unlocked his phone and opened the messages to see a new text from Barbara, their neighbor. In their entire time living in the neighborhood, the old lady had never texted them. They exchanged phone numbers when they first moved in, doing the neighborly service expected of them. Outside of a phone call to complain about her dog chasing after Holly, they never talked on the phone. They rarely even talked face to face when they saw each other. Anthony disliked her so much that he had her name saved in his phone as

"Bitchy Barbara." So, to get a text from her wasn't normal. Anthony read the message three times.

BITCHY BARBARA: HELLO ANTHONY. I JUST WANTED TO LET YOU KNOW, A COUPLE FELLOWS IN A BLACK SUV CAME BY YOUR HOUSE THIS MORNING. I CAUGHT THEM SNOOPING IN YOUR SHED OUT BACK. THEY TOOK SOME-THING AND LEFT.

"Fuck," Anthony whispered.

It wasn't until he read the text that he remembered sticking the property folder in there. At first, he prayed they hadn't found it, but he knew better. They were trained professionals; there was a very slim chance they left his house without the address to the campground. And if they had found it, the odds of them coming tonight were high. The way he saw it, he had two options. He could tell Holly, who would want to leave before they showed up, or he could keep it from her, and take care of business tonight when they arrived. It was a decision much more difficult than it had any right to be.

Anthony stood and walked to the sink. He almost jumped back when he spotted his reflection: his eyes were bloodshot, the pupils a lighter shade of brown than normal. His back was still throbbing, so he unbuttoned his shirt to get a look. He turned around and glanced over his shoulder in the mirror. A gash started between his shoulder blades and ran down to the center of his back. It wasn't just one scratch but four bloody trails. The skin around each scratch had begun to swell, but Anthony noticed the claw marks didn't look like typical scratches. The blood had mostly dried, showing the early stages of scabbing. Within that scabbing was a strange green texture mixed in with the crimson. It appeared infected. Anthony grabbed a piece of toilet paper and dabbed the middle of his back. Not only was it dead center and hard to reach, but he was reminded painfully of the bullet that'd ripped through his arm when he stretched the muscle.

"Fuck!" he muttered.

When he pulled the toilet paper away, the green sludge painting the edge of his scratch marks stuck to the paper, a glue-like substance. Without thinking, Anthony held it up to his nose and sniffed. He instantly regretted it; the slime smelled like a can of spoiled sardines. When he looked back to the mirror, he stifled a scream. Alister Burns stood behind him.

Except he wasn't really there, he was transparent. His eyes were not the white orbs, or even the green that Anthony had seen in his nightmares. Instead, blank eye sockets that resembled two black holes more than eyes stared back at him.

"We are connected now, Anthony. Whether you want it or not, you are part of us. There is no use fighting the urge to join..." Alister said, but his mouth wasn't moving.

"What's happening to me?" Anthony asked, spinning to face Alister.

Alister wasn't there.

When he returned his focus to the mirror, the reflection was gone. He turned the sink on and splashed water on his face, now feeling sick to his stomach. *Keep your shit together, man*, he thought. After turning the sink off, he tossed the green toilet paper in the toilet and flushed it down. There was no way he could let the others see this. He put his shirt back on and buttoned it up, shaking his head as he walked out of the bathroom. The decision was made. He would take care of the problem tonight, get rid of Vincent's crew. He needed to prepare, and time was running out.

––––––––––

Holly sat on the edge of Spencer's bed, rubbing his back while fighting away tears. After he spoke his one, ominous sentence, he'd fallen back into silence. *What is happening to my baby?* She wondered. He appeared to be getting better, but every time she thought he was coming back to reality, he returned to his catatonic state. It was hard to imagine the shock he went through on the dock. Quite frankly, she didn't *want* to imagine it. Her heart broke at the thought of their family falling apart; she wasn't sure she could add any more weight to the strain holding her sanity together. *Be their rock.* That phrase brought her thoughts back to Cole. As much as she'd wanted to tear him apart just a few hours ago, she found herself believing what he said—or at least *wanting* to believe him. Every bone in her body told her that he was a good person, and she wanted to latch on to that hope.

It was Anthony she deemed truly responsible. There was no doubt in Holly's mind he thought he was doing what was best for them. That he was hiding things to protect his family. Unfortunately, it'd become a slippery slope he was getting far too comfortable with. He hid the agreement with Vincent. He hid the story Cole told him about the cult's history. What else wasn't he telling her that might possibly be putting them in danger? Holly still wasn't sure what they would do when they left tomorrow. Where would they go? Who would they reach out to for help? All she knew was this place was not the answer. She got up carefully, so as to not disturb her boy who apparently needed more rest. After taking one final glance back at him, she silently left the room to start packing. When she entered the bedroom her and Anthony had shared, she couldn't help but feel relieved to see he was no longer in there. She was sick of the lies. Sick of hearing him try to talk himself out of a corner. At the moment, she just didn't have the energy to deal with it. Her eyes started to water up, but she forced herself through it and tossed clothes back into the suitcases she had put out. Holly pushed the dirty clothes down to make more room and felt a hard bulge under the bottom layer of clothing. *The gun.* With all the craziness, she forgot she'd packed it. What good would the gun even do? She hadn't seen anything in the water, in the end, but based on how Spencer was acting, how serious Cole was about getting close to the water, and how strange Anthony had behaved, she felt a small amount of relief knowing it was there.

After getting all the clothes packed, Holly walked over to the window and gazed out at the land. The sun was starting to take its place behind the treetops, giving off beautiful pink and orange hues. *Pink skies at night, sailors delight*, she thought. She laughed to herself as she looked in the opposite direction and saw dark clouds on the horizon.

"That's more like it."

There had been terrible storms over the last few weeks in the area, and it appeared tonight would bring another. As long as it wasn't raining when they left tomorrow, she didn't care. Driving half a day in torrential downpours would be the icing on the cake of one of the worst weeks of her life. She heard a motor outside and shifted her attention from the sky to the path. Anthony sat behind the driver's seat of the van, driving it down the trail toward the woods. Why would he be going out there after what just happened? When the van was out of sight, she started to walk away, but saw Cole sitting down at the picnic table with Teagan and Allie. She decided it was time to apologize to Cole: he *had* saved Anthony after all. If he was truly evil, would he have put his own life on the line to pull someone from the danger in the pond? It seemed unlikely. She took a deep breath and walked downstairs, prepared to eat some crow.

20

ANTHONY PARKED the van and hopped out. Hiding the vehicle in the forest would buy some more time when Vincent's men showed up. If they arrived and didn't see the van, *maybe* they would just turn around and leave. Highly unlikely after driving all this way, but it would at least give them some doubt about the family hiding here. This was step one of the plan he and Cole discussed earlier. Give the appearance of nobody home. Holly wouldn't like it, but eventually Anthony would tell her that she and the kids would need to hide in the basement to stay safe while they got rid of the problem.

He walked back toward the house, his experience in the bathroom swirling through his thoughts. A sliver of hope remained that it was all due to him being off his meds, seeing delusional visions as a result of withdrawal or his mind's fucked up chemistry. Deep down, he knew that wasn't true. Anthony could sense his body going through a transformation—not just the visible changes to his back and eyes—but inside, almost like a cancer patient knowing something was altering the normality within. He could feel his anger hibernating in his core, waiting to come out. As if his subconscious was allowing him to get these last few things done before it inevitably exploded.

You are connected with us now...

What exactly did Alister mean by that statement? The words brought back flashes of what he saw under the water. When his body sank to the murkiness below, he couldn't help but open his eyes wide in surprise, unsure of what the pond water would do to his vision. As his eyes shot open, he saw things worse than any nightmare could ever conjure. A green haze as though he were swimming in pure poison. The corpses of a young man and woman who appeared to have just recently been drained of life.

And worse, he saw *them*. This time, in the flesh.

Their bodies lay scattered along the bottom of the pond's floor, reminding him of vampires asleep for a thousand years in their coffins. Except instead of coffins, the pond itself was their chamber. Not all of them remained dormant—a few around Anthony were awoken by his plunge into the water. He watched as their eyes fluttered open, and their bodies moved much faster than he would have expected physically possible. They came for him, reaching up toward him with their mouths open wide, ready to feed. Farther back, through the cloudy green haze, he spotted Alister, floating in the center of the water and watching it all while flashing a toothy smile.

Anthony shook the thought away, bringing his attention back to what needed to be done to stop Vincent. Barbara was a nosey old bitch, but she might have just saved their lives by gawking out her window. On a regular basis he'd found himself hoping she croaked, and that her stupid little dog would get flattened by a studded tire. Now he was thankful that didn't happen. In fact, he felt like he could actively kiss Flower on his doggie lips next time he saw him if it meant this crisis was finally over.

The house came back into view after walking for a few minutes. The storm clouds made it seem as if nightfall was close, but he still couldn't help the sense he was running out of time.

A jolt of pain shot from his back, up through the center of his chest, bringing him to his knees. Something was happening inside his body, the agony forcing him to cry out.

"What the fuck! What is happening to me?"

Anthony keeled over, holding his stomach as if that would stop the pain from throbbing.

Bring us Allie... We can protect you tonight...

He looked around, trying to see where the voice was coming from. After he did a full circle, he realized it was inside his head. He also realized that the pond was close by. The voice was Alister. *How is he doing this?* Anthony wondered. Bolts of pain blasted through his entire body, like the finale of some professional fireworks display. It hurt *so* badly he thought he surely should have passed out.

Anthony lifted his chin, staring through squinting eyes toward the pond. Why do they want Allie? Why can't they just take Vincent and his men? That could kill two birds with one stone. He gritted his teeth and forced himself to his feet. There was no time to talk to voices in his head or pout. Cloudiness came over his vision. He squeezed his eyes shut, trying to adjust them back to normal, but when he opened them, Alister and his followers stood in front of him. Anthony jumped back, falling on his backside and watched as they approached. Just like in the bathroom, they were there but not *really there*, transparent in the gloominess of the oncoming storm. Alister led the way, his eyes radiating a bright green glow, his face carrying a blank expression. He tilted his head to the side, looking closely at Anthony as he backed up on the dirt path, now oblivious to the pain ripping through his body.

Alister's mouth opened wide, revealing a set of grimy teeth covered in sludge; his jaw continued to lower until the opening in his mouth was at least a foot wide.

"You will do as we say, Anthony. I am not one to ask twice. If you don't willingly bring her to us, we will do it for you. And then we will offer no such protection..."

Anthony couldn't talk. He found himself glued to Alister and his lurkers—walking in unison behind their leader like an assembly line. As they got closer, the pain in Anthony's body intensified, ravaging his brain. It felt like something was swimming around inside him, working its way upward.

Holding the sides of his head, his temples throbbing like someone injecting a hundred needles into his skull, he said, "Why? Why do you want my daughter so much?"

Alister was now a mere three feet from Anthony, towering over him. His sadistic smile faded away, switching to pure resentment. *"Because... that is who he wants. We do not question Vodyanoy, and we surely won't let a cynic doubt his choice."*

A sudden intensity stabbed the back of Anthony's head, bringing the sensation of being stung by a horde of wasps. He dropped from his crawling position, rolling to his stomach, and curled up into a ball. For a moment, he lost all consciousness of the horrors in front of him. Moisture trickled from his ear, and his first thought was blood, that he must be experiencing a brain hemorrhage, dying right here in the dirt. He wiped away the liquid and looked at his hand. Instead of the dark crimson of blood, his fingers were covered in a green liquid. Before he had a chance to comprehend, the thundering voice of Alister roared out like it was being shouted inches from his ear.

BRING HER TO US!

He looked up, prepared for Alister, prepared for death. Instead, the trail was empty, only the rocky dirt path and the swaying trees on each side remained. For a while, Anthony was unable to move. He slowly sat up and hugged his knees, crying and praying it would just be over.

Unfortunately, it was just getting started.

21

ALLIE WAS STRUGGLING to keep it together. She'd been hiding so many secrets from her parents, afraid to add to the stress they found themselves in. But she needed her mom, needed the comfort of telling someone what she was hiding. She couldn't hold it in anymore, regardless of what it might do to their crumbling family. After Cole and Teagan went off to tend to some jobs on the property, Allie decided to find her mom and have a sit-down talk, just the two of them.

She entered through the back door, listening for any commotion in the house. Listening for an argument between her mom and dad. The silence was a welcoming sound as she climbed the stairs. The door to the room she and Spencer were sharing remained shut, just a sliver of space giving a small view into the room. Before entering, Allie stood outside the door and watched her mom, sitting on the edge of Spencer's bed and crying by herself. Maybe now really wasn't the best time to throw more stressful news her way. Her brother almost drowned, or worse, got torn apart by whatever those things were in the water. Her dad came even closer to death.

Allie started to have second thoughts of telling her mom everything, debating whether to turn and walk away. But as she took a step back, a floorboard creaked, giving her away. Her mom turned to the door with shimmering eyes.

"Allie?"

"Hi, Mom. Can we talk?"

"Of course, hon. What's on your mind? Not like we have anything exciting going on," Holly said with a forced smile.

"How's he doing?" Allie nodded toward Spencer.

"I think he'll be okay. The poor kid's been through a lot though. I can only imagine what's going on in that mind of his. Your mind too, for that matter. How are *you* doing?"

"I'm fine..." she started, then reminded herself why she was there. "That's not true. I'm a wreck, Mom. There's so much I need to tell you, I just don't know where to begin." Her eyes glistened as tears fought to escape.

"Hon, I know you've been put in a situation no kid should ever have to go through. Not just these last few days on the run and dealing with this creepy ass campground. But even *before* that. I want you to know your father and I have been working hard on fixing this relationship, fixing our family."

"I know, Mom... That's not it though. That might be why I haven't come to talk with you about things sooner, but this isn't about that stuff." Allie noticed the perplexed look on her mom's face.

"What else in the world could be going on worse than any of that?"

Allie considered coming right out and saying it but thought it may be best to ease into the bombshell. "Well, I know things have been rough with you and Dad for a while. So... any time something bad happens in my own life, I try not to bother you with it. You guys think I'm just some grouchy teen when deep down I'm falling apart." Allie paused, seeing the shame in Holly's face at the realization she hadn't been there for her. "First off, I tried to say this when we got back from the pond. Something happened to me, Mom. I don't think it was Cole anymore, but I woke up in the forest last night with no idea how I got there. I saw things... heard things. The way

Spencer was acting on the dock makes me think someone did it to him too, or that it's at least all related somehow. Are you experiencing any strange occurrences since we got here?"

"I've had some strange dreams, but nothing like that. Do you think maybe you were sleep walking out there?"

"Seriously, Mom? I've never sleepwalked in my life, why would it start here? And how would that explain what happened to Spencer? I'm telling you, somebody did this to us. And that picture you showed Teagan? I saw the lady in that picture holding him as a baby when I was in the woods. I didn't know who it was when I saw her, but after looking at it, everything connected. She told me they want me to be with them, that I had no choice."

"Allie... Are you sure you didn't see the picture first and *then* envision her in the woods? That doesn't make any sense, how would you imagine her when you didn't even know what she looked like?"

"No! I know this sounds crazy, but she was there!"

"Well, we are leaving first thing tomorrow, we won't have to worry about it anymore. Whatever this place is, it will all be behind us," Holly said, clearly hoping that would help comfort Allie.

"I just wish Spence would come out of this so I could talk to him," Allie said. "If he saw the same things I did, it would explain why he was about to give himself to the water."

"We won't speak about this with him, you understand me? He's been through enough, the last thing I want to do is stress him when he wakes up and send him into another panic attack."

"I just want to know what's going on..." Allie whispered, fighting back more tears.

Holly got up and hugged her. Her mother's embrace felt so much better than she expected. As affectionate as her parents were with her when she was younger, they rarely showed it anymore. She understood that was mostly her doing, but in this moment, she welcomed the warm embrace of her mother. Which made the next part of her confession that much harder.

"I keep pretending like I actually care about prom, when the truth is I don't want to go anywhere near the place—"

"What? That's all you've cared about this entire school year," Holly said.

"Let me finish, Mom. Please. I don't care about prom because Troy dumped me..."

Holly gave her a look as if she felt awful for her, understood her pain. "I'm so sorry, Allie. It's part of life, but that doesn't make it any easier to live through—"

"Mom... none of that matters," Allie choked up, forcing herself to get out the next sentence. "I... I'm pregnant."

22

CLOE SAT OUT BACK, watching Teagan ride away on his 4-wheeler as the storm clouds rolled in to block out the day's remaining sun. The conversation went about as well as he expected it to. He'd asked to speak with Allie and Teagan separately to make amends with them. After everything that happened earlier, he didn't think the Grahams would allow him to talk with their daughter, but his explanation must have brought back at least some of the trust he'd earned upon their arrival.

Allie told him she had trust issues, and that she could tell deep down he was a good man. But she had no explanation as to what happened to her. He asked her about what she saw in the woods, more specifically, *who* she saw. It didn't take long for her description to scream Rebecca. Cole's heart skipped a few beats at the thought of seeing her again, but he reminded himself she wasn't really the Rebecca he fell in love with.

From the way Allie explained her foggy brain when awaking in the woods, it sounded an awful lot like the effects of the concoction Alister used to give those about to be sacrificed. In truth, the liquid in the cups had always been water from the pond mixed with a shot of whiskey to help ease the nerves. Something in the water numbed the body, preparing it for the transition of life from body to pond, which in turn fed them, made them more powerful. Cole figured out that not only was Alister losing his powers, leading him to want younger blood, but so was the entity he worshipped. Cole refused to call it a god. Allie said it was as if Rebecca was a ghost, her body not fully visible. That gave Cole hope. It meant they still weren't powerful enough to leave the pond, acting as some type of specter, only able to show themselves for small amounts of time. That would all change if they got the kids. He had a feeling they wanted Spencer too—Cole didn't believe for a second the boy would willingly jump in the water—especially in such a robotic stride. Again, it brought back memories of those sacrifices about to give themselves to the water.

He wanted to help the Graham family stay safe and had to agree that leaving was their best bet at survival. During the entire stretch of time Cole had been back at the campground, he hadn't seen any signs of Alister or his group. No sightings, no unexplained occurrences. But the feeling that they were around never left. For a time, he thought he was paranoid, just going through a form of PTSD about the cult. Deep down, he knew they would return some day. Alister's whole intention was to eventually sacrifice them all to the waters and become forever connected to his "god." He once told Cole that they would all live on in eternity. He also referred to the body of water as a powerful source of energy, but he never got into the detail about why this spot was so special. What gave the water its power? Why had the entity chosen this place to reside specifically? And how the hell had Alister known to come here in the first place? Those were questions that Cole never got the answers to in his time with Mr. Burns.

When he first came back, after finding the compound absent of the cult, Cole tried to get rid of the pond. He called a company to come out and drain the body of water, but once the local businesses found out where he was located, they all turned the job down. He wasn't even so sure that draining the pond would have solved the problem anyway—just led to new ones. And then when he went days, weeks, months, and eventually a few years without seeing or hearing from them, he decided to let it rest—at least for the time being. He had a son to focus on, and the last thing he wanted Teagan to think was that he was some lunatic out to hunt something living in the water that wasn't there.

A sense of dread overcame Cole at the idea he might cross paths with Alister again. He wanted to end his reign of terror once and for all, but he also knew the power behind those convincing eyes. After years of being in the water, who knew what new powers he possessed. Although clearly not at full strength, that didn't mean he wasn't strong enough to convince Cole to do something terrible, like sacrifice his kid and complete the ceremony Cole prevented on Teagan's second birthday. The thought sent fear coursing through his body.

Teagan sat mostly in silence while listening to Cole dig himself out of a hole, explaining his past. He told Teagan it was for his own good. He told him he didn't want to hurt him by revealing the whole story while he was too young to understand. It wasn't just hiding his mother from him; it was what the entire cult was all about. The story Cole told strangers about being a groundskeeper for the campground was the same lie he told his own son. He expected more of a reaction from Teagan. Hatred. Anger. *Anything.* Instead, all the boy gave him was the silent treatment, with one word answers when he finally did decide to respond. It was a lot harder to build back trust with your own flesh and blood after years of lies compared to a family that didn't depend on you and had only known you a few days. He could only imagine what Teagan was thinking on the inside. He'd never seen him so quiet.

Teagan was now out of sight, the dust kicked up from the speeding ATV settling back down on the path. Cole had no idea where he was going, but he didn't feel like pushing it too far. He assumed the boy needed some time to think about everything by himself. If the incoming storm was anything like the last few that had plowed through the area, he wouldn't have much time to think before getting stuck in a torrential downpour. Cole would give it some time, but if Teagan didn't return rather soon, he'd have no choice but to go after him and get him back. The storms were far more violent than anyone in New England was used to, more than your typical thunderstorm. The weatherman on the radio said it was a result of an out of season tropical storm system working its way up the coast, leading to intense weather all through New England.

After a few more moments of contemplation, a crack of thunder brought Cole alert. He needed to warn the others to stay indoors until it passed, however long that may be. But first, he wanted to find Anthony and make sure he was okay. He appeared to be in a great deal of pain after Cole pulled him out of the water. He seemed agitated, and after Spencer spoke, Anthony stormed out of the room and went upstairs before eventually taking his van down in the south field. It was the same direction Teagan was headed.

Cole hadn't cried since the day he escaped with Teagan years ago, but as he sat watching the coming storm, it was a struggle to fight back the tears. So much had gone wrong in the past two days.

He loosened the strap on his prosthetic leg, massaging the nub. While Alister had taken away the pain Cole lived with every day, storms still brought aches and pains back to his joints. That was likely due to Father Time, not the explosion that took his leg.

The flashback of the car bomb made him flinch. When the vehicle exploded, it sent him flying and knocked him unconscious. When he woke, his body was strapped to a hospital bed, and he was disabled.

He never wanted anyone's pity. The truth was: he was supposed to be leading the way that day but held back for a moment to give a command. One of his men didn't hear the orders and kept going, triggering the bomb, and killing him and others around him instantly. Had Cole not stopped, it would have been him that got sent home in a bag. It *should* have been him. It was his job to protect his fellow soldiers, and he failed them. He wouldn't fail the Graham family. Slowly, he strapped his leg back on and got up. It was time to prepare.

23

SPENCER OPENED his eyes to discover his head throbbing like it had just been stomped on by an elephant. He blinked a few times, trying to regain clear vision. Attempting to sit up, he saw Allie and his mom sitting in the corner of the room, hugging each other and crying. So much crying these last few days. It hurt to hold his head up for more than a few seconds, so he dropped back to the pillow, taking a deep breath. The movement grabbed the attention of his family, they ended their embrace and rushed to his bedside.

"Spence!" Allie yelled.

"Hi, guys. Did I miss anything?" he asked with a smile.

Holly knelt and hugged him, squeezing harder than Spencer would have preferred after waking up and feeling like his body had been in a car wreck. He let her hug though, the comfort of his mom's strength, of her familiar scent, helped ease some of the fear.

"Oh, thank God you're okay, buddy. How are you feeling?" his mom asked.

"Sore... I could use some of that lemonade that Cole made."

Holly eagerly jumped to her feet and headed to the door. "Talk with your sister, I'll get that for you right now, kiddo." She left the room and Spencer heard her footsteps thumping down the stairs two at a time.

"Spence... I'm so sorry about the way I've been treating you. None of this is your fault. I've been such an awful sister to you lately..." Allie trailed off, her voice trembling.

"It's okay. I know you don't mean a lot of the stuff you've said. And you're the best sister, I wouldn't want anyone else."

Allie wiped a tear away with the back of her hand. "I love you so much. I'll be different from now on, I promise. I thought we lost you and all I could think about was how mean I was to you the last time we talked."

Holly rushed back into the room with a cup in hand. The ice clinking off the glass was the most satisfying sound Spencer had heard in his life. His throat felt rough and dry, like he'd inhaled a bunch of sand and it still clung to the back of his lungs. He grabbed the glass, which was already starting to perspire from the humidity the storm brought with it. Before saying anything, he drank the entire glass in four giant gulps, the cold liquid instantly soothing his insides. Spencer let out a loud belch, which made them all laugh.

"Only time I can get away with that and not get yelled at," he said with a grin.

"We're leaving in the morning. Hopefully this storm passes in time so we can get out of here. I won't let you out of my sight the rest of the time we are here, okay sweetie?" Holly asked.

Spencer nodded, relieved to hear that. Everything that happened leading up to falling in the water was a blur to him. He heard the voices, saw the kids, and once he made eye contact with them, everything got fuzzy. He shrank back in fear at the thought of almost dying. He wasn't even sure how he got out of the water. Brief, rapid bursts from his memory were there, but it was as if they were in fast-forward and half the film was missing.

"How'd I get back here? I don't remember anything."

Allie and Holly shared a concerned look with one another, and he knew they were probably trying to figure out how much to tell him. His mom spoke, "Your dad jumped in the water after you and pulled you out. We dragged you to the side, and I thought... I thought you drowned in the water because you weren't moving. But I saw you breathing, and then you randomly fluttered your eyes here and there." She leaned in and hugged him again before continuing. "We thought you were coming back to us when you spoke earlier. You said something, then went back into a deep sleep..."

Hearing that brought back some of his memories like a gust of wind blowing right through him. Some of them could have been dreams while he was sleeping, but either way, panic struck him at once. He took deep breaths, trying to calm himself, but it wasn't working. Spencer reached up and held onto his mom's shirt, something he often did when he was having one of his attacks. She closed her eyes, shaking her head.

"I shouldn't have gotten you worked up like that, I'm sorry. Take deep breaths, just like Dr. Goodman taught us... In... and out."

After a few rounds of concentrated breathing, Spencer felt himself calming down. But that didn't erase the images stuck in his mind. When he fell in the water, he saw *them*. Ripping and clawing at his dad while he tried to pull Spencer to safety. The look in his dad's eyes before he got Spencer up on the dock would be burned into his mind forever. There had been a transition, where his eyes went from worrying and scared to pained, and then completely foreign. It was a wonder that Spencer got to safety before they reached him, unharmed.

"Mom, there were so many of them in the water... I saw one of them grab Dad... Then I like, passed out or something." Holly's eyes sank with sadness. They sat in silence for a few moments before he spoke again. "Dad's changing, I saw it in his eyes. They did something to him, Mom..."

"Oh, Spence. Your dad is just stressed with everything going on. He's doing what he thinks is best for us all, whether we agree or not. All we want is to keep you safe..."

It was frustrating that, once again, a grownup had pushed aside his fears. There wasn't much he felt he could say to make her believe him, but he recognized the doubt in her voice. Maybe she believed some of what he was saying and only said what she thought was the right thing to make him feel better.

Whether she believed or not, his dad was starting to scare him. Even before the water incident, he'd struggled to control his mood since they arrived here. His dad had promised to work on the short temper. Things had been better between them, at least when his dad was around. He was always at the office, or showing off a listing somewhere, getting home at late hours. When Spencer and Allie were younger, he was around a lot more. He would be at their sporting events, dance recitals, and even teacher conferences. But now, the odds were high that he would show up late, even to their birthday parties. Spencer was just grateful that his dad had started joking around more with him again and took his eyes off his phone for two seconds to play with him in his room. That all changed when they got here.

"I wish you would believe me; he's scaring me—"

He stopped talking when he looked over his mom's shoulder toward the door. Anthony stood, sweat dripping down his grimacing face. *Did he hear me?* Spencer thought.

The room went silent, everyone staring at Anthony. When Anthony realized Spencer was alert, he walked into the room and smiled.

"I thought I heard his voice! How are you buddy?"

"Good…"

"You seem quiet, what'd I just walk in to here?" Anthony surveyed the room. "You're *all* quiet…"

"Spencer still feels off, but we're just glad to have him back. I think he needs more rest before he's at full strength, poor kid," Holly said.

Anthony winced, clutching his stomach before speaking again. "Yeah… About that, we have to start preparing for Vincent's crew. We're lucky to have made it this far."

Holly shook her head. "And how do you suppose we do that, Anthony? I just said Spencer can't do anything right now."

"He doesn't have to do a damn thing, Holly. I spoke with Cole earlier to come up with a plan. It's why I moved the van out of view. He suggested everyone hide in the basement and he would answer the door as if he was the only one here. If we keep it dark down there, they likely won't even look."

"*That's* the big plan? Hide in the fucking basement? I'd rather leave tonight," Holly snapped.

Spencer couldn't believe it took less than five minutes after he woke up before they started fighting again. Allie sat on the bed next to him and gave him a knowing smile. The thought of finally being on the same page with her helped him feel a little better. He watched his dad getting angrier by the second, his patience thinner than his grampa's hairline.

"I don't know if you've looked around, Holly, but we are about to be in the center of a brutal storm. Our best bet's to wait out the storm and leave in the morning like we planned," Anthony said.

Something in his eyes told another story. Anthony went to say something else, but once again clutched his stomach, this time dropping to his knees in pain. A cry of agony escaped; his face blocked by his hanging bangs.

"Are you okay?" Holly asked in a tone lacking any real empathy.

Anthony vomited on the carpet, a green sludge shooting out of his mouth and spreading across the floor. He lifted his head, breathing heavily, and looked around at his family. Spencer wanted to crawl back under the blankets and hide: his dad's face looked worse than any boogeyman ever could. His eyes had gone bloodshot, but instead of red lines webbing throughout, they were bright green.

"Oh my God," Holly said, covering her mouth.

Anthony wiped the green drool from his chin and looked back down at the floor.

"Something in that water poisoned me... I'm not right..."

As frightened of his dad as he was right now, Spencer found himself wanting to get up and hug him. He battled different emotions inside, debating on what he should do. Whatever was happening to his dad, it wasn't his choice. The good man that raised him and used to build giant Lego forts around his bed was still buried deep within, fighting to get out.

"We need to get you to a doctor, Anthony. Protecting us from these people won't do any good if you're killing yourself in the process," Holly said.

Anthony shook his head. "No. I'll get help as soon as this is over, Holly. Let Cole and I take care of this, then we can go wherever your heart desires tomorrow, got it?"

"And what makes you so sure they'll be here tonight? What if we hide out in the basement and they don't even show up? Are we just going to live our life in a dark room, waiting?"

"Can you *please*, stop with the sarcastic shit?" Anthony snapped, looking at the rest of his family before speaking again. "I know they'll be coming… because Barbara texted me saying she saw them snooping through our back yard this morning."

Holly raised her brow in irritation. "Another thing you decided to hold from us, huh? Didn't you say they would be going through our house? Why do you assume that means they know where to go?"

"Because I threw the folder with the campground info in the shed with some junk mail. There's no guarantee they found it, but I promise you they ripped the place apart searching. Please, trust me on this."

Spencer wanted his mom to say no. He *wanted* her to say let's get out of here right this second. But he kept his mouth shut, afraid it would set his dad off again. Allie tensed up next to him, her posture letting Spencer know she was just as afraid.

"There has to be another way… I want what's best for the kids, if that's what Cole thinks is safest… then fine," Holly said unconvincingly.

No, no, no! Spencer thought. This place was getting in all their heads, making them see things that weren't really there, forcing them do things that they would never do. Allie again grabbed his hand and held it firm. She looked at him and mouthed, "It will be okay."

"I would like a word with you in private, Anthony," Holly said before looking back at the kids. "Hang tight guys, everything will be okay."

Somehow, all of these empty promises only made Spencer feel worse.

———————————

"It's over... Do you hear me? *Over!*" Holly said, sneering at the sight of her sickly-looking husband. "I've watched you put us all in danger for the last time. When we get back to the city tomorrow, we can get someone to watch the kids so we can figure out the best way to approach this."

It was hard to feel bad for him when this was all his own doing. She expected him to beg, to say things would change and they would talk more with the therapist, but his reaction was somehow worse. He *laughed.*

When they'd left the kids in their bedroom, they walked down to the kitchen, trying to make sure they were out of earshot so the kids wouldn't hear them. *As if it matters at this point,* Holly thought. The damage had been done. Now, not only would she need to continue seeing a therapist, but their kids would also likely require some help to correct years of mistakes. It broke her heart to think of what impact this would have on them while they were still molding into grown adults.

"And what's your plan, Holly? To take the kids to Guatemala and live in some hut, going about each day in fear and looking out your straw window to make sure nobody's coming? You can hate me all you want. But I'm keeping us safe. *I* am the one providing for us and giving you what you need. Instead of being thankful for everything, you sit there continuing to be ungrateful and judging everything I do, commenting on every fucking thing I say. So, I really suggest thinking this over before you make a stupid decision."

Holly shook her head, tears sliding down her cheeks. "What happened to you, Tony? You used to be such a good man. To me. To them. We can blame things on this situation for breaking the glass floor beneath our marriage, but this place didn't do this to you... It just brought out the worst in you. And I... I can't ever let this just go. You have to understand that. We've done enough damage to the kids, if we have any chance to salvage their future, we need to end this..."

Anthony closed his eyes and took a deep breath, sending a rancid fishy odor in Holly's direction. She wanted to gag.

"And you need to see a doctor, whether you think you do or not. It's obviously not normal to throw up green sludge, Tony. The water must've given you some sort of infection."

"Seeing a doctor will do me no good if we all get killed tonight. Let me handle this situation first. If they don't show up tonight, we can still leave tomorrow. You can still figure out whatever it is you think is better than being with me. I know in my gut, they are going to come tonight," Anthony said.

"What I still don't understand, is how you think the two of you can take them down. You don't even know how many will show up. Cole is handicapped, and you... you aren't exactly the assassin type. I don't see how you even stand a chance with them. Meanwhile, I'm supposed to hide with the kids like sitting ducks if they do something to you. I don't like any of this!"

Anthony clutched his stomach, but Holly could tell he was trying to hide the pain. She knew he was getting agitated with her, but she wasn't exactly sure what he was envisioning in his head. If something was to ever happen to the kids, she would never forgive him.

"Holly... I don't have time to argue anymore. There are things I need to do before nightfall. And this fucking storm is putting a damper on all that. The rain's already started, I need to prepare. Whenever Cole gets back, he will show you the basement and get you guys set up. Whether you feel the same way or not, I still love you. But please, get the fuck out of my way..." He blasted past her. His face looked deathly, his eyes sunken and dark. Holly stood in the hallway and cried for a moment, then took a deep breath and headed back upstairs to her kids. *Be their rock.*

24

COLE HOPPED on the remaining 4-wheeler and started it up. The rain had picked up intensity over the last twenty minutes, no longer just a light sprinkle. Dark clouds hogged the sky, warning him it was only going to get worse. He needed to find Teagan and tell him it was time to get to safety. Not just because of the incoming storm, but also because Anthony told him about the text message he got earlier. He knew there was a very high likelihood the men coming for the Graham family would show up tonight.

When Anthony got back from parking the van down in the woods, he sat Cole aside and told him everything. In that moment, all Cole cared about was going after his son, catching up with the boy, and talking more about all the secrets he'd hid from him over the years. Rain splashed against his exposed face as he sped off down the trail searching for Teagan. He had an idea exactly where the boy was. The crackling of a thunderbolt shot off in the distance, making Cole's heart jump into his throat. He was on edge, pushing a level he hadn't felt since the night he left the cult. A gust of wind forced the rain to momentarily fall sideways, obscuring anything more than a few feet in front of Cole.

Up ahead, a flash of lightning popped off in the horizon, as if to say, "He's over here." Cole saw the other 4-wheeler sitting at the edge of the forest. He parked next to it and walked along the trail. The tall, wet grass slid against his good leg like a batch of slithering snakes. Through the trees he spotted Teagan sitting at the water's edge, facing the pond with his back to Cole. The boy didn't hear him coming, which surprised Cole considering the 4-wheeler wasn't exactly quiet. Teagan was talking to himself. With the intensity of the rain peppering down on the water, he couldn't make out what his son was saying. He reached the bottom of the wooded trail and approached the water. Teagan whirled around, seeing Cole for the first time. He was crying and wiped the tears away.

"What do you want?"

"Can I come sit with you for a few?" Cole asked.

Teagan's eyes turned to angry slits, but he nodded anyway. Cole appreciated the boy at least giving him a chance to redeem himself.

"I know that no matter how many times I say I'm sorry, it won't make a difference. I just hope you can see *why* I didn't say anything about how things went down with your mom. But... I know that's no excuse. We've built our relationship on honesty and trust, and I ruined that. The weight on my shoulders all these years is finally lifted, I just wish it was on my own terms..."

"I get why you did it," Teagan said, catching Cole off guard.

"You do?"

"Yeah... Doesn't make it any easier, but I'll be okay."

Cole wanted to ask what Teagan was saying to himself before he interrupted but thought he should just let it be. The boy needed to digest it his own way. They sat for a few minutes in silence. It was something Cole wished could go on longer, but they were running out of time.

"Bud, do you remember why I told you the Grahams were staying here?"

Teagan nodded.

"Well, there's a really good chance that those men coming for them will show up tonight. Now I know you, and I know you'll want to help. I've trained you to the best of my ability to handle yourself. But what I need from you, is to protect those kids and Holly. Leave the rest to Anthony and me. Can you do that for me?"

"What are we going to do?"

"Hopefully nothing. Anthony parked the van further down the trail to hide it. You will all be hiding in the basement. *If* they knock, it will only be me at the door. If they don't, well… Then we have to go with plan B."

Teagan scrunched his eyes in confusion. "What's plan B?"

"Let's hope it doesn't come to that. Anthony will be hiding in the woods, waiting. He's setting up a tarp to keep him out of the rain, but this damn storm is going to make his life a living hell out there," Cole said.

"Okay, whatever you need from me to help."

"Thank you so much, Son. Once this is all over, we can leave if you want, okay? I should've never put this place above our relationship."

Teagan nodded again but said nothing. Cole expected some fight from him, more anger. He was relieved to get none of that, but he had a feeling the boy was burying it deep inside.

"Let's head back to the house, get everybody situated. I promise, from here on out, it's all honesty between us, deal?" Cole asked.

"Deal."

Cole rubbed Teagan's wet head. They got up as another crack of thunder echoed through the woods. The sky continued to darken. Cole was determined to make this right, and it started by protecting the Graham family like they were his own.

25

THE RAIN PICKED up intensity as Anthony set up the tarp in the woods. From his location, he would be able to see the house and driveway but remain hidden to the naked eye. If Vincent's goons decided to get physical with Cole, he would come from behind them and attack. At this point, he cared little if the old groundskeeper survived the night. His top priority was getting his family to safety. Once that was handled, he would get Holly and the kids to stay with him—by any means necessary. This wasn't the first time she'd threatened to leave him. One thought of how it would impact the kids, of them walking down on Christmas morning to only have one parent there to greet them, would send her into a deep depression and have her crawling back to the therapist asking how to fix it. She was ungrateful, but he would fix that... *by any means necessary*.

After throwing up and dealing with the excruciating pain in his stomach, Anthony finally sensed his body was on the rebound. Things were coming to him clearly: what he had to do, what he had to sacrifice. Throughout their entire marriage, he'd been the one sacrificing. Hanging out with friends was a thing of the past. Going out for a drink after a long day at the office didn't exist. And what did he get for those sacrifices? An ungrateful bitch of a wife who wanted to take the kids from him, when all he ever wanted to do was protect his family and provide for them. For the first time since the day they'd both said "*I do*," Anthony saw things with the clarity of a powerful telescope, all the cracks and imperfections of a distant star. He now knew what had to be done.

The rain continued to soak his clothes as he tied a thick rope around a large tree trunk. He'd already done this to three other trees, which now stretched the tarp out, providing him shelter from the storm. Cole asked him if he was sure about staying out here all night without knowing for sure if Vincent's crew would come. But Anthony knew they would come, and even if they didn't, he enjoyed the peace and quiet outside where he could be away from the nagging and bitching. While the pain had finally lowered to a level where he could function, he still knew something was different inside him. He was okay with that. The wound on his back still throbbed, but the sensation was morphing into a satisfying pulsing, almost like a constant ejaculation. Before he left the house, he stopped by the bathroom one more time to inspect the wound only to find it was no longer bleeding and the green fluid had sealed the gash.

He sat below the tarp, thinking through everything that'd led to this. What could he have done differently? The answer was nothing. It was easy for Holly to play driver from the passenger seat—as she always did—but she didn't find herself forced to make a decision that could ruin the family. He did. The pattering of the rain off the tarp got louder as the storm continued to ramp up. Anthony sat, staring toward the house, envisioning what he would do to these men who believed they could take out his family. A smile spread across his face at the thought.

The sun was long gone, the storm clouds going from grey to black as nightfall settled in. He looked down to the gun in his hand and thought it wasn't really a satisfying way to take them out. They deserved to suffer. They needed to suffer. When he looked up from the weapon, Alister's transparent figure towered over him, only this time Anthony didn't flinch. He'd expected this moment.

"We are one now, Anthony. This was no accident; do you hear me? That power you are feeling is my power, and it's fading. We need to correct that, and the only way to do so is by bringing us the girl…"

"I know… It's the only way to keep her safe," Anthony said.

Alister nodded but said nothing. There was a plan in place, now it just needed to be executed properly, and Anthony knew his family would be safe. One thing he was sure about, was that he had no intention of leaving this place. And now that this power was flowing through him, he had no intention of letting his family leave either.

———————————

Cole opened the basement door, releasing the earthy smell of the unfinished room. He flicked the light on, revealing the dirt floor below, and took in the years of clutter still making itself at home. It was rare for him to visit the basement, as it brought back too many bad memories of his days with Alister. This was the location that Alister held those who went on to be sacrificed. It was disguised as a makeshift bedroom for the "chosen" to stay in before they brought themselves to the water to end their own life. But in actuality, it was a damn prison. Alister tricked his followers to believing they could enjoy one last night of comfort while they were still on Earth. For years, Cole had shared that belief. It was treated like part of the ritual. When his time with the group ended, he realized it was really just a way for Alister to keep tabs on the chosen ones, to make sure they didn't second guess the sacrifice and try to flee the compound.

Most of the stuff the cult had set up for the chosen was still in place. A ratty ass bed that even a homeless person would debate sleeping on sat propped in the corner. Cobwebs decorated the wooden beams in the ceiling, the dim light adding to their eeriness. The storm windows that gave the room its only source of natural light during the day were covered in years' worth of grime on the outside, an unfortunate effect of the sloped driveway leading down to the house. Any time it rained with any intensity, the water rushed down the driveway against the side of the house, slapping a layer of mud along the glass's exterior.

He turned to Holly and the kids, who stood behind him at the top of the stairs and gave them an apologetic look. "I'm sorry you have to spend even a minute down there, let alone the night."

Holly faked a smile. "Is this really the best option for us, Cole? Do you truly believe Anthony's plan makes any sense at all?"

"Honestly, I don't know what to think. All I know is that the way he explains these fellas coming after him... after all of you, they're not people you want to take lightly. And if you leave here to go somewhere else, you may not have someone like me to try and help you when they find you. And Holly... they *will* find you." Cole let out a big sigh. "Come on down, I'll get you set up as best I can down here."

Cole noticed the concern in Spencer's face as he looked around the creepy room. He rubbed the boy's head, hoping it would comfort him some. Allie and Teagan followed them down the stairs.

"Oh my God, this is disgusting," Allie said.

Cole chuckled. "Yeah, I hear that. Teagan will be down here with you guys. And I'll bring some food and drinks down, so you're stocked up. Listen... I don't know for sure if anything will happen tonight, but until these men are taken care of, your family will be in danger."

Silence suffocated them all in the tightly packed area. Even with the dim light hanging above, the dull illumination of it struggled to show the room in its entirety. Spencer sat on the bed, and it creaked loudly.

"With these basement windows right here, don't we have to worry about them seeing the light if they pull in?" Holly asked.

Cole nodded. "Yep. Which means our best option is to leave the lights off. You don't have to get down here until we know if some-one's coming, but we need to be close so you guys can get down here quickly at the first sign of them. I want to show you something over here, follow me."

He walked to the back corner of the room and moved some boxes out of the way. Behind them, a rusted handle sat on the wall. He dusted the area off, revealing a small sliding door. Spencer came up behind him in excitement.

"Woah! Is that a secret door?"

"It is. And if things get out of hand up there, I want you all to go out through this way. It's a tight tunnel, but it leads out to the back yard and comes out inside the shed. Alister had us build this. I never knew why until years later. He was worried that if we needed to make a quick escape, that we needed to have another option. In truth, we never needed it for that, but he used to lock children in here as a punishment. He called it the 'thinking hole.' Imagine twenty-four hours locked in that tunnel with no light or food... Those that got put in there didn't come out the same."

At that comment, Spencer backed up, no longer appearing fascinated by the hole, but terrified. Cole immediately regretted saying it aloud. Holly gave him a glance that made him want to cower like an abused dog. He provided an understanding nod and looked down at Spencer.

"Don't worry about that stuff though, kid. That was a long time ago. And you probably won't need to use the tunnel anyways, it's just here as a backup if needed," he said while looking to Holly for approval. She didn't appear much happier, but it would have to do. "Teagan knows these parts well; I've taught him how to get out through here in a hurry. I promise you I'll do everything in my power to make sure you guys stay safe, you have my word."

"I'm really sorry Anthony brought this on you, Cole. It's not fair to you or Teagan," Holly said.

Cole contemplated his response. Part of him was bitter about it all. Another part saw it as a chance for redemption, for not only failing to save his brothers and sisters in the war but failing to stop Alister from rotting Rebecca's brain. It was as if this whole situation was fate, allowing him to see that the cult had in fact stayed and sacrificed themselves. In a way, it brought him a sense of peace. Once he helped Anthony dispose of these thugs, he would do whatever he had to do to get rid of the pond once and for all. Drain it, fill it, light the fucker on fire.

"Life isn't always fair. I want to help you guys. You're a good family, and I'll treat you like my own." He looked at Teagan, hoping the boy could find it inside himself to forgive him for the lies.

"So now what?" Allie asked while peering into the tunnel.

Cole looked at her with concern. "We wait."

26

ANTHONY HADN'T MOVED for a few hours. He sat in a trance; eyes locked on the driveway. His inner clock told him it was just a matter of time before they showed up. From the point he got the text from the old bitch across the street, he'd assumed Vincent's cronies would time it to make sure they arrived at night. It was now as dark as tar in the sky, and the dismal weather continued to soak the forest around him. The occasional gust of wind blew swathes of water across his face, even under the protection of the tarp. He didn't care though; his mind was on one thing and one thing only: ending this headache once and for all. If Vincent didn't show up with his crew, the odds of this ending tonight were slim. He would just send more men after them if the first crew didn't get the job done. But he knew the boss. Knew how controlling he could be, that he would want to be involved in the bloodbath he intended to bring Anthony.

Anthony no longer felt sorry for Hank. If it wasn't for the stupid kid, none of this would have ever happened. But then again, if it hadn't happened, his family would have never come to the campground, and he wouldn't have obtained this sensation surging through his body. It was amazing how over just a few hours, he went from feeling like he was knocking on Death's door, his stomach eating him away from the inside out, to feeling an inhuman strength. And for the first time in a very long time, he felt a purpose. *Bring the girl to us*, Alister had said. The ghost of the enigmatic leader continued to burrow inside him, making itself at home within Anthony's mind.

The pistol felt comfortable in his hand, fully loaded and ready to go. Cole showed him how to load it and refreshed him on the basics before handing it over. A loud explosion of thunder crashed close by, followed quickly by a flicker of lightning. When the lightning flashed, Anthony faintly caught a glimpse of Alister's followers, encircling the forest. They were ready to feast. *Those fuckers won't know what hit them*, he thought. As soon as the sky went dark again, they disappeared.

Through the battering of rain, another sound loomed in the distance. His grip tightened on the pistol. Slowly approaching down the long dirt driveway, a black SUV came into view. The headlights enhanced the severity of the storm; the rain poured down like it was being continuously dumped from a large bucket over the property. Water rushed down the sides of the driveway, moving so fast that one could mistake the stream as a river running along the land. It continued to flood the area around the house with the sloped driveway creating a waterslide that ended with it crashing into the foundation of the home.

The headlights turned off as the SUV got closer.

The vehicle crept forward in silence.

Anthony crouched, holding the gun. The SUV came to a stop and the vehicle's engine was turned off. As the driver's side door inched open, his heartbeat began pulsating from head to toe. He waited in anticipation.

———————————

Allie watched out the window as the headlights approached. Before she could warn the others of the advancing vehicle, Cole was there to greet them. With all the lights in the house turned off, she struggled to see where she was going. Only the sporadic flashes of lightning provided momentary relief to the darkness.

"Get them to the basement, now!" Cole said to Teagan.

The boy did as he was told, not saying a word. As they followed him to the basement door, Allie realized he hadn't really talked at all since seeing the picture of his mom. She felt bad for him. As much as her parents fought, at least she *knew* her mom and dad. She couldn't even imagine what must be going through his head. And now he was in charge of keeping them safe, something no teenager should be responsible for.

"Be careful following me down the stairs. We can't turn on any lights or it'll give us away," he said.

Allie was scared. It was one thing to prepare for a moment like this, but to actually live it brought on a whole new level of stress. Teagan opened the basement door and quickly descended the stairs, which groaned with the weight of pounding footsteps. Holly was right behind him, holding Spencer's hand to try and keep him calm. She turned to Allie and kissed her on the forehead.

"I love you, Allie. We got this." She turned and walked down without another word.

Watching Spencer follow her down into the darkness, Allie's heart broke. The thought of carrying a baby inside her was terrifying. She watched her mother and how she handled this situation, protecting Spencer and keeping him close. Knowing that one wrong move could lead to a panic attack, or worse.

Her mother did it with such confidence. Allie felt sick at the thought of having to be in her shoes. When she told her mom about the baby, she didn't know what to expect. But her mom just hugged her and said everything would be okay, that it would all work out. She didn't know what that meant. Was she supposed to keep the baby? She had considered an abortion, but only for a brief moment. Even if she did have the guts to carry through with it, she would have needed to tell her parents, which is something she had avoided until earlier. In that moment, watching the strength her mom showed with Spencer, she knew she would keep the baby.

Allie shut the door behind her, robbing them of any remaining light. She threw out her hands to the narrow walls, using them to steady herself while going down the stairs in complete darkness. Grime and cobwebs immediately caked in her fingernails, but she didn't have time to be grossed out. She stood in place for a moment, allowing her eyes to adjust to the black hole in front of her, taking in the musty smell. Teagan clearly knew his way around, as he had already led Spencer and her mom to the bed. Allie heard the old, rusty springs cry as they sat down on the weathered mattress. Even from the basement, the storm was so loud, the rain crashed against the ground outside the storm windows. It wasn't until she felt the dirt under her feet that she realized she didn't have shoes on. In all the commotion, it didn't even cross her mind. Hopefully they could just lay low in the basement until the problem was over.

"Allie, are you okay?" Holly asked.

"Yeah, just waiting a second until I can see. Where's Teagan?"

From over in the corner near the secret door, he said "Over here. Be careful where you step, the dirt floor has some uneven spots."

Finally, she made it to the bed and sat next to her family. The storm windows were right above their heads, close to the front porch. A vehicle door shut, followed by muffled voices approaching.

The bad men were coming for them.

————————

Cole crouched low, peeking through the office window at the men approaching the porch. There were two of them, and both appeared to be armed. The shotgun felt comfortable in his hands as they closed in on the home. The rain hid their features, but they clearly weren't coming to politely ask for directions. When they were close, he backed away from the window to avoid being seen.

The thumping of footsteps climbed the porch, approaching the front door.

He waited in silence for what felt like an eternity.

Dinggggg.

Even expecting them, the sound of the doorbell startled him. Holding onto the shotgun with one hand, he took a deep breath and cracked the door open.

"Can I help you fellas?"

One of the men, his dark hair soaked, wiped away the water dripping down his face. Cole noticed the hair product leaving slimy streaks on the man's forehead. He appeared to be the one in charge. The other—a tall, pale, brute of a man—stood quietly behind him.

"Hey there, Sir. We was just wondering if we could come in and use the phone? This storm seems to have us lost and we're about to run out of gas," he said with a greasy smile.

"Sorry to say it, but I don't have no phone anymore. All those damn bill collectors calling and what not... If you need gas, the closest gas station is about twenty minutes the other way, although they're closed this time of night. You might have to stay at the motel over in Newport."

The thug's smile shifted, he tried to maintain it, but Cole sensed his irritation that it wasn't going to be so easy. The man looked at his counterpart, then back to Cole.

"Listen, it would be kind of you to let us in for a few. We were actually out this way looking for a man. He owns this place. Name's Anthony. That's not you, is it?"

Nice try playing stupid, Cole thought.

"No, no. My name's Cole Springer. I look after this place and keep it maintained until Mr. Graham sells it. I've only met that man twice in my life—once when he came to check the place out, the other when he came to sign the official papers to buy it. He asked me to stay on and keep it looking nice for any potential buyers."

"So, you're saying he hasn't shown his face around here lately?"

"No, Sir. I'd hope he would give me a heads up before doing so, on account of it being a bit of a mess in here," Cole chuckled. He knew it was a game of chicken, that both understood they were waiting for the other to crack, but he kept up the front—for now. A flash of lightning momentarily lit up the SUV behind them, and Cole could have sworn a shadow shifted behind the wipers whipping across the windshield full blast. *Is there someone else in the vehicle?*

"Old man, we don't want any trouble. So, we suggest you tell us the truth. I see you're already handicapped there," the man said, pointing to his leg. "I'd hate to do that to your other leg..."

The mood instantly shifted; the tension was as thick as the humidity in the air.

"I've dealt with scum like you many times in my life, I think you ought to watch what you say, boy. And get off my property before I call the cops." He knew the threat was empty, but he was trying to buy some time so he could get a good look at the vehicle again. Cole liked to find all targets before getting into combat.

"Boy? You don't fucking know who we are, do ya? And this ain't your property, Grandpa, hence why we're here looking for Anthony. If he isn't here, I suppose you don't mind us coming in to take a look around?"

Cole got the shotgun ready behind the door and gave the man a cold stare. "I don't let people in the house that I don't even know the name of."

"Name's Christopher, and this here's Birdman. Now let us in the house, you fucking gimp." The man—Christopher—pushed the door, sending Cole off balance, but he was prepared for confrontation, and quickly regained his footing. He swung the door open all the way. The thugs looked down to the shotgun, which Cole raised and aimed toward them, and quickly backed up.

"I suggest you do as I say, or I'll blow a hole in your stomach the size of a bowling ball, pretty boy."

"You just made a big mistake, asshole," the taller pale man said.

It was as if time froze, none of them moved while the storm ravaged on behind them.

Again, something moved in their vehicle, drawing Cole's attention for just a brief second. That was all the time they needed. Christopher charged at him, and Cole fired wildly, the shot cracking by Birdman's ear and dropping him to the ground. He wasn't hit, but the feedback exploding past his head forced him to his knees. Christopher rammed his shoulder into Cole's midsection, taking the wind out of him. They fell inward to the floor and began to scuffle on the hardwood, fighting for position. Cole spun on top of him and mounted the hitman. With the shotgun still firmly in his grip, he drove the butt of it into Christopher's skull, receiving a loud pop of bone and skin beneath the impact. Blood quickly trickled down the pretty-boy's face. Cole was prepared for them to show up, but he never expected full blown violence within a matter of minutes. He lifted the shotgun again, ready to drive it down for the killing blow—when a shot from behind him echoed through the house.

The impact sent him off Christopher and he landed side by side with the ailing henchman. Looking to his shoulder he saw what he already felt, a newly formed crimson hole where a bullet had entered and then escaped near his collarbone on the other side. Cole looked toward the front door, watching as Birdman came out of his daze, holding a gun of his own. He approached the entrance, lifting the weapon to fire again as he got closer. *Where the fuck are you, Anthony? Can I get a little help here?* It wasn't until Birdman was stepping foot in the door that Cole realized he'd dropped his shotgun when falling to the floor.

Birdman looked down at him with a sneer, exposing a set of crooked teeth. "Bye bye, old man."

— — — — — — — —

Anthony observed the fight breaking out between Cole and Christopher, feeling helpless as they disappeared into the house. After firing his gun, Birdman got to his feet, wiping the rainwater out of his eyes, and marched toward the house. It was now or never. Anthony aimed the pistol, trying his best to see in the sheets of rain falling. His lack of skills, along with the pitch-black night would make it hard enough to aim in the first place. The storm made it impossible. He had to try. Squeezing one of his eyes shut, he took a deep breath and held it, trying to steady his aim. Just as Birdman said something that he couldn't make out, Anthony fired the gun.

His arm jerked, the gun producing much more kickback than he would have expected. The bullet missed by a wide margin, exploding through one of the storm windows on the house's foundation. The window to the basement. Where his family hid. Nerves clenched in his stomach at the thought that his stray bullet may have hit one of them. He didn't have time to think about it though. When he looked back to the door, Birdman had turned, facing his direction, confused by the surprise ambush. If he had just hit him, this whole thing could have ended much sooner than expected. But with the missed shot, they now knew someone else was here. Anthony had no choice but to approach the house.

He crouched down and ran out of the woods, trying to maintain as much cover as he could. A loud crack of thunder rang out, or a gun shot, Anthony wasn't sure of which. Maybe it was both. But with it, Birdman dropped out of sight, giving him a wide-open path to sprint to the house. A muffled voice came from somewhere within the house, the storm blocking out what was said. For all Anthony knew, Cole could be dead on the floor, the two goons waiting for him to come in and fall for their trap.

Anthony climbed the steps, intentionally staying to one side to remain in the entrance's blind spot. He leaned against the side of the house and listened.

"Get out there and check for him! I'll take care of the old man," Christopher said.

A few seconds later, Birdman came through the front door. He had just enough time to look over and see Anthony pistol whip him in the temple. Birdman fell off the porch, landing in a large puddle. Anthony jumped off the porch, landing on top of him and punched him with everything he had. He felt more powerful than he ever had in his life, as if he was being assisted in the fight. Birdman's head snapped back into the puddle after the third blow and Anthony didn't waste the opportunity. He pushed down on his head, holding it under the water. His hands squeezed into the windpipe, the bone beneath his fingertips giving in to the vice-like grip.

Birdman coughed up water, attempting to save himself from drowning, but Anthony held firm. Anthony raised the gun, aiming it point blank at his forehead, ready to fire just like they did to Hank. Like they wanted to do to his family.

His finger found the trigger, prepared to pull.

"Drop the gun, you piece of shit!"

Anthony spun toward the house and saw Christopher standing on the porch, aiming his own gun. He hesitated, not wanting to give up his advantage, but realized he had no choice. He tossed it into the puddle and raised his hands.

"Good, now get up."

Birdman remained in a bloody daze, rolling to his side when Anthony got to his feet.

"Why'd you have to go fucking up a good thing, Tony? Vincent actually liked you. I can't say that for many of his business partners," Christopher said.

"We both know as soon as I saw that body that I was a dead man. You would've done the same thing…"

"Hey… I put myself in a position where I don't have to worry about that, eh? Now shut the fuck up and drop to your knees, keep your hands up…"

"If you're going to kill me, just fucking do it. Why are you doing this?"

Christopher laughed. "Boss wants you to suffer, Mr. Real Estate. First you kill one of us, then you put another in the hospital. Then, you think you can sneak off and hide the rest of your life? You must be fucking stupid. We. *Always*. Find. You."

Anthony tried to remain calm on the surface, but inside he was frantically trying to come up with a plan. He needed to keep Christopher talking longer.

"What'd you do with Cole? He had nothing to do with this."

"Neither did the kid at the office building, but you left us no choice. Both stuck their nose in our business."

If he could just make a run for it before Christopher got a shot off, he might stand a chance. Vincent's first in command still stood in the doorway, so he didn't have the best shot unless he came outside to the edge of the steps. Even in a moment of stress, Anthony still found himself laughing inside at the thought of this slick fuck not wanting to come out and get his hair messed up in the rain.

"Boss wants to do this himself, so as much as I want to put a bullet in your face, I have to follow the rules. Once Birdman is ready, he's going to tie you up and then the real fun begins. How does that—"

Something behind Christopher clubbed him in the back of the head, dropping him to the floor. Anthony let out a sigh of relief as Cole appeared, stepping over Christopher's limp body. Anthony glanced down at Birdman who was starting to get to his feet. He kicked him in the head, dropping him back down. When he approached to strike again, Birdman swept his feet out from under him with cat-like speed. The air escaped out of his lungs as his back slammed into the ground, landing in the puddle next to the fallen thug. He attempted to take deep breaths, but a sensation like someone pressing a cement block into his chest made it all but impossible. Birdman rolled over and climbed on top of him, punching him in the mouth. Stars flashed in Anthony's vision, and he didn't have time to blink them away before the fist came back into his nose. He heard a crack, followed swiftly by blood pumping down into his throat from his busted nose. The pain soon followed, and Anthony screamed out in rage.

"What the fuck? What's wrong with you?" Birdman asked, backing away.

Anthony shook his head, trying to clear the fog that had tightened its grip around his brain. When his vision came back into focus, he saw Birdman staring at his own fist in horror. Instead of blood dripping down his knuckles, it was a slimy, green fluid. Anthony took advantage, kicking Birdman in the knee. The leg buckled before forcing itself backwards, completely bending it in the wrong direction. Birdman screamed and fell back in the pool of water.

Something consumed Anthony; he no longer had control over the rage. He got to his feet and towered over Vincent's piece of shit stooge, his blood boiling—or whatever the hell was inside him eating away at his blood. With a predatory howl, he slammed the heel of his shoe into the helpless skull of Birdman, feeling the bone give slightly, but not all the way. That was okay, he would fix that. Again, he lifted his foot and drove down the heel, this time into the eye cavity. A disgusting crunch stopped the screams of agony, but Anthony didn't stop. Thoughts of them trying to kill him, kill his *family*, swam through his mind like a shoal of piranhas as he stomped repeatedly like he was trying to put out a fire. Birdman's head was now unrecognizable, the puddle clouded with blood and skull fragments. Anthony watched the body twitch with satisfaction until it came to a stop.

He turned back to the house, an uncomfortable whistling escaping through his busted nose with each forced breath. Cole sat on the floor next to Christopher's body. The groundskeeper was wincing, holding his hand over a wound near his shoulder. Anthony wasn't sure if Christopher was dead, or unconscious. Before he could ask the question, Cole's eyes went wide.

"Anthony, there's someone else in the vehicle!"

He turned just in time to see Vincent getting out with some type of machine gun in hand. Instinct kicked in, Anthony took off in a sprint as the mob boss opened fire, a barrage of bullets striking the side of the house. Anthony heard windows shattering, wood cracking, and Vincent, yelling over the bullets and the pouring rain.

"You mother fucker! I'm going to kill you and your entire fucking family!"

Anthony dove down over an embankment behind the house, desperate for cover. He saw the shed a few hundred feet away and needed to find a way to get there without Vincent seeing him. After the bullets stopped, he heard the screams. They were coming from the basement.

27

HOLLY SQUEEZED SPENCER TIGHT, trying to calm him after bullets blasted the house, forcing him to scream. A few moments ago, muffled voices on the porch above quickly escalated to something more, but they couldn't see what was going on. The poor boy was shaking in fear, and she was doing everything she could to comfort him. They had been in the dark long enough that their vision adjusted as best it could, and she looked over to Allie who, just like her, hid most of her concerns on the inside. She knew though: her daughter was terrified. How could she not be?

"It's okay, Spence. They don't know we're down here," Holly said, knowing full well that it was a matter of time before they *did* know.

A stray bullet had come through one of the windows, ricocheting off the cement foundation inside. They were lucky it didn't hit one of them. The bigger concern now was the rainwater coming in through the window. The bullet hole quickly splintered with the force of the water pressing against it, and then completely shattered, providing a perfect relief for the strain of the water pushing against the house. With it raining so hard, it was a continuous stream of river-like force dumping into the basement, and the floor was quickly flooding. At the moment, the water was already a foot deep, and rising by the second.

"We have to make a decision, Holly," Teagan said.

She wasn't sure what he meant, but then looked to the secret door leading to the tunnel, which was not much taller than a crawl space. The longer they waited, the less chance they had of escaping through there, which would force them to go up through the main house and likely be discovered. They still had no idea if someone had been shot. Holly thought there was a good chance at least one person was dead in the driveway, especially after the rapid fire of a machine gun a few moments ago.

"So, this tunnel… it leads to the shed out back?" Holly asked.

Teagan nodded. "Yes, and if we don't go now, it'll flood completely, and we won't be able to use it. We need to go now."

"And where exactly is safer than here in the dark?"

"If we go further into the woods, they may not look for us. And even if they do, I know these woods far better than some out-of-state assholes do."

Holly considered it, knowing she had to make a decision quickly. "Okay," she said. She looked down at Spencer, who was curled against her, still trembling. "Buddy, we're going to need to crawl through that door and get to safety, okay?"

Spencer violently shook his head, not wanting to move from the bed. "Mom, that hole scares me…"

"Pal, we don't have time to think about it, we need to go now," Teagan said.

The boy wasn't budging. Holly sighed and kissed his forehead. "Get Allie to safety, I'll talk with Spencer some more."

"Mom, I don't want to leave you guys alone…" Allie said, her voice cracking.

"Hon, we'll be right behind, just do whatever Teagan says and we'll catch up."

They embraced, and Holly didn't want it to end. Holding both her kids tight, she would have gone through a whole army to protect them. The thought of letting her daughter go out on her own, even with the help of Teagan, scared her to death.

"Go, sweetie. I love you."

"I love you too, Mom. And Spence, you're stronger than you think. Just listen to Mom, buddy," Allie said, and before Holly or Spencer could respond, she was following Teagan to the secret door.

The pressure of the water pushing against the door made it a struggle for Teagan to slide it aside. Holly heard him straining as he pried it open. With no lights on, the opening looked like a black hole. Water rushed through the newly exposed space; Teagan was right, it would be completely flooded soon. She had to get Spencer moving.

Teagan dropped down and started crawling through the tight space. Water splashed up off the dirt walls, obstructing what little view they had ahead of them. Holly's chest began to tighten at the thought of the walls collapsing down on them once enough water entered. With Teagan out of view, Allie glanced back at Holly and Spencer one last time, tears pouring down her cheeks. Finally, she crouched down and crawled into the hole. A few seconds later, she too was out of sight.

———————————

Anthony remained hidden behind the bank but decided to risk a peek at the backyard. Vincent came into view, holding his gun like a madman. Even with the poor visibility afforded by the storm, Anthony could see the crime boss's eyes. He'd always heard stories about Vincent—how you didn't want to make him angry—that if you did, he wouldn't just kill you, he would brutally take away your desire to live. The look in those eyes confirmed everything Anthony had heard was true.

Vincent's hair fell into his face, his expensive business suit clinging to his body like an extra layer of skin. "Where are you, you fucking pussy? Show your god-damn face!"

A snap of lightning again lit the sky, giving the momentary appearance of daylight. Behind Vincent, Anthony spotted Cole approaching. He was getting close enough to grab ahold of Vincent. The boss now stood only ten feet from Anthony's hiding spot, and for a moment, Anthony thought he'd spotted him. If he had, Vincent would have lit him up with his machine gun.

"I said… where are you, mother fuck—"

Moonlight poked through the haze of the sky.

And Cole jumped on Vincent's back, wrapping his bicep around Vincent's neck. The veins in Cole's neck bulged as he tightened his grip. Vincent dropped to his knees, prying the arm wrapped around his neck loose, like one would the death-grip of a python. *He's going to fucking do it*, Anthony thought. He barely finished the thought when a gun shot went off, and Cole dropped to the ground behind Vincent, clutching his leg. Christopher limped up behind him, aiming the gun at Cole, and prepared to fire again.

Vincent turned and kicked Cole in the stomach, the momentum flipping Cole to his back.

"What's with you people getting in my fucking business?" he yelled, then kicked again. Vincent knelt over Cole, watching the pain in his eyes, and aimed the machine gun at his face.

Christopher's shot had obliterated Cole's calf. *I need to help him*, Anthony thought. But Cole wasn't the only one who had been shot. Christopher's gun slipped from his fingers, and he clutched his stomach. Blood poured out of a wound in his midsection, his white dress shirt now stained a dark red. The moonlight did him no favors, his skin losing its color.

"Where is he? Tell me where the fuck Anthony is!" Vincent shouted, his face only inches from Cole's dazed expression.

"Fuck… you," Cole said in a whisper.

While all of this was going on, Anthony had slowly inched closer to the shed. He needed to find another weapon after losing his gun out front. A loud rapping sound came from inside the shed. *What the hell is that?* Then he heard voices, one that sounded too familiar… it was Allie. He wasn't the only one that heard it. Vincent and Christopher took their attention off Cole, looking toward the commotion.

Vincent marched toward the shed. Christopher still had his attention on his boss, giving Cole a chance to attack. Cole grabbed the gun Christopher dropped and fired, hitting Chris in the stomach again. With the shot only a few feet from its target, the bullet tore a large hole through Christopher, dropping him to the ground. His eyes went wide with shock. He looked down at the new wound. Blood pumped out at a much more aggressive rate, leaking between his pale fingers. He tried to say something to Vincent, but nothing came. Christopher's eyes went blank. Vincent turned back to see what had happened, and Anthony made his move. He ran from the bushes, tackling Costello to the ground, sending the machine gun tumbling into the mud.

The door to the shed burst open. Allie looked on in horror at the sight of she and Teagan's dads, bloody and beaten, still struggling with the intruders. Without a word, Teagan grabbed Allie's arm and pulled her toward the path heading to the woods. Anthony saw their movement in his peripheral vision and did everything he could to keep Vincent from spotting them. He squeezed Vincent's throat, watching the mob boss's eyes bulge out of their sockets with grim satisfaction. All the trouble this asshole had caused him, it was his turn to repay the favor.

Cole lay on the ground next to Christopher's limp body, and from Anthony's viewpoint, it appeared they were both dead or on the verge of it. Both had been shot more than once and were bleeding out. Vincent's face turned purple under the power of Anthony's hands. He was desperate, ripping and clawing at Anthony's iron tight grip to get him off.

Anthony looked up. The figures of Alister and a few of his followers now stood like a set of lurking statues, just waiting for the moment to act. His grip loosened at the sight of them, and his attention zoned in on Alister, who, in spite of the rain hammering down, approached him without flinching as the water splashed off his ghostly face.

"You can feel us inside you, can't you, Anthony? You must know, the sacrifice is now underway already..."

"What? What do you mean underway?"

The menacing smile that Anthony saw in his nightmares returned, a set of sharp, algae-covered teeth flashing before him. Was he really here this time? Or was this another vision?

"Please... take care of business and then come join us at the water. I would hate *for you to miss the ceremony..."*

Anthony was confused, but then remembered Allie and Teagan heading toward the woods. Toward the *pond*. He found the entity tightening its grip on him, unsure of what he was supposed to do. Whatever was inside him had grabbed hold, driving him to accept the rage, accept that his daughter was better off with them. He was, after all, doing this to protect her and the family. All he wanted to do was scream at the top of his lungs, willing the invisible demons out of his body.

Apparently, he had stalled long enough for Vincent to regain some of his breath, because with his eyes locked on Alister, Anthony didn't see the fist driving into his already broken nose. His head jerked back, taking with it his advantage, and sending him sprawling to the ground. Vincent stood, trying to correct his balance. When he did, he stomped toward Anthony, who was getting to his feet.

"You know, kid... You got some balls; I give you that! No fucking real estate agent should be able to take down some of my best guys..."

"Yeah, well what would you do if it was *your* family in danger, Vincent? Sit there and let it happen?"

Vincent chuckled. "No... I'd be doing the same thing you were, Tony. That's what makes the fact that I'm forced to kill you so sad," he said, then lowered his shoulder and rammed it into Anthony's chest, slamming him into the side of the shed. The metal gave way, bending inward on impact.

Vincent punched him in the stomach repeatedly, driving his fist into Anthony's ribs. Something cracked inside with the last punch.

But with it, something else cracked in Anthony. The anger came back. He kneed Vincent in the stomach, providing enough distance between them for him to push off the warped metal wall. As he attempted to throw a punch of his own, Vincent blocked it, then pushed him back into the shed, only this time it dropped Anthony to the ground on impact. He rolled to his side—and spotted the ax he'd used earlier to split the firewood. Vincent stomped on his ribs, sending fireworks across Anthony's vision. If his ribs weren't broken before, they were now. Once again, Costello stomped down, nailing his target. Anthony reached for the ax with his outstretched hand, feeling the grip of its handle in his fingertips. He spun around as Vincent went to stomp on him again and swung the ax, wedging it into the mob boss's shin.

Vincent screamed, clutching his leg and falling to the ground. He tried to pull the ax out, but it was imbedded in the shin-bone. Anthony didn't mind giving it some extra force for good measure. He yanked the handle and felt the grinding of blade sliding back through the bone. Vincent's screams intensified. He stared up at Anthony, lumbering toward him, breathing heavy, with the ax in hand. He looked like a madman about to slaughter a bunch of teens, not some real estate agent in fear of his life. Vincent crawled through the puddles and mud, trying to reach his gun. He was so close to making it, but Anthony had no intention of letting him get to it. Lifting the ax up high, he drove it down through Costello's forearm, severing it in one swing. Vincent's eyes went wide. A sound Anthony had never heard before gargled out of his mouth.

"FUCK! FUCK FUCK FUCK FUCK!" Vincent screamed incoherently. "You realize... realize they'll come for you if I don't return, you son of a bitch?"

"Oh, but you are the big, bad boss, right? You wanted to kill my fucking wife and kids... All to... prove a point? Well, I have a few points of my own to prove!"

With his ribs sending bolts of sharp pain through his body, Anthony raised the ax again.

"DON'T..." Anthony bellowed.

He swung the ax down, lodging it into Vincent's other arm. This time, it didn't take the arm off with the first try.

"FUCK..."

So, he swung again, separating the arm at the elbow.

"WITH..."

Panting, he lifted again and lodged the blade in Castillo's left leg, right below the knee. A sickening crunch as metal and bone came together. As Anthony lifted the weapon once more, ready to strike down on the other leg, a flash of lightning lit up the sky. He saw terror in Vincent's eyes, and not just because of Anthony. He looked past him toward the woods. Anthony turned and saw the figures of Alister's family watching him.

"Wha... what the fuck are they?" Vincent cried out.

Rage consumed Anthony, ignoring the question. He lifted the ax up again, zoning in on the remaining limb.

"ME!"

28

THE WATER CONTINUED to rise in the basement at an alarming rate, and Holly knew she had to get Spencer up and moving. As it was, they were already going to have to swim through the tunnel—in complete darkness—to escape through the shed. The thought scared her to death; she couldn't even imagine how an eight-year-old was feeling about it.

"Spence, we need to go, okay? Do you trust me?"

He looked at her, remaining in his curled-up position on the bed, terrified of moving. The water was now at least two feet deep. The tunnel couldn't be more than three feet tall and would soon be closed to them.

"I don't want to go near the water, Mom. *They* might be in there."

"*Who* might be in there?"

Spencer hesitated.

"There were kids who made me follow them through the woods, they told me to come play with them. When I got to the water, they looked like monsters..."

With everything they'd been through, Holly was the only one in the family who hadn't seen these ghosts, or whatever they were. The place scared her, but it was mostly just a feeling she had manifesting inside; she had no real evidence that made her believe anything else existed. But the scene at the water, and how bizarre Anthony had been acting since... The green vomit. All of it was so strange. She wanted to tell her son that what he saw wasn't real, but that might just push him further away, and if she was being honest, she didn't know what to believe anymore.

"I'll keep you safe. From any monsters, bad guys, you name it. But to do that, I *need* you to listen to me, and trust me..."

After a moment, he nodded and sat up. Holly picked him up and carried him to the hole in the wall. The smell of fetid earth and dampness wafted out. The water flowing into the hole disappeared into an empty void. Its force was strong, raging like an angry river. She pulled Spencer close and hugged him. After kissing him on the head, she set him down and got face to face with him.

"Okay, let's go."

—————————————

Spencer felt his chest tighten as he approached the darkness. His feet locked into place; his knees shook. The water pushing against the back of his legs into the tunnel urged him forward like it was trying to suck him in and never let him go. He closed his eyes and took a deep breath, just like his doctor told him to do when practicing relaxation exercises. It wasn't bravery that forced him to move, it was the fact that he didn't want his mom getting too far ahead of him in the tunnel.

"Stay close to me... I'll go first to make sure it's safe, okay?" Holly asked.

Spencer nodded, watching as she disappeared into the darkness; he had no choice but to follow.

If he had a say in it, they would have waited in the basement, curled up on the bed until everything was resolved. He would rather chance them being discovered than going into a deep, dark, nothingness. Spencer crouched. The minimal light peeking through the grimy storm windows had now diminished to a memory. He reached his arms out to each side, searching for anything to hold on to. When his hands hit the walls, he immediately felt better, digging his fingers into the packed dirt for grip.

"How're you doing?" his mom asked, her voice echoing ahead, letting Spencer realize how much further they had to go.

"I'm okay," he lied.

There was approximately a foot not submerged in water, leaving barely enough room for their heads to remain above the surface. His mom was too tall to crouch and forced to crawl ahead while he walked blindly in a hunched posture.

A noise in the water, coming from behind, jolted him upright and he smacked his head off the dirt ceiling.

Spencer spun around to see what it was.

It was impossible to *see* anything, but he knew he heard it. Squeezing his eyes near-shut, he attempted to adjust them as best he could to make out anything where the sound had come from. When he still didn't see anything, he turned back and continued moving through the water. He reached for his mom, who promised she wouldn't go too far ahead, and was relieved when his hand landed on her back. A sick thought came to him that it might not be his mom at all, that it was some mud monster living in the tunnel waiting for him. He forced the idea from his head.

"I'm scared…"

"I know, sweetie. We're almost there…"

Again, a splash from behind, much louder this time.

He looked over his shoulder, and what he saw sent fear trickling down his spine. The kids from the woods were swimming toward him. Their white eyes glowed in the darkness, providing enough light to reveal their hideous faces. Spencer screamed and started splashing around, trying to increase the distance between him and them.

"What's wrong?" his mom yelled.

"They're here, Mom! They are coming behind us!"

The illumination of their eyes allowed him to see his mom's face as she turned and looked back in fear. It was the first time she'd seen any of them, and she could no longer keep up her strong front for the sake of her children.

"Quick! Let's go!"

She yanked on his arm, pulling him close.

"*Come play with us, Spencer... You can bring your mommy too...*"

He wasn't sure which of them said it, not that it mattered. Cackling laughter reverberated in the dark, claustrophobic tunnel as they continued swimming closer. Spencer struggled to concentrate on moving forward, his eyes locked behind him on their white orbs. His mom tugged at him some more, forcing him to come with her.

"*Let's play hide and seek...*" one of them said.

Their heads disappeared below the surface, returning the tunnel to complete darkness. Spencer's chest began to tighten again, the thought of those things coming for him under the water sending chills through his body.

"We're almost there! I can hear the rain up ahead!" his mom said while picking up the pace.

They were so close to the exit. The moon forced some of its light through the shed, providing them with a dull image of the opening. Holly reached it, poking her head up through, leaving only her legs visible to Spencer. She climbed out, flipping over to her stomach and reaching down to grab him as he got closer. Her hand latched onto his, ready to pull him to safety, when something pulled at his leg in the water. His bones turned to jelly.

"Help! Mom! Something has me!"

Holly squeezed with all her strength, her fingers digging into Spencer's forearms, refusing to let go. Her nails scraped along his arms as her grip loosened.

A head popped up right behind Spencer; breath slithered along the back of his neck.

"*Found you!*"

Spencer screamed so loud he could feel his lungs vibrating inside. The water created a slick layer on his arm, and no matter how hard Holly tried to keep hold, it was like trying to grab a handful of night crawlers squirming to get away. With one final tug, the children pulled him down below.

"Spencer!" Holly yelled.

He fell below the surface, water filling his lungs. He was with the kids below, and they smiled. His mouth opened wide, and he screamed, sending a fit of bubbles to the water's surface. The boy stopped smiling at him, and at first Spencer thought he had frozen in place. But then the boy's mouth began to slowly open wide, and it moved closer to Spencer's face like it was about to swallow him whole.

Spencer closed his eyes, too afraid to do anything else.

Something ripped him up out of the water. He opened his eyes to see his mom holding him, tears flowing down her face. There was no time to let relief settle in. The boy with the white eyes came up and grabbed ahold of his leg again, pulling with an inhuman strength.

"Don't leave us!"

Holly stood in the opening, pulling Spencer with her. She kicked at the monster child, her foot connecting with his face and sending him backward into the water. The first thing she did was push Spencer up to safety, then she climbed out after him. For a moment, they lay on the floor of the shed, regaining their breath. Spencer coughed up some of the water, but he was otherwise okay. Echoes of the children below continued to ring throughout the tunnel.

Holly grabbed hold of the secret door attached to the floor of the shed and slammed it shut, silencing the voices. She hugged Spencer so tight that he thought he might lose his breath again.

"I got you, baby. I won't let anything happen to you..."

The storm continued its path of destruction outside the shed, the rain slamming off the tin roof above them. Holly got to her feet and helped Spencer up. Beyond the rain, beyond the loud rumbling of thunder, Spencer heard something else outside.

The sounds of a crazed lunatic.

His mom heard it too. She brought her finger to her lips, telling him to remain quiet. Slowly, they approached the exit, noticing the wall bent in next to the door. Both looked out and were not prepared for what they saw.

Anthony stood over someone, swinging an ax over and over into their defenseless body. It was an image that Spencer would have etched into his mind for the rest of his life: his dad covered in blood, the body laying limply below him in a puddle of mud and gore. Holly again pulled Spencer close as they watched in terror.

When Anthony was done, he stood with his back to them, still unaware he was being watched. Slowly, he turned around, seeing his family hiding together, staring at him like he was some kind of monster. His face softened.

"I did it guys... I took care of the bad men."

Unable to speak, unable to take his eyes off his dad panting before them like a rabid dog, Spencer had one thought. *You're the bad man, Daddy...*

29

ALLIE SHIVERED as she wrapped her arms around herself to try and keep warm. Her clothes were soaked, her bare feet making squishing noises with each step she took deeper into the trail. Teagan continued to lead the way, moving in silence down the path. He hadn't said a word since they reached the end of the tunnel. Allie wanted to have her family back by her side. After telling her mom about the baby, it was as if a connection between them, dormant for years, had finally been rekindled. She didn't want to judge Teagan, but his expressions and the way he moved were starting to concern her.

"Teagan, where are you taking me? Don't you think we can just stay in this area so my family can find us?"

He stopped, and for the first time since they entered the basement, he made eye contact with her. His eyes were different now. They no longer contained softness. With everything they had been through, she couldn't blame him. But Allie thought the shift had happened before the bad men showed up, when Holly showed him the picture of his mom.

"We have to keep going. The further away from them we get, the less of a chance there is they'll track us down."

Allie hesitated for a moment, but what he was saying made sense. If Cole and her father weren't able to stop the bad men, then they needed to keep running.

They approached the end of the path: they could either go straight, take a right down the next path, or head straight into the woods—toward the pond. Teagan grabbed her hand firmly, something that no longer felt protecting. She tried to veer right and head deeper into the campground, but Teagan wouldn't let go of her. He forced her to go toward the woods in front of them.

"Teagan, let *go*! I don't want to go down there."

He stopped at the tree-line and sighed. His expression now cold.

"Sorry... It's what he wants..."

"What? What who—"

Teagan struck her face with his elbow, sending her into blackness.

———————————

Cole opened his eyes. He tried to sit up but the pain in his leg was excruciating. A passing thought that he would need to get his remaining leg amputated crossed his mind, as the bullet swam around through his muscles and tendons. A scream coming from the shed forced him to sit up. He spotted Holly and Spencer huddled together in the doorway. They were looking at Anthony, who was covered in blood standing over the dead body of one of the men they killed.

He looked like the last ounce of sanity inside him had perished.

They'd taken them all out. But instead of relief, dread filled Cole. Along with pain, fear, and uncertainty.

"Anthony... *Anthony!*" he yelled.

Anthony turned to face him. Something shifted behind his eyes, bringing him back to reality. Looking down at the dismembered body below him, then back to his family, it was as if it all clicked at once—how horrific the scene was.

"Guys... I'm sorry..."

Holly and Spencer said nothing, continuing to hold one another.

"*Please...*" he pleaded.

"You're a monster! Stay away from us..." Holly screamed.

"I... I did it to protect you," he said, shaking his head. He attempted to walk toward them but stopped when he saw them back further into the shed as he approached.

"Anthony... let them be. Please, come help me up," Cole said through clenched teeth.

Seeing that his family wasn't coming to him, Anthony walked to Cole, holding out his hand. Cole grabbed it and pulled himself up, a shot of pain going through his calf in the process. He'd been through a lot over the years, but outside of the explosion in the war —which he didn't even fully remember—he had never felt so much pain.

"You need to take a minute, Anthony. Go sit down, take some breaths. Your body's in shock right now. When it wears off, it'll all come crashing down on you. Believe me, I've been here before. Your family just needs time to process this."

Anthony looked back to them one last time, and without another word he headed into the house. Cole limped over toward the shed, grimacing at the pain with each step.

"It's okay, guys. Come on out of there now. It's over."

"It's not over until we're far away from *him*," Holly said.

"He did what he thought he had to do, Holly. They would have killed us all; he was protecting you."

"Protecting us? Hacking a body to pieces is *protecting* us? He's a monster, Cole!"

Cole knew she was right, but he also knew it was important to keep Spencer calm. He just watched his dad going ballistic with an ax. Instead of talking, he reached his hand out, hoping either Holly or Spencer would grab hold of it. Holly whispered something in her son's ear. After he nodded, she reached out and Cole helped her out of the shed. Spencer followed her, clinging to her side like Velcro.

"Where are Teagan and Allie?" he asked.

"They went ahead of us through the tunnel. We were about to go looking for them when we came up to this."

"We best go look in the woods then. Let's take my truck, I'm not so sure I can walk that far with my leg like this."

Holly nodded, then put Cole's arm over her shoulder and helped him as they walked around the front of the house. The body of the first man Anthony killed lay sprawled in the puddle, his head caved in. Cole nudged Holly so she would make sure her son didn't see it. Without a word, she freed herself from Cole and directed Spencer around the other side of the truck.

Cole swiped the cluttered seats, sweeping everything to the floor, and hopped in the passenger seat. Holly and Spencer climbed in the other side, immediately hit with the scent of stale cigars.

"Keys are above the visor," he said.

Holly pulled them out and started the truck.

"Any idea where to look for them?" she asked.

"Well, let's just take it slow, keep our eyes out. If they hear a vehicle coming, they may go for cover, unsure if it's us or not."

An unsettling feeling overcame Cole as Holly drove. Something felt wrong, but he wasn't sure what it was. The truck eased down the path with the wipers going full blast. Even though there was plenty of landscape to search, his eyes were locked on one spot. The headlights provided a laser beam of light, aimed right at the woods overlooking the pond. Cole's heart sank when he noticed his son dragging Allie through the trees.

Toward the water.

———————

Teagan pulled the unconscious body with all his strength. The dead weight was a struggle to get over the tall grass and down through the trees. It was important he didn't accidentally kill Allie before the sacrifice. It had been so hard to maintain a loving personality toward Cole. The dumb bastard thought he was protecting Teagan from the evil of Alister and his followers. He *really* thought he was his father too. Even before they came back to Bird's Nest, his *real* father talked to him. So did his mother. Alister connected with Teagan in a way that Cole never could.

The truth was, when Teagan's mom was pregnant with him, Cole had experienced doubts. Every woman in the group had to spend time with Alister on a regular basis. He was trying to expand the family.

Cole actually thought his pathetic human seed would be strong enough to overpower someone like Alister. It was ridiculous. And then there was the fact that the old man thought he was *saving* Teagan from death as a baby. What he really did was ruin the ceremony. Teagan's youth was supposed to bridge them all, to make them powerful and connected to Vodyanoy. Alister's power was fading, and the One in the Water had told him what it would take to get that power back. When it didn't happen, the only way to keep their God happy was to proceed with the Great Baptism, to sacrifice the entire group. The reward, they were told, would take time to come. That reward was now here, with him.

Earlier, Teagan thought he'd been caught talking to them when Cole stuck his damn nose where it didn't belong. Then he remembered that Cole couldn't see them anymore. Once he stopped believing, they no longer showed themselves to him. So, the crippled prick thought Teagan was just talking to himself, processing the fact he had just seen a picture of his mom. He chuckled. The fact that Cole trusted him enough to have the pictures just sitting on the computer, available for anyone to click on, no password lock, was pitiful.

Cole trusted Teagan so much that he just let him wander out into the woods to clean campsites and mow all day, when in reality that work took half the time he was gone. The rest of the time he spent at the pond, talking with his true family. They could only show themselves for a short period of time until they regained their strength.

Teagan put on a front with Holly. He could see why Anthony hated her. She was a know-it-all, nosey bitch. He'd been forced to pretend he hadn't seen his mother before she showed him the picture, and almost ruined the whole plan.

They sensed the anger brewing inside Anthony and wanted to use him to bring the girl. But they were hungry. Vodyanoy was hungry. And they were getting sick of waiting for Anthony to battle his inner demons. The scared little shit, Spencer, gave him the perfect opportunity to bring her to them himself, which he'd already attempted once before. The horny couple sneaking into the woods forced him to leave Allie behind and make sure they were taken care of first. When he got back to the spot where he left Allie's body, she was gone. The drugs he'd slipped in her drink wore off. This time, he wouldn't make that mistake again.

"Whaaa… What's happening?" Allie moaned. She was still dazed, but he had to hurry.

"Sorry it had to be this way, sweetie pie. You're just too valuable to them. I really did like you though," he said with a smile.

He pulled her down the hill, dodging trees on the way down, until finally they came to the clearing. The pond was pulsating, the green glow lighting up the dark sky as the followers awaited the power they would soon absorb. Cole had been right about one thing: they did want youth. Spencer was the youngest, and they did want him as well. But what Cole didn't know was this whore was pregnant. She was carrying something far younger than Spencer. For them to get not only Allie, but the young soul inside her, *that* was power.

Teagan dragged her across the dock. The water crashed against the platform, eager to be fed. He dropped her body and looked out at the water. This was finally it. He was going to join his family and give them exactly what they wanted. They would all be one step closer to their destiny.

———————

Holly parked the truck at the edge of the path. The storm was starting to let up some, but the rain was still coming down at a decent clip. She opened the door, feeling the water splashing on her face. Spencer sat between her and Cole, nuzzled up to her side. She looked down at him and kissed him on top of the head.

"Stay here, we'll be right back."

He raised his face from her shoulder and shook his head. "No! Don't leave me alone, please..."

She didn't have time to waste; she needed to get to her daughter. Cole gave her a nod and pushed the door open, wincing in pain as he did.

"Okay, but we have to be quick, buddy. Stay behind me and don't leave us, no matter what."

Holly kept her calm tone with him, but inside she was screaming. She needed to get to Allie. They left the truck with the doors still ajar and headed straight for the woods. As they got closer, she saw Teagan standing over her daughter on the dock. The water was going crazy, glowing so bright she had to squint to keep her focus on them. *What is he doing with her?* She wasn't going to wait to find out. Holly took off in a sprint the rest of the way. Spencer struggled to keep up and found himself closer to limping Cole as they both tried to catch her.

When Holly got to the opening, she choked. Teagan was cradling Allie, who appeared to be dazed or hurt. She couldn't hold herself up on her own. Teagan heard them running and looked around, a smile on his face.

"Hey there, Holly! I was just taking Allie for a swim."

"Put her down! What's going on, Teagan?" she yelled.

Cole and Spencer reached Holly, now standing at her side.

"Son... what in God's name are you doing?" Cole asked.

"Oh, Cole... I'm doing nothing in God's name. I'm doing it in *Vodyanoy's*."

Cole swallowed hard. The look in Teagan's eyes was unlike any he'd ever known.

"Please, Son. I don't know—"

"Stop calling me *Son*! I'm not your fucking kid, old man. Don't you get that? I've been holding it in all these years. Pretending to love you. Pretending that I didn't know who my own flesh and blood was. Do you know how *hard* that was?"

Allie started to move, slowly coming to her senses, but Teagan tightened his grip around her throat, holding her in a modified sleeper hold.

"I... I don't care what lies you're being fed, Teagan. You *are* my kid. I raised you. I saved you, I..."

"I... I... I... shut the fuck up. You didn't save me from *anything*. You ruined my special ceremony, and then took me away to make sure it could never happen. All these years, the questions I asked about Mom, about where you used to live, that was all just me planting the seeds to get you back here. And you fell for it. Hook, line, and sinker. But you know what?" He smiled. "It was worth the wait. Because now, when I join them, they will be even more powerful."

"Please... You don't have to do this, Teagan," Cole said.

"Let go of my daughter!" Holly screamed, charging toward the dock.

Teagan backed up, now standing at the edge of the platform. "I wouldn't do that, Holly. Allie and her precious baby are going to join us whether you want them to or not. If you come any closer, they will just rip you apart and leave poor Spencer as an orphan."

Holly stopped, bursting out in tears. She wanted to strangle him. She was their rock; she could not let anything happen to her kids.

"I'm begging you, please don't do this, Teagan. My kids are everything to me."

She was desperate. Scared. A sense of defeat hit her at once, dropping her to her knees. Allie lifted her head, her eyes clearing. It was as if the water sensed her awakening, crashing harder against the dock the moment she raised her face to look at her mom. Holly watched her daughter, who locked eyes with hers, mouthing the words "I love you." Allie attempted to push off from Teagan, one last effort to get away. It caught him off-guard, making him lose his balance on the edge of the dock. His grip loosened on her as he tried to prevent himself from falling in. Allie elbowed him in the stomach, coming completely free and ran toward her mom. A disfigured hand shot out of the water, reaching up toward the dock. Allie didn't see it in time. It grabbed ahold of her foot.

She went crashing down, face first onto the wood. Holly screamed. Allie kicked at the hand, trying to loosen its grip. From behind, Teagan stalked toward her, no longer smiling. Holly charged toward the dock, not caring if something tried to stop her. She had to get to Allie. As she got closer, the water around the dock shifted on both sides, arms reaching up and grabbing hold of the platform, blocking her.

"No, get up, Allie!" Holly yelled.

Teagan grabbed Allie by the hair and hauled her to her feet. Holly heard the rip of hair torn from scalp. She looked back to Spencer, who was clinging to Cole, burying his face against the leg of a man he hardly knew. She wanted to run to Allie, to risk everything. As if the water could read her mind, the dark figures below the surface got closer... waiting for her to make that mistake.

Cole walked toward the water but dropped in pain. The gunshot wound was too much, he had lost pints of blood from the wound.

"Teagan don't do it!" Cole yelled from the ground, spittle flying from his mouth.

Ignoring his former father figure, Teagan dragged Allie back to the end of the dock by her hair. He pulled something out of his pocket, and it took a second for Holly to register what she was looking at.

He held a knife.

Teagan pulled back on Allie's hair, exposing her bare neck. Allie reached for her mom, her fingers uselessly clawing the air between them.

"Thank you for your sacrifice," Teagan said.

He took the knife and swiftly slid it across Allie's throat, a fountain of blood shooting out of the newly opened gash. Allie's eyes bulged; she continued looking at her mother.

"NO! Allie!" Holly screamed, reaching out for her daughter.

Allie choked up bloody phlegm as her reaching hand dropped

limply to her side, her eyes rolling into the back of her head. Teagan again lifted the blade, this time to his own throat.

"See you on the other side," he said, then swiped the blade across his jugular. They fell back into the water, splashing on impact and sinking below the surface.

Holly sobbed uncontrollably. She buried her face in the mud and trembled, saying Allie's name over and over, letting the water roll over her shaking body. After everything they had been through, how hard Holly had gone out of her way to keep the kids safe, she had failed her daughter.

30

ANTHONY LOOKED at himself in the mirror, wiping off the last streaks of blood that had lathered his skin. He understood why his family was scared by what they saw, but they were simply being ungrateful. He saved them. Now, they could live on in peace and quiet. Whatever was consuming him from the inside had eased after he took care of Costello. For the first time since they arrived, he felt a sense of clarity in his foggy brain. His eyes, however, still looked odd, green peeking through his normally brown irises.

The buzz of something crawling through his back caused him to jerk upright. Anthony turned and looked at the wound in the mirror, it had mostly healed, and the green scabbing had begun to peel off. It itched so badly, he wanted to scratch it, but he couldn't reach it. He threw his shirt back on and walked out of the bathroom. The house was eerily quiet with nobody else around. Looking at the clock on the wall, he realized he hadn't seen anyone in at least an hour. When he came inside, he heard the truck start up and saw it driving slowly down the path. He assumed they were going to get Allie and Teagan. But they should have been back by now.

With his adrenaline now subsiding, the pain started to ramp up.

His body felt as if it had been hit by a bus. His nose was bent, looking as if someone had taken a baseball bat to it. The agony when trying to simply blow his nose to get out the congestion and stop the annoying fucking whistling sound coming from his nostrils, brought tears to his eyes. He took a deep breath and walked downstairs. Whether his family wanted to see him or not, it was probably best that he looked for them to make sure everything was okay.

Anthony walked out onto the front porch, noticing the rain had finally stopped. *Thank God for small favors*, he thought. Even with the weather improving, he really didn't feel like walking all the way down the path to find them. He was exhausted. The van was still parked down in the woods, and they had taken Cole's truck. That left him with either Vincent's SUV, or one of the 4-wheelers. He decided to check out the SUV and stepped over Birdman's bashed skull to walk around to the driver's side. The door was still ajar from their arrival. When he sat in the driver's seat, he pushed the keyless start button on the dash, but nothing happened. The words "KEY FOB NOT DETECTED," lit up the screen on the dashboard.

"Son of a bitch."

The key could be anywhere. He climbed out of the vehicle and walked around the side of the house to where the 4-wheelers were parked. Anthony hopped on one and started it up. A sharp pain shot through his organs, forcing him to grab at his side. He looked around frantically, trying to find Alister. Every single time he experienced this phantom pain, they were close by. This time, however, none of them showed their faces. He sped off on the 4-wheeler down the path, an overwhelming sense of uneasiness starting to roll in.

—————————

Cole couldn't grasp everything that'd just happened. He still held Spencer close, in the exact same posture when his own son—or the boy whom he *thought* was his son—sacrificed himself and Allie. This was all his own doing. Taking the kid back here and giving him access to them. It was selfish. Getting Teagan out of the cult all those years ago and living a normal life should have been the end of it all. To hell with Alister and his followers. But that wasn't how Cole lived his life. He had a mission to finish, and he was determined to do just that when coming back to Goshen.

Holly remained crumpled in the mud, crying incoherently. He wanted to comfort her but didn't feel that was the best idea, given her current state. She probably wanted to rip his head off for all the trouble he'd brought on their family. Instead, he cried silently and held Spencer close as if he was his own. He hated himself for not seeing the signs with Teagan. In retrospect, it was as clear as night and day. The long days of the boy gone by himself out in the woods. Talking to himself by the water. Showing almost no emotion at all when he saw a picture of his mom with Alister. Cole felt like he got punched in the gut, and the urge to throw up was real, but he held it together for Spencer. The kid had been put through the wringer the last few days.

The engine of one of the ATVs revved close by, approaching the end of the path above. He sighed, knowing it was Anthony. When Cole came home from the war, he visited the spouses of all the dead soldiers killed when the car bomb went off. He had to look each of them in the eye and say he was sorry that their loved ones wouldn't be coming home. Yet, no matter how many times he did it, it never got any easier. Now, he found himself in the same position with Allie's dad. Anthony appeared at the top of the hill through the trees, starting his descent down towards them. Cole decided to intercept him halfway, so Holly had more time to grieve to herself. She didn't need to hear him telling her husband that their daughter was dead.

"Anthony, can I talk with you for a moment?" he asked, looking back over his shoulder to make sure Spencer was okay by himself for a minute. The boy ran to his mom and hugged her.

"What is it? Why's everyone crying?" Anthony asked, panic in his eyes.

"It's Allie and Teagan. They... they're gone, Anthony."

Anthony grabbed him by the collar, enraged eyes searing into Cole.

"Gone? What the fuck do you mean, *gone?*"

Cole glanced back at Anthony's family again, making sure they were out of earshot. They likely heard Anthony yelling, but hopefully with it being dark out they couldn't read his lips to know what he was saying.

"Teagan, he got poisoned by Alister's persuasion. He sacrificed himself and Allie to them. Your poor wife and son watched it all happen," Cole said, choking back tears. Speaking it aloud made it real.

"Wha... What? She's *dead?*"

"I'm afraid so. I'm so sorry, man." Cole attempted to put a hand on Anthony's shoulder, but Anthony leaned over and vomited, green fluid splashing on the ground.

Anthony stood back up, wiping the remaining dribble away from his mouth. His eyes went cold, and he pushed past Cole and walked to the water, ignoring his grieving family.

"Are you happy now? You got what you want! All of you fucking monsters!"

He looked at the sky and screamed, allowing the anger inside to blast and rage. Then Anthony sat at the edge of the water, putting his head between his knees, and wept. Cole surveyed the Graham family. He had to do something to try and help, even though he was grieving himself. The water's glow had dimmed, bringing nightfall back to its normal state. He walked to Anthony, unsure of what to say.

"Anthony—"

"Get the fuck away from me! Leave me alone..."

Cole turned to Holly and Spencer, who were still embracing, and letting out all the tears that came.

"Guys... we should go..."

Holly looked up at him and, after hesitating a moment, got to her feet. She stormed toward him and got a few inches from his face.

"This is your fault! My baby's gone! She's *gone*, and I'll never see her again!" She screamed and started pounding his chest with both hands.

Cole knew better than to respond. She needed to get this out, and if he had to be the punching bag for it, so be it. Anthony wasn't exactly in the mindset to take the brunt of it. Cole wrapped his arms around Holly and hugged her. At first, she struggled to break free. Eventually she gave in and rested her head on his chest, crying harder than before. He rubbed her back and cried with her.

"My baby girl... my baby girl," she said, over and over.

"I know." It was all Cole could think to say. Spencer got up and came to them, hugging both. After a few minutes, Cole said, "Let's go back."

Holly instinctively looked at her husband, and for a second, Cole thought she intended to comfort him. She turned her back on him without a word and walked away from the pond. The three of them trudged back through the woods, leaving Anthony to digest it all in his own way. Every step Cole took was like being jabbed with a knife in the calf, but that pain had been overtaken by heartache. They had all lost someone tonight. Now more than ever, Cole was determined to rid the world of this fucking cult.

31

ANTHONY SAT at the edge of the pond, staring straight ahead. The rain had stopped, bringing with it a thick fog that suffocated the water's surface. Allie was gone. His first-born kid. Everything seemed so petty in retrospect. All the pointless arguments with Holly, the white lies he kept from her just so he didn't have to listen to her bicker at him. All the useless hours in the office, trying to give them a life of luxury. This whole time they were worried about tearing the family apart—now they were actually destroyed. Alister told him the sacrifice would happen, whether he helped it happen or not. Now he saw firsthand how true that was.

The soggy ground continued to soak through his pants as he sat, but he didn't care. He thought about his wife and kid, watching him butcher Vincent like a maniac. He thought of Spencer—who normally would cling to his leg after a bad nightmare—backing into the shadows to keep the distance between them. Alister had taken hold of Anthony's sanity for the good part of the past few days, but now that he had what he wanted, he appeared to be done with Anthony. It brought a clarity to his thoughts he was ashamed hadn't been there before. He hated it took his daughter being killed to make him realize the truth. And now, Holly would likely never speak to him again. Spencer wouldn't even want to come visit during the holidays. He hadn't just lost his daughter; he'd lost his entire family. His *life*.

The usual sounds of night were still absent, leaving him in silence to bathe in self-pity. Anthony put his hands over his eyes and continued crying. He decided in that moment, he had to let his family go. All the thoughts Alister put in his head to keep them there, to make him feel they were protected, it was all a bunch of manipulative bullshit designed to gain more power for himself and his God.

"*Daddy?*"

It couldn't be. Allie's voice, somewhere close by. Was she still alive? Could he save her?

"*Daddy...*"

Anthony looked around in the darkness of the woods, hoping he wasn't losing his mind any more than he already had.

"Allie? Where are you?"

The water shifted, bringing his focus back to the pond. Once again, it let off a dull glow, not nearly as bright as it had previously. The fog trapped some of the brightness. He stared at the water, waiting for something to happen.

Below the surface, something started to rise close to the dock. He would have recognized the face anywhere; it was his Allie. The crown of her head rose above the surface and continued to ascend until the top half of her mouth sat on top of the water. It was her, but she looked different. Her eyes glowed white, burning through the dense fog and staring directly into his. He didn't care that her eyes were different. He didn't care that her voice sounded off, like something was crawling around in her throat and clawing at her vocal cords. It was her, standing in front of him, talking to him. He leapt to his feet and got closer to the water.

"Allie! Please, tell me you're okay. Come to me, oh my God... I thought I lost you."

"*I'm okay, Daddy. I'm better than okay. But I can't come to you, not yet...*"

"What do you mean? You need to get out of there. Your mother and brother will be so happy to see you... *I'm* so happy to see you. I can't believe this..."

"Everything Alister said to you, it was all true, Daddy. I feel so good, so strong. We can all be together again. We can all be safe together..."

He realized what she was telling him. She wouldn't come out of the water; she wanted them to come to *her*. Anthony stared into her eyes, crying tears of joy. The white glow began to change, at first getting brighter. Then, the color transitioned, converting to a bright green. He couldn't take his eyes off the glowing beauty.

"If you come, we will all be together again. Do it for me, Daddy. Do it for Alister, and all of us," she said, the top half of a smile reflecting off the water's surface. The smile both chilled him to the bone and filled him with warmness at the same time.

Pain ravaged his insides, the warmness he felt now boiling hot in his stomach. He tore at his shirt, desperate to get it off and see what was causing the sensation. The fabric ripped, exposing his skin. Something was moving under his flesh, pressing against the wall of his stomach like it was trying to escape. The pain was unbearable. Anthony hunched over, praying for the discomfort to go away.

"What's happening?"

"Don't worry, Daddy... It takes time to adjust to your body. You aren't fully converted yet... It's trying to get back to its master..."

"What? Who—"

Whatever it was, the pain continued to get worse. Like a shark slamming its ravenous maw into a shark cage at the scent of blood, this thing inside him rammed against the walls of his stomach lining. Anthony recalled the pain arriving every time Alister was near. It was trying to get back to Alister. Which meant...

"He wants to help you, Daddy," Allie whispered, her voice now sounding like she was gargling on razor blades.

Anthony wiped tears away and glanced back to his daughter, who was now rising further out of the water, to a standing position. He screamed at the sight; her throat split open like a second mouth. Green ooze trickled out of the hole, sliding down her neck and into her dress. Anthony snapped out of the daze her eyes had held him in and jumped up, ignoring the pain in his abdomen.

His foot landed on something, and he looked down to see a boney white foot with green veins throbbing beneath the sole of his shoe. He stepped off it and turned, knowing before he even looked up that it was Alister. The tall man smelled of rotten swamp. He let out a maniacal laugh and shot his arm out with such speed that Anthony didn't have time to react. Alister locked his sludge covered fingers into Anthony's shoulder, squeezing with a strength that sent Anthony back to his knees. Alister removed his webbed hands from Anthony's shoulders, his clawed fingers dropping to his side.

"Hello, Anthony. We are taking care of your daughter, just like we promised. Now, we want the boy... If you can convince your wife, we can make an exception and allow her to join. As far as Cole, I think you know what needs to happen to that traitor."

The thing inside Anthony was going crazy. With Alister so close, it could sense him.

"Please... Make this stop inside me, it hurts so fucking bad!"

They locked eyes, and he saw the green fire behind them.

"I can make it so you never hurt again, Anthony..."

Alister opened his mouth wide, the bones in his jaw cracking and popping as his chin continued to lower. It was just like Anthony had seen in his nightmare, but worse. He stood and tried to back up, to keep Alister away from him. He remained so focused on the monster in front of him, that he forgot about the monsters *behind* him. The splash of the water at his feet warned him that he was against the edge of the dock. He risked a look down—only to see a set of hands reaching from the water. They latched onto his ankles, clenching around with a vice-like grip. Anthony tried to break free, but he was stuck.

"Don't worry, Daddy... It will only hurt for a minute," Allie whispered.

Anthony brought his attention back to Alister, the leader's mouth now two feet wide. A dry, clicking sound came from somewhere inside Alister's throat, getting louder as the distance between them shrank. Anthony had nowhere to go. His daughter kept telling him it would be okay; the clicking sound intensified. He couldn't hear his own screams, but he was screaming now. His throat begged the screams to stop, but he didn't even realize he was doing it. Alister's mouth was inches from his face now, and Anthony got a clear look inside, seeing things move and shift in Alister's throat. He could have sworn he saw another set of eyes *inside* Alister. Red, burning eyes.

He threw up his arms in a pathetic attempt to stop whatever was happening. Alister's hands shot up like two snakes pouncing on their prey, forcing them down and leaving Anthony's face exposed. Anthony wanted to shut his eyes, but a fearful curiosity got the better of him. The mouth pulled Anthony closer. Then the mouth closed completely around the top of his head and slid down his face like a python devouring its meal whole. Everything went black, but he was still awake. Panic set in as he began to suffocate; each attempt at a breath was like swallowing a mouthful of dirt. Something squirmed past his ears and latched on. His screams were muffled. His body twitched trying to reject the foreign substances entering his mouth. Anthony saw stars floating as his lungs struggled for oxygen. He thought he might be dying, that his daughter had tricked him and that this was his punishment for not helping them when they asked. He thought of his wife. His son. And how all he ever wanted was to protect them. Anthony was sorry for everything he'd brought on them. Sorry for ruining their lives. If he could just have another minute with them, a second chance, he would make it right.

"It will all be okay, Daddy…"

32

THE MEDICAL TRAINING Cole received when serving in the Army proved to be his saving grace. He was able to get the bullet from his calf, stop the bleeding, and stitch up the wound. He'd need a trip to the doctor to make sure there was no infection, but for now, he appeared to have saved his leg. Doing it all himself had seemed like an impossible task, but he'd fought through the pain. Now he had what felt like a massive Charlie horse in his leg and a pounding headache as well.

He sat at the kitchen table, looking at the bottle of whiskey sitting in front of him. It sure as hell didn't feel good pouring it onto the wound, but he'd be lying if he said the thought of pouring it down his throat didn't sound nice. When he'd told Anthony that he didn't crave it anymore, he meant it. But with how the last twenty-four hours had gone, he found his eyes looking at the glass bottle with a desire he'd never thought would return.

His fingers slid along the grooves in the elaborate design of the bottle. Just one shot wouldn't hurt, right? He'd lost his son tonight, killed someone after he never thought he would have to do it again, and watched everything be yanked out from under him, proving the cult was far from gone. *Just one shot...* He cried, wiping away the tears. Whether Teagan was his own or not, he'd raised the kid. And he'd loved Rebecca unconditionally before Alister got in her head. The doubts he'd carried that the boy was his faded with the years, but it sucker-punched him today to hear those words from Teagan. For all this time, the weight he'd borne on his shoulders, hiding stuff from Teagan, was all for nothing. The kid knew everything and was playing Cole like a banjo the entire time. How early did they get in Teagan's head? When he was still a baby? Recently? Did he expedite the process by coming back here? Of that he had no doubt. At this point, none of that really mattered anymore. The damage had been done.

His hand wrapped around the neck of the bottle. With the cap already off, it would be a quick, swift gulp of the burning sensation hitting his tongue and sliding down into his belly. Floorboards creaked above him, reminding him that he wasn't the only one here dealing with loss. What kind of coward would he be if he got plastered off his ass and left the Graham family to fend for themselves? There was a lot that needed to be done before dawn approached. He needed to take care of the bodies outside, clean up as much of the mess as he could. Spencer didn't need to be reminded of the events any more than his brain was already forcing him to remember.

Cole got up from the table with the whiskey bottle in hand and limped to the sink. It was his first attempt at walking since taking the bullet out, and it hurt like hell. *Maybe I would be better off cutting the thing off and having two prosthetic legs*, he thought bitterly. Taking one last glance at the bottle, he dumped the remaining contents of the booze down the drain, inhaling deeply to get one last smell of the liquor before it was gone forever. It was time to get to work.

———————

HOLLY HELD IT TOGETHER JUST LONG ENOUGH TO GET SPENCER TO sleep. It wasn't a deep sleep, and she knew he would likely wake with some sort of nightmare, but she was selfishly relieved that he'd passed out. She wasn't sure how much longer she could hold it all in. Holly snuck out of the bedroom and shut the door, leaving it open a crack to keep some light from the hallway shining in for him. She walked down the hall to the bathroom and shut the door behind her. Before she'd even sat on the toilet lid, she burst into tears. She sat and wailed, so many horrible snapshots flashing in her head. They always said no parent should have to bury their own kid, but she wouldn't even get to do *that* after losing Allie. Allie had stared right into her eyes with a look of defeat, knowing she was about to die and that her mom wouldn't be able to save her. A mother spends their life telling their children they will keep them safe, protect them, love them. She failed in that. Her baby girl was gone.

Holly couldn't even begin to think about all the issues Spencer would have to cope with after this. In the span of forty-eight hours, he'd been put through Hell and back, all topped off by his sister's throat being slit right in front of him while he clung to a stranger instead of one of his own parents.

She didn't know how to handle the situation with Anthony. It was clear their marriage was over, but could Spencer be put through a divorce after all this? His sister gets killed, he's haunted by some fucking demon children, sees dead bodies littering the lawn like weeds that were never plucked away, and then gets to go home to be told his parents are splitting up? The poor boy was going to need years of help to get through this, and she feared it was already too late.

There was a moment where she'd wanted to hug Anthony at the pond. No matter how much of this was his fault, he also lost a kid. They may have their differences, and their own ways of dealing with loss, but Allie was theirs together.

But she just couldn't bring herself to do it, afraid if she got close to him, she would be just as likely to strike him as hug him. That was the last thing Spencer needed to see. One thing she knew for sure: she would do everything in her power to recover the body of her daughter. They had no phones with them, thanks to Anthony forcing them to leave all electronics behind, but she would ask Cole to use his and call the police. What she would tell them, she had no idea. Would they believe something lived in the water and possessed Teagan to sacrifice her? Should she just say he had mental issues and killed her because he had something wrong with him? Quite frankly she didn't care what the police thought, as long as they could pull the body from the water. The thought of Allie sinking to the bottom of the pond brought on another wave of tears.

Holly decided to let Spencer sleep for a bit before leaving, but she had no intention of waiting until morning anymore. Her stomach dropped when she remembered the van was parked deep in the woods, and that Anthony had the keys. She needed to talk with him; whether he planned to leave with them or not was up to him. As soon as they got back in the city, she was going her separate way. The thought of living under Witness Protection was not appealing, but with the position Anthony had put them in, they might have no choice.

She got up from the toilet and gave one last look at herself in the mirror. Dark circles had caved in her cheeks, giving her the appearance of someone who hadn't slept in days. She shook her head and walked out of the bathroom, stopping outside Spencer's door, and peeking in at him. He looked to be at peace, his chest rising up and down like a calm boat at sea. But behind his closed eyelids was a different story. His eyes darted side to side looking around each corner of his mind for the next monster. She wanted to go hug him and tell him everything would be alright. But she was sick of lying to him.

33

Cole threw the last of the bodies into the back of his truck. He felt like a state worker who'd drawn the short straw and got stuck with roadkill duty, stacking mutilated bodies scraped from the roadside. The one with his brains smashed in was especially disgusting. Cole threw a tarp over them to hide them from plain sight, then twisted bungee cords through the tarp's loops and fastened them to the bed of the truck. The last thing he wanted was the tarp blowing off and Spencer coming out to see a set of dead eyes staring back at him.

He wasn't really sure what he wanted to do with the SUV yet. Hiding it deeper in the woods made sense, just in the off-chance others from the crime family came looking for them. It wasn't like Cole needed to worry about local authorities coming, for they wanted nothing to do with this place. Basically, if something happened here, then so be it in their eyes. Anyone dumb enough to step foot on the property was putting their own life on the line, and the police weren't going to waste their time trying to save anyone.

With the bodies taken care of, Cole planned to make one last lap around the house to be sure it was as tidy as it could be before bringing the bodies out in the woods and burying them. In a way, keeping himself busy was taking his mind off what had happened tonight. He worried that his battle with alcohol wouldn't end well once the Graham family was gone. There were just too many demons buried inside him. He needed to fight through it, one minute at a time. *At least until Alister was dealt with.* Once that was taken care of, he didn't see further purpose. He'd lost Rebecca. Lost Teagan. What else was left? Once the family was safely away from the campground, he would get rid of Alister and the Vodyanoy.

He slammed the tailgate shut and stretched his back. That was when he heard the squishing sound of footsteps through the muddy terrain. Cole spun around and came face to face with Anthony. The expression looking back at him was terrifying. It looked like something was using his skin as a mask, disfigured and contorted. There were movements, something shifting beneath his skin. And his irises were now completely green, the whites of his eyes bloodshot.

"Hi, Cole. We missed you while you were gone..." The voice was Anthony's, but there was something else with it. A nest of multiple voices all fighting to get out. It sent chills through Cole's body.

Anthony struck Cole, sending him flying into the tailgate of his truck and dropping to the ground. Anthony marched toward him, with one intention in mind. Cole saw it in the eyes, heard it in the voice. He was staring at more than just Anthony. The gap between them was shrinking, he needed to react quickly. He grabbed the bumper of the truck and pulled himself to his feet.

"Anthony... I know you're still in there. You need to stop this; your family has been through enough. *Fight* it, Anthony!"

A glimmer of hope flashed across those crazed eyes, but it quickly vanished and was overtaken by madness. Cole limped around the side of his truck, keeping the vehicle between them.

"Think about what you're doing... I know you don't want this."

"You have no fucking idea what we want! Teagan says hi, you pathetic cripple!"

Cole needed to get as far away from him as he could; he had nothing to defend himself with. Whatever had taken over Anthony had inhuman abilities. He needed his gun, which was inside the house.

"Are you in there, Alister? Are you the one fucking with Anthony's mind? Or is it your so-called god, Vodyanoy?"

The skin around Anthony's face tightened, stretching like someone was pulling back on his ears until they were about to tear off his face. Green veins bulged up his neck, spearing into his jawline and mouth. Cole heard a squirming sound beneath the skin as the poison spread throughout Anthony. The green eyes burned brighter, then narrowed to tiny slits as Anthony focused on Cole.

"You could have joined us, Cole. You are no better than the rest of the world. Thinking you are too good for us, that what we're doing is a *bad* thing. Now we have no choice but to take your life… But don't worry, it won't be lost for nothing. We will feed on you and leave you at the bottom of the pond to rot along with all the others who got in our way."

While it was Anthony's voice, it sure sounded like Alister talking. Not only did Cole need to kill him, but he also needed to warn Holly and Spencer before it was too late. He needed to buy more time. He looked around for anything that could help, but there was nothing within reach. The shovel he'd used to scoop up some of the loose body parts leaned against the porch, maybe he could grab it before Anthony reached him? With one leg, and injured at that, he doubted he could outrun something from the depths of that pond.

"I could've joined you. I could've let you kill an innocent child, and then what? Waited for you to do it again? You are pure evil, and don't think for a second that I'll give up before I end you."

Anthony lifted his upper lip in a snarl, revealing not only his teeth, but his gums, which had started to change color. Green veins spread like a spiderweb through the inside of his mouth. Cole continued keeping the attention on the conversation, edging closer to the porch as he talked.

"The only thing that will be ending is your sorry attempt at being a hero. We should have let you die at the bottom of the pond instead of helping you get better."

It was odd hearing Anthony speaking words from Alister's mind. Cole was almost close enough to grab the shovel. He just needed to get his hands on it. He hoped he would be able to land a blow and give himself long enough to get away. Holly and Spencer hadn't even had enough time to recover from what happened at the pond, but if he didn't do something soon, they would be thrust into a situation far worse.

"You are pathetic, you know that?" Cole said. "Still too weak to handle this on your own. You *need* his body to carry out whatever sick shit you think makes the world a better place." As he said it, he realized how true that statement was. If he could destroy Anthony's body with Alister controlling it, maybe that would get rid of Alister all together.

"If only you really knew the way... We've been around for centuries, before your kind even existed, and we have no desire to take advice from someone who couldn't even protect his own people."

He was trying to do exactly what Cole was doing—get under his skin in hopes that he would falter. As much as hearing those words stung, he forced himself to push them aside. Just a few more steps and he would reach the porch.

"You brag about being around for centuries, when you spent most of that fucking time hiding below a puddle in the earth, waiting for *your time*. You feed off our blood to survive and suck out *our* souls to gain power. So let me ask: If you're so special, why in hell do you need us to survive?"

Anthony's jaw looked as if it might shatter from clenching so hard. His brow furrowed as he picked up his pace toward Cole.

"For prey!" he snapped, sending spit through the air like bullets.

He was enraged, and Cole knew he had him where he wanted him. Anthony charged, moving in an unnatural dash. Cole grabbed the shovel by its handle, swinging it like a baseball bat as Anthony lunged at him. The metal clanged off the side of his head, sending vibrations down Cole's arms and Anthony to the ground. The sharp edge of the metal left a gash in Anthony's head; green fluid gushed out of the wound down over his eyes. With it, something squirmed in the green pus, which frantically tried to reenter the hole in his forehead. It was such a disgusting sight that Cole hesitated too long, giving Anthony time to get up. Cole attempted to swing the shovel again, but Anthony sprung from the ground, slamming into Cole's chest, and sending them both through a pillar on the porch, snapping it in half and sending shards of wood flying around them. They crashed to the floor as the porch roof began to moan without the support beam holding it in place.

Anthony, or Alister, was on Cole within seconds, squeezing the sides of his head and slamming it down into the porch repeatedly. Cole struggled to see, his vision diminishing with each blow of his head. Desperate to break free, Cole reached up and forced his fingers into the new wound on Anthony's forehead, pushing in and tearing at the hole. A scream erupted from Anthony and his eyes shimmered with a green glow. Cole flipped their positions, landing punches of his own against Anthony's already broken nose. He grabbed ahold of a long piece of wood that'd broken free from the pillar. The edge was sharp, like a makeshift spear. Cole drove it into Anthony's chest, bringing out another roar of anger and pain. With the stake still sticking out of Anthony, Cole got to his feet, intent on getting into the house and grabbing his shotgun to finish the job.

His hand touched the doorknob, getting the door open a few inches before Anthony had ahold of his leg. The demented figure crawled toward him, locked on to the prosthetic leg and wouldn't let go. Anthony dragged himself closer, pulling on the artificial limb. Cole kicked at him with his other leg, trying to break him free but lacked any true power in the hurt leg. His shotgun was just inside the office. He heard shuffling upstairs and glanced up to see Holly at the top, looking down at him in terror.

"Run! Get Spencer and go!" He didn't have time to say anymore. Anthony twisted the fake leg, snapping it off Cole's body. Cole felt his balance shift and knew there was no stopping his fall. Holly screamed as he crashed down. He landed inside the doorway sending the door slamming against the wall. Unless he could get Anthony away from the entrance, there was nowhere for Holly and Spencer to go. The front door was blocked, and they would have to go down the stairs to reach the backdoor, risking getting close to Anthony.

Cole rolled over to his back and saw Anthony towering over him in the doorway. Anthony looked at the leg in his hand and smiled. With his free hand, he grabbed the end of the wood sticking out of his chest and ripped it out, throwing it to the floor.

"Who's depending on something now, huh old man?" Anthony kneeled and struck Cole with the leg, over and over. Cole covered his face in defense, but he was losing strength. Each strike hit with a bone-jarring force. Welts quickly started to form on Cole's face and forearms. The leg wouldn't kill him. Anthony—*Alister*—was simply toying with him, making him suffer.

"Anthony! Stop it! You're going to kill him!" Holly screamed.

What was left of her husband jerked his head up, looking to the top of the stairs like a feral savage. "That's the point, *honey!*"

Cole kicked him in the stomach, sending Anthony backward out the door. *The shotgun,* he thought. He jumped up, hopping on his leg, a sharp pain shooting through his calf with each sudden impact. His calf felt like it was on fire, but he had no choice. He reached the desk, the shotgun leaning against it. It never felt so good in his hands as it did in that moment. He turned, prepared to pull the trigger at the first sign of Anthony. What he saw instead made him tremble.

Rebecca stood in the doorway.

The love of his life, the mother of his child. At first, she remained in the darkness of the porch, her face hidden in shadow. He would have recognized that hair from anywhere, those beautiful blonde locks.

"Rebecca…" he whispered.

"*Hi, Cole. Did you miss me?*"

He knew it couldn't really be her—she was dead at the bottom of the pond. But part of him didn't give a shit. Even if he got to see her just one last time, it filled his empty heart. On a day where he didn't think he could shed anymore tears, he did just that. He slowly hopped toward her, using the shotgun as a makeshift crutch.

"Come to me, baby. I'm sorry things went the way they did... I've missed you," she said.

"I missed you so much, Bec."

He reached the door, prepared to embrace her. She stepped forward, allowing the light from the house to expose her bloated face, full of squirming parasites under the skin. Her eyes were a dull white, like someone scraped the pigment out of them with a knife, just leaving the eyeballs.

"You fucking pathetic traitor!" she screamed in a demonic voice, and leapt at him.

Cole fell back, instinctively closing his eyes as he fought to stay upright. When he opened them, she had vanished.

"Cole, look out!" Holly yelled from the top of the stairs. She had been too afraid to move, watching everything happen from the safety of the second floor.

Before he realized what she was warning him about, Anthony charged through the doorway with the ax in hand, driving it into Cole's midsection. It stuck into the meat of his stomach, wedging between organs. Cole's eyes went wide. He clawed at the ax handle sticking out of him, dropping the shotgun. Anthony's hand was still gripped tightly around the handle, holding up Cole's weak body.

"Hurts, doesn't it? Don't worry, I don't have time to waste on making this take long..." Anthony said, then snapped his attention up at Holly. "Hi, honey. I'll be right with you!"

Holly had seen enough, running to the bedroom where Spencer was hiding.

"You... you've lost your fucking m-m-mind," Cole struggled to say with blood pouring through his teeth.

"That's not very nice to say now, is it? Here, let me help you get that out," Anthony said, ripping the ax from Cole's body.

Cole dropped to the ground in a heap. He could feel his life draining away, and knew he was about to die. *Once a failure, always a failure*, he thought. His body hardly had the strength to lift his head, but he forced it up and saw the blood pumping out of his stomach like a geyser. His fingers and toes had gone numb, and for a brief second, he thought he had his other leg back, the phantom pain forcing out an ill-timed smile.

"What the hell are you smiling about? You're dying."

Cole knew his hand was near the gun, but he couldn't feel it in his grip. He willed his hand closer, turning his head and saw that his finger was so close to the trigger. He tried to lift the gun, but he might as well have been trying to pick up a Mack truck. Anthony cackled watching his last-ditch effort to defend himself.

"Y-y-you will... rot in Hell for this," Cole spit out with blood.

"Hell has no place for our kind," Anthony said, then drove the ax into the center of Cole's face.

34

HOLLY SLAMMED the door shut and locked it, as if that would do any good. She looked into Anthony's eyes while he attacked Cole: any ounce of sanity he had been clinging to had now been erased from existence. Spencer sat on the corner of the bed, hugging his knees, and staring straight ahead at the door.

"Daddy's a bad man now..." he whispered, rocking back and forth.

Holly took her eyes off the door and stared at her son. He appeared to be in some sort of nervous trance, watching the door and waiting for the inevitable.

"Listen, buddy... That's not your real daddy inside there, we have to stay away from him, okay? We can't get downstairs, so we need to find another way out."

Spencer slowly turned toward her, but his eyes remained unfocused, staring through her like she wasn't even there.

"He wants us to go to the pond with him, Mommy. Just like the kids wanted."

His tone scared her. But what scared her even more was the way he called her *Mommy*. He hadn't called her that since he was five—it appeared he had mentally regressed over the past two days. She shook him violently, more than she meant to, but he needed to understand the importance of the situation.

"Spencer! I need you to listen to me… We need to find a way out of here before he gets to us."

He blinked, then stared into her eyes. Without a word, he nodded in agreement. Holly looked around the room for anything to help block the door. She wasn't sure she could move the dresser on her own, but she needed to try. It was only a matter of time before Anthony came up after them. The dresser sat against the wall adjacent to the door, so she just had to move it a short distance to block it. She crouched, put both hands on the edge, and pushed. It only moved a few inches before catching on one of the floorboards.

"Damn it!"

Quickly going to the other side, she lifted the legs over the gap in the floorboards and backed up. The scraping noise of the legs grinding across the hardwood was like nails on a chalkboard. Any chance of Anthony wondering what room they were hiding in went out the window.

Out the window. It was pretty high up, but one of the two windows in the room overlooked the porch roof below. They might be able to jump down and climb off to escape.

Holly again switched sides, shimmying the dresser inch by dreadful inch across the door. With one last push, she got it in place. She wiped sweat away from her eyes and ran back to the window, all while Spencer sat on the bed awaiting instruction. When she opened the window and looked out, a knot formed in her stomach. She had never been a fan of heights, and the fall looked farther than she was hoping. But then she heard the thudding of Anthony marching up the stairs. Any fear of heights she had dissolved with each approaching step.

"Oh family, oh family, where are *you?*" Anthony sang in a strange melody.

Holly lifted her finger to her mouth, telling Spencer to remain quiet. She motioned for him to get closer to her so they could climb out the window. He slid off the bed and his first step landed on a weak floorboard. A creak that might as well have been a car alarm sounding off gave away their location.

"I *heard* that… There's nothing to hide from, guys. I just want us to be together. All the bad men are gone. Allie's waiting for us…"

His voice was right outside the door. Holly imagined him resting his cheek on the other side, caressing the door like some intimate serial killer. The mention of Allie twisted an imaginary knife in her heart. Light coming in from underneath the door shifted, and then the door handle jiggled.

"Get away from us! You're crazy, Anthony! Something happened to you…" Holly yelled.

"You're right. Something *did* happen to me. I now realize what this family needs to stay together. With the help of Allie, and Alister, the picture has never been so clear. Can you *please* let me in, so we don't have to play this game?"

A moment of silence followed. Holly and Spencer stood at the window; the moonlight helped them see the slick surface on the porch roof. Holly's muscles tightened, her body rejecting the idea of going out there even as her mind was bent towards it. She had no choice, she needed to get Spencer to safety and put her fears behind her. Holly lowered face-to-face with Spencer.

"Okay, Spence. I'm going to get you out first. Stay against the house until I get out there to help you down."

He nodded.

As his first leg stepped out of the window, a loud crack exploded at the door. Holly glanced back and her blood went cold. The door was splintering already, after just one strike. It wouldn't take Anthony long to break in. She went to lift Spencer's other leg out the window when Anthony struck again, this time much harder. Spencer slipped from her grip and fell the rest of the way out the window, sliding down the roof halfway before getting hold of a raised shingle. He screamed in terror as his grip began to slip.

CRACK!

"Where the fuck do you think you're going? You ungrateful *cunt!*" Anthony screamed.

Holly ran to her suitcase, throwing clothes to the floor. The gun glistened in the light. She grabbed it and prepared to aim it at the door.

"Don't come near us, or... or I'll pull the trigger, Anthony. You will not touch Spencer!"

She dared a final look to the door, and saw a jagged hole blasted in the center of it. Anthony locked eyes with her through the hole, flashing his teeth which were stained green. He heaved and struck the door a third time with the ax, this time expanding the hole wide enough to climb through.

"You're only making this harder on yourself, Holly... If I have to kill you to get to him, so fucking be it!"

"No, leave us alone! What's happening to you, Tony?" Holly cried.

"All I've ever done is take care of your sorry ass. Given you all everything you need... And still, all you do is *fucking* complain!"

Anthony started to climb through the hole with the dresser blocking the bottom half of the door. He backed his head out of the hole and with a strength Holly had never seen, he kicked the door in, sending the dresser toppling over to its side. She screamed again.

"Help, Mom! I'm slipping!" Spencer yelled from the roof.

The drop from this high up wouldn't likely kill him, but it would very likely break bones—something they could not afford to deal with right now. Anthony kicked the remaining pieces of the door out of the way and bulldozed into the room. Holly backed away from the door, getting out of his reach, aiming the gun with trembling hands.

"You have nowhere to go out there, fucking dumb bitch! I don't have time to wait for you, get back in here..."

She fired the gun, exploding Anthony's right ear into mist. Green and red splattered onto the wall next to him and he dropped to the floor holding the side of his head. She aimed again and pulled the trigger.

The gun clicked on an empty chamber.

The suitcase containing the box of bullets was on the floor next to a thrashing Anthony.

"Mom, help!"

Holly looked to the suitcase, then back to the window. She had to help Spencer before he fell below. She threw the gun to the floor and ran to the window. Spencer's grip was loosening, his eyes open wide as he held on like his life depended on it. She climbed out the window; she was too afraid of losing her balance to walk, so she slid down the roof until she reached him. She grabbed hold of his hands and pulled him to her, briefly hugging him to ease his stress.

"I got you, baby," she whispered in his ear with a panting breath, feeling him tremble in her arms.

Anthony appeared at the window, taking labored breaths through his shattered nose. He started to climb out after them. They had to move, but where to she had no idea. She looked down below but didn't see any soft spots she felt comfortable jumping to.

"I'm going to break your damn neck, Holly!"

Anthony was almost out of the window.

"We have to move, now!"

Holly stood and pulled Spencer to his feet. The roof moved slightly, followed by a drawn-out groan of wood too stressed underneath weight it could no longer support. She had no idea what was happening. The collapsed pillar from earlier would have been located right below them, but without it, the roof was beginning to collapse. Anthony realized what was happening and backed into the house, watching it unfold.

"Oh, Holly bear. Looks like you are in a bit of a mess there. Guess you have no choice but to come back to the love of your life, hmm?"

His expression was sinister, his tone filled the air with poison. She looked around for any other way in or down. It was either climb back to a killer, or jump off.

"We have to jump, Spencer. Do you trust me?"

He hesitated but nodded again.

They moved closer to the edge with Anthony laughing in the

background. Holly again looked over the side, planning to help Spencer down first somehow, and then worry about herself. As she inched closer to the edge, the roof shifted another few inches, followed by a loud crack. And then they were falling, the roof collapsing below. She had just enough time to scream before they hit the ground.

35

SPENCER OPENED HIS EYES, confused where he was. He tried to sit up, but a rush of pain shot through his body. His mom lay next to him, and she appeared to be sleeping. But that couldn't be, they were just... the fall. They were trapped under a section of the roof that collapsed on top of them. He shook his mom, trying to wake her up, but she just moaned. The look on his dad's face before they fell reminded him of the boogeyman in some of the YouTube videos he watched when his parents weren't paying attention. If they didn't hide, Anthony would come find them, just *like* the boogeyman.

"Mom," Spencer said, his voice coming out raspy. He cleared his throat. "Mom!"

Holly opened her eyes, squinting at her son, and he felt a wave of relief knowing she was alive. She forced a half smile and tried to sit up.

"Oh... I can't move, Spence. This heavy piece is pushing down on me."

"I can help move it. We'll get you out..."

As she came back to reality, her eyes sparked with fear.

"You need to hide, get away from here, Spencer. He'll be out any second..."

Spencer shook his head, his eyes welling up. He didn't want to leave her. He didn't want her to end up like Allie, or Cole. "I'm too afraid to go by myself, we need to stay together, remember?"

"I'll get out, but I need you safe first. Find a place to hide, just like when we play hide and seek, right? Pick the best spot you can find, *quickly!*"

He understood the sense of urgency in her voice and didn't question it. He was able to army crawl out of the wreckage and the cool night air hit him like a slap in the face. His leg hurt, but not enough to stop him from pushing on. He heard movement in the house and knew he didn't have time to run down the trail and hide, he needed to find a spot close by. Cole's truck and the big black vehicle the bad men came in both sat in the driveway. Spencer jogged around the truck and noticed the door was still open on the SUV. His dad would hear him shut the door if he climbed in there. He glanced back to the truck. A large tarp covered the bed of the truck; the odds of his dad checking under there were less than inside the vehicles.

Crouching low, Spencer climbed the bumper of the truck, so he didn't have to open the tailgate. He grabbed the edge of the tarp and lifted it.

The dead eyes of Vincent Costello's decapitated head stared back at him.

Spencer covered his mouth to block the scream. He dropped the tarp back down, desperate to find another spot to hide. That's when the front door to the house opened. With no other option, Spencer hopped in the bed of the truck, pulling the tarp over him like he did with a blanket when he hid from the monsters in his closet. Except this time, the monsters were dead and lying next to him. He crawled farther, reaching the end of the bed against the truck's back window. He refused to look at the dead bodies, but he could sense their eyes lifelessly staring at him. Curling into a fetal position, he held his breath and waited. Half of a cut up arm sat inches from his face, forcing him to hold the bile down in his throat.

"You guys had quite the fall! I hope you're okay?" Anthony said while approaching the collapsed roof.

Spencer heard his squishy footsteps in the mud. They were getting louder. He closed his eyes and hoped his dad wouldn't find him.

The footsteps stopped next to the truck.

A faint whistling noise broke the silence. It was his dad's broken nose as he forced air through crushed bones. Spencer wished he could peek out and see what was going on, but he knew that would blow his cover. His head rested against a gas can; the fumes burned his nostrils. When he was smaller, he always liked the smell of gas, inhaling deeply whenever his parents would stop to fill up the tank. His mom told him how bad the fumes were for him, and that they would kill his braincells. He supposed killing a few braincells was better than his dad killing him.

Boards were being moved, sounding like they were being thrown aside with ease thanks to his dad's newfound strength.

"Oh, hey there honey. You know, I really wanted you to join us..."

It was his dad's voice, but different. Something else was powering him, using his body. The tarp moved slightly, and Spencer saw his dad's hand gripping the truck while he talked. Fear clawed its way from Spencer's stomach up to his throat—it was becoming a struggle to hold his breath. The hand moved away from the truck, bringing a momentary sense of relief. After another moment of silence, his mom cried out in pain. Spencer couldn't help himself, he needed to see what was happening to her. He slowly climbed over the mangled body next to him and lifted the tarp just enough to peek out.

Anthony held Holly by the hair. Blood decorated her shirt like crimson tie-dye. His back was to the truck, but Holly locked eyes with her son briefly before focusing on something different to avoid giving his location away.

"Where is he?" Anthony asked.

Holly clenched her mouth shut, letting him know she had no intention of giving her son up.

"I said, where the fuck is he?" He yanked her hair, snapping her head back.

"Anthony... I know this isn't really you. You know we can't let them take our boy. They... they already got our daughter," she said, struggling to get the words out.

"You can think I'm whoever you want to, but we will have him. Clearly your time has run out," Anthony scoffed. "Now, I'll just use your blood for more strength and leave your body to decay away in the mud."

Her neck was still exposed in the moonlight. He lifted his hand, preparing to rip her throat out. Spencer couldn't let this happen, he had to distract him. He threw the tarp up and jumped over the side, landing a few feet behind Anthony.

"Leave her alone!"

Anthony's head tilted in curiosity. He slowly turned, a grisly smile infesting his face.

"There he is..."

He dropped Holly to the ground in a heap and kicked her in the face, then brought his attention to his son. Spencer's legs felt like rubber. He feared panic would prevent him from running away. But he needed to get this monster away from his mom.

"You aren't my dad, you're a monster. My dad would never hurt us!"

"I assure you, that thought crossed his mind on numerous occasions, you little shit. Now, get over here."

Spencer didn't think, he *ran*. He made sure he had a wide enough distance so Anthony couldn't lunge and get him. His feet slammed hard on the path, and he had no idea where to go, but he ran deeper and deeper into the campground.

"You're making this harder than it needs to be, Spency boy!"

As much as he didn't want to look back, something compelled his eyes to look back and see if he was being pursued. His dad was following, but he appeared to be taking his time. He looked way too calm for someone losing sight of their desired target. That thought disturbed Spencer, but he didn't feel he had a choice. This was about saving his mom. He continued to run at full speed until his lungs burned so bad, he thought he needed an icepack to cool the inside of his throat—and then he pushed through that feeling and ran some more. He didn't stop until he reached the end of the path and came to the woods blocking the pond. There was no way he was going back down there after what happened earlier.

"Keep on going, you're almost there!" Anthony yelled from fifty yards back. Again, he sounded confident. *Too* confident.

Spencer turned right, prepared to follow the next path—and stopped in his tracks. The two children, who had made his life a living nightmare since getting here, stood in the middle of the road, the moon giving their pale skin an even brighter glow. Those white eyes were glued to him, and even in the dark, from this distance, he could see they were smiling. Spencer looked back toward the house. Anthony was now only thirty yards away and gaining ground. Spencer was trapped, and now realized why his dad was so calm.

He was right where he wanted him to be.

36

HOLLY SAT UP, an excruciating pain in her back. One of the roof's support beams had landed on her in the fall, and she was lucky not to have broken her spine. As if that wasn't enough, the force of Anthony's kick had knocked her out cold. Even if she did have a broken spine, she would fight through it to protect her son. Spencer saved her life but put his own on the line in return. Such an act of bravery from the panic-ridden boy would normally make her the proudest mom in the world. That wasn't the case when he had a possessed lunatic trying to drown him. The fact that Anthony didn't finish her off before going after Spencer showed just how important —and perhaps time-sensitive—their sacrifice was. She had no intention of letting them see that through.

She forced herself to her feet and tried to see down the trail, but it was too dark to make anything out. Spencer and Anthony were already long gone. That scared her.

As if one fear birthed another, Holly suddenly felt herself over-come by the fear that her husband may not have taken off, after all, that he was hiding around the corner, waiting for her to come so he could finish his little game with her before having Spencer all to himself. Her eyes scanned the woods surrounding her, looking for him, looking for any of those *things* that wanted their souls.

She needed to face this nightmare side-by-side with her son.

Holly ran to the driver's side door of Cole's truck and got in. The stale smell of cigar smoke filled her lungs. She desperately looked around for the keys and then remembered Cole stuck them above the visor. Ripping it down, the keys fell into her lap. She latched onto them and shoved the key into the ignition. She pictured the truck not starting, turning over until it chugged to a dead stop. But the vehicle started right up. The passenger floor was littered with papers, Cole's lighter, a box of cigars, and a pair of work gloves. She pushed it all to the side, looking for a gun, *anything* that could help her. The only thing remotely useful was Cole's pocketknife. It wouldn't exactly scream "threatening". But she didn't have time to run back in the house and grab a gun, she needed to hurry. Besides, she wasn't a killer. What would she do if forced to hold a gun to her husband again? Shoot him? She wasn't sure she had it in her after the last mishap, but she also knew her motherly instincts would kick in when needed. If her son's life was on the line—which by all accounts, it was—she would do whatever she needed to. Madness lived behind Anthony's eyes. She couldn't treat Anthony like it was him, even though it was his flesh, his *blood* in front of her. Holly threw the headlights on, cut the wheel, and sped off down the path toward the pond.

————————

This little shit. Anthony was fed up with the game of cat and mouse. It was time to start the sacrifice. Alister had a vice-like grip on his mind, and any wrong decision on Anthony's part was greeted with a needle-like stab to his temples. As if he needed another reason to be pissed off. All these years, taking meds, going to therapy, controlling the anger—it had all been a waste of time. He felt so free just letting the anger out into the wild and not trying to tame it.

He continued his march down the washed-out path, the woods

not too far ahead. Spencer had run right into the mouth of the forest—right where he was supposed to go. *Good little boy*, he thought.

It was unfortunate Holly wouldn't be uniting with them, but then again, he really had no desire to listen to her bitching for all of eternity. He smiled at that image, living the life of gods, and *still* having to deal with her telling him he was doing something wrong. Once this ceremony was complete with Spencer, he would finish her, and then feed her to the rest of them. They could have all of her, he'd already had enough.

————————————

It was dark in the center of the forest, the moon blocked from providing light by the thick canopy. Spencer couldn't see anything. The pond provided minimal illumination with its emerald glow, but not enough to help him. Maybe that was a good thing. If he could hide somewhere in here, his dad might not be able to see him. At the moment, he hid behind a tree, his eyes glued to the hill for any sign of his dad. He couldn't be far now. Spencer clung to the tree, holding onto it like it was somehow protecting him. *Please don't find me, please—*

A crack behind him broke the silence. He whirled around and saw the ghost kids coming for him. They had spread out, protecting the perimeter like some kind of guard dogs.

"*Hi, Spencer... Did you come back to play with us?*" the girl asked.

They were getting closer on each side. Up top, he heard his dad approaching. There was nowhere to go. The dark figure of his father appeared, right outside the tree line, the tall pine trees criss-crossing above, his eyes letting off a dull green spark. Whatever was inside him now had full control.

"Nowhere to run, kiddo. Just give up already, come say hi to your sister with me—"

Something lit up behind Anthony, growing brighter. Anthony spun around to face back toward the house, saying something that

Spencer couldn't hear. Then the sound of a vehicle approached. Spencer's heart ramped up; his mom had come to save him. Anthony looked back down to the woods.

"Grab him and hold off until I'm back!" Anthony shouted to the kids.

Spencer turned to break for the woods, but he was too late. They were on him, grabbing ahold of his arms and not letting go. Their white eyes gave off a warmth that hit his face like a grill fire. The boy squeezed Spencer's wrist, digging his claws into the skin. And they *were* claws, any sign of regular fingernails long gone.

"Let go, you're hurting me!"

"*Sorry, Spencer... We must do as Father tells us, we don't want to get locked in the thinking hole again,*" the girl whispered.

He tried to break free, but it was pointless. They easily overpowered him, dragging him through the wet forest toward the pond. He screamed for help, but there was nobody left to save him. The fingers penetrated his skin, firmly holding his arms. His legs dragged behind, unable to get any traction on the wet leaves. Spencer spotted the water ahead, its brightness intensifying the closer they got.

"No! *Please!*"

Dark shadows rose from the pond, breaking the surface one after another, exposing their terrifying faces to him. He wet himself, the urine spreading down his leg with uncomfortable warmth. The first head to reveal itself was a lady, her hair tied up in a tight bun. She didn't say anything, but she didn't have to. Just one look at her and his blood froze in his veins. Behind her, a second figure rose, and he was hit with an invisible gut punch.

Allie.

"*Hi, Spence... Soon, you will join me, and we can be together again...*"

He couldn't concentrate on what she was saying, his eyes locked onto the gash in her throat, green fluids sliding slowly down her skin like a thick syrup. Her throat was fully exposed, and muscles squirmed around inside, living a life of their own. Allie's eyes glowed brighter than the rest, the white light forcing Spencer to squint.

"Allie, please tell them to let me go!"

"*I can't do that, Spencer. I think you know what has to happen.*"

And then, the kids dragged him to the dock—a place he never wanted to step foot again—but here he was. They held him in place with the water crashing against the wooden beams beneath. All of Alister's followers now surrounded the area. Watching. Waiting for their newest member to come join them.

The ceremony was about to begin.

37

HOLLY PARKED THE TRUCK, and without hesitation climbed out of it and marched straight toward the woods, clutching the handle of the knife tightly. She would have liked to have run Anthony over, but the trees blocked the way. Anthony turned around at the sight of the headlights casting their glow over the forest. He stood between her and her baby.

"Holly, so glad you could join us. We are just about to begin!"

Something thrashed under the surface of his skin, traveling around while he spoke. The headlights illuminated his writhing face. He provided a smile that scared the shit out of her, but she would not let him see that. She was done cowering under him.

"Where's Spencer? What the fuck did you do with him, Anthony?"

"Always questioning everything. Nothing's ever good enough for the perfect Holly. I know you want to ruin this for me, just like you do everything else. You could've been part of this! We could have stayed together! You ungrateful *bitch*," he snarled.

"Stop saying that stuff! You sound crazy, Tony!" She knew he had every intention of killing her before drowning their son. There was no stopping him with words. She had to act.

"Crazy? *Crazy* was marrying you. Crazy was trying to make it work with you when clearly, you won't ever change. There's nothing crazy about what's going to happen tonight. He's in good hands down there, you have nothing to worry about... as for you, well, I'm done talking—"

Anthony sprinted toward her, his eyes piercing. She almost didn't have time to react, he was so *fast*. Holly flinched, preparing for impact. Her hand tightened on the knife. He bowled into her with the sudden impact of a plow truck taking out a mailbox. She dropped to the ground, fumbling around with the knife. Hoping she would at least have a chance to use it before she died. His hands found her throat. Pressure tightened around her windpipe and panic set in. Veins bulged in his neck as he squeezed with everything he had. She gasped for breath, but nothing would come out. Her left hand came up, helplessly slapping at his face. Trying to claw, gouge, do whatever she could to break free. Everything was turning black.

"Help me! Please, help me!"

It was Spencer, yelling from the pond. She knew he couldn't see her, but it was as if he could sense her. He wanted his mother for protection. Anthony's eyes widened, a fiery green rage staring down at her. *I. Need. To. Save. Him.* Holly felt for the knife in her right hand. It was still there, but her fingers were tingling as she sensed herself losing consciousness. She squeezed the handle while he squeezed her throat. The hole where his missing ear used to sit was oozing down the side of his neck and onto her hands. She jabbed the thumb of her free hand into the missing earhole, and Anthony growled in pain, but his grip loosened just a little. With the remaining strength she had left, she swung the knife up, puncturing his neck. He fell backwards on the ground, reaching for the foreign object sticking out of him.

"Oww, you *CUNT!*"

He blinked repeatedly. He shook his head, as if doing so would shake the pain away. Holly watched him attempt to stand, only to fall back again a few feet further away. His eyes briefly rolled into the back of his head, but then they came back, staring right at her with pure hatred.

"I'm going to fucking kill you!"

Spencer continued to scream through the woods; she was running out of time. Holly still sensed a set of invisible hands wrapped around her neck, the pain throbbing with each breath she took. She got to her feet, coughing up the iron taste of blood.

Anthony ripped the knife from his neck, the sound of the blade sliding out giving Holly the chills. He moaned in pain. She needed to do something before he was on her again.

He started to climb to his feet, his legs fighting him to stay down.

Holly ran to the driver's side of the truck and jumped in. She slammed the door shut and punched the gas, watching the distance between the truck and her husband shrink. *Pedal to the metal*, she thought. His head shot up and he glared directly into the windshield. Holly screamed in anger, flaring up the pain in her throat.

The truck slammed into Anthony. Metal and flesh collided with a disturbing crunch. She kept the gas to the floor, picking up speed as his upper body fell against the hood while his legs flailed around beneath the fender. His hands clawed at the hood, scraping, searching for grip. His wild-eyed face and body blocked her view, not that she would have stopped anyway. They continued to pick up speed, and all she wanted was for his hands to slip and send him to the ground beneath the studded tires.

"Holly! Stop the fucking—"

The truck smashed into a tree. Glass shattered. Metal crunched. A loud pop forced out the airbag, puffing it into Holly's face, sending her head snapping back into the seat. The night went silent.

38

HOLLY OPENED her eyes to the sound of the truck engine sizzling, a cloud of smoke coming from beneath the hood. For a minute, she forgot where she was. Then she heard Anthony screaming and it all came back to her. She ripped at the airbag to get a better look. When the fabric was out of the way, she saw him. He was pinned between the truck and the tree, the metal wrapping around the base of the massive pine, trapping him. Holly couldn't believe he was still alive. He should have died on impact, but whatever was inside him was not going to let that happen.

"You bitch! I'm going to rip your throat out and watch them suck you dry!"

Her head was pounding, and she was pretty sure she felt something cracking in her neck. The pain was excruciating when she turned to open the door. She opened it as far as it would go and fell to the ground. It hurt to crawl, let alone walk, but she forced herself to try. She pulled herself up using the truck to lean on. Even with Anthony trapped, she still feared getting too close to him.

"You think you're so fucking clever, don't you? Why don't you get me out of here so I can show you how *clever* you really are? I can't wait to end your life," he sneered. He grinned at her, a mix of blood and green fluid running through his teeth and down his jaw.

Holly gave a wide berth around the truck and looked down toward the pond. Terror stole her focus at the sight of Spencer being held down by a number of Alister's followers. They were terrifying in their ragged clothes, skin wrinkled and bloated, but most of all, their white eyes, all staring down at Spencer with a predatory urge to kill. *No, worse, to sacrifice him.* He was being held against his will, lying on the dock in a mock crucifix position. She could hear him crying, but the screams had stopped. The thought of leaving Anthony pinned against the tree to go save her son was a hard one to let go, but she knew she needed to take care of her deranged husband before going down there. To risk him getting out would end in sure death for both her and Spencer. As if he could read her mind, he forced out a cackling laugh.

"You know they're just waiting on my command, right? Whether I'm down there or not, I can have them slice his tiny little throat open and drink the blood from his baby Adam's apple..."

The fear suffocating Holly quickly dissolved, replaced with a hatred she didn't know she possessed. She ignored the pain pounding through every inch of her body and walked back to Anthony. A desire to bash the smile from his lunatic face had never been greater.

"I know you won't do that... I know because you're too selfish. Because whatever is making itself at home inside you, wants to be part of it all. If you die... It dies. They *all* die."

She saw it. A flash of doubt fought through the confidence of a madman. His green eyes flicked from side to side, looking for a way out. He let out a furious growl, slamming his hands down on the bent-up hood of the truck. The vehicle moved, just a little. She couldn't let him escape. She turned her back to him and walked to the back of the truck.

"Where the fuck do you think you're going? Can't save the little shit if you leave now, can you?"

"Who said I was leaving?"

She threw back the tarp, revealing the dead bodies of the men he butchered earlier. The sight of them didn't even faze her anymore. She was hoping to find a weapon, anything that could end the nightmare. A gas can sat against the back of the truck bed. She walked to the side and grabbed it. The sound of gas sloshing around against the metallic wall of the can got Anthony's attention.

"What are you doing?"

She ignored him and opened the passenger door. Tossing the loose papers and food wrappers to the ground, she found what she was looking for. When she backed out of the truck, she sat the gas can on the hood, then climbed up after it.

"What are you fucking *doing*?"

Holly took the protective lid cap off the nozzle of the can. She stood on the hood, looking down at Anthony. She fought back tears, thinking of everything they had been through as a family. Thinking about how she still loved him after all that happened. But this wasn't him, she had to realize that. She lifted the can and started dumping the gasoline onto his trapped body.

"Stop that! You goddamn bitch! STOP!" His voice altered, deepening to a demonic level.

His body started to shift, the skin expanding. She watched his mouth open wide. His jaw cracked as it opened beyond its normal capacity. Something was trying to get out of his body. Tears rolled down his cheeks, and she realized they were real tears, not the green fluid he'd been releasing. His eyes looked at her with his mouth locked open at an unnatural angle. He couldn't talk.

He nodded.

It was him. For a brief second, it was *her* Anthony. And then a ripping sound came from within his throat as something began to claw its way out. He screamed. Holly saw something climbing out of his mouth. A slimy green hand with webbing that was covered in grime started ripping at his cheek.

She opened the top of the lighter and flicked the switch, emitting a small flame.

"I love you, Anthony," she sobbed.

Holly threw the lighter at the body, and he was instantly engulfed in flames. He flailed, the sounds coming from him more like squeals than actual screams. Anthony's head snapped back, a hole splitting in the center of his throat. Another clawed hand forced its way from the hole. Ripping. Tearing. Trying to get out before the body was burned to a crisp. The smell of her husband's burning corpse was too much to handle. Holly slid off the hood and threw up while listening to his screams of desperation.

The body continued to bend at odd angles, the skin peeling off in layers. The flame was intensifying, spreading, and not letting up. Holly backed away from the heat, holding her hand up to block the burning sensation from hitting her face. A set of red-hot eyes stared out from the open cavity in his neck. The entity inside Anthony slowed its movements. His head stopped whipping side to side. The green glow in his eyes extinguished. And then, his body went limp. The screams stopped, only to be replaced by the crackling of the fire as it continued to consume his charred body.

Holly dropped to her knees, crying so hard it brought back all the pain her body had sustained in the last few hours. She had just killed her husband.

But there was no time to reflect on it. Spencer screamed from the dock, yelling for his mom.

39

SPENCER HAD NEVER BEEN SO scared in his life. The monsters held him down, and the scariest of them all was his sister. Allie's throat was wide open, and he could see *inside* her. The water was so bright now that it was hurting his eyes. He heard his dad screaming at his mom through the woods and hoped he wouldn't hurt her. He'd never touched his mom before tonight, but he was different now. He was the bad man.

Spencer heard a crash. After a few minutes there was more screaming.

The screams turned to angry growls. A fire lit up the woods, but he still couldn't see them while being held down. Spencer badly wanted to know if his mom was okay. That was when the monsters all started crying out, their voices sounding like echoes in a tin can. The hands holding him down let go, and he immediately jumped to his feet. He looked at his sister, then the older lady with her hair in a bun. Something was happening to their bodies. The water splashed around, almost as if *it* too was in pain. Fear paralyzed him, locking him in place. His brain was screaming to run to his mom, but the monsters still surrounded the dock, though howling in agony. *What is happening to them?*

Allie fell face-first to the dock, giving Spencer a closeup view of the horrors ravaging her. He screamed at the top of his lungs. Her skin was pale white, with green lines branching out under the skin. She lifted her head, gasping for air, and something crawled out of the hole in her throat. Long, algae-like strands slithered around her face before curling up and going still.

Spencer screamed again.

Holly appeared at the top of the hill, and for a second Spencer thought she was one of them. But she was coming to save him. Determination was etched on her face as she hopped over fallen branches and got to the clearing.

"Mom! Help me!"

———————————

Holly ran to the dock, taking in the destruction around her as she approached him. Then she noticed Allie, reaching for them with her hands outstretched as far as they could. Her white eyes went dull and rolled into the back of her head.

"*Mommm... He-help me...*"

Holly screamed Allie's name, pulling Spencer out of her reach as they watched together. The bodies of Alister's followers were breaking down, as if years of decomposition had been held back by his powers that were now fading away with the fire. She squeezed Spencer, holding him close while her daughter—what was left of her—stopped trying to crawl. Allie's body went still. All of them did. The water calmed, the bright green colors fading to an ordinary-looking pond.

For a while, Holly and Spencer just stood, holding each other. Eventually they sat down on the dock, too drained of the energy to do anything different. They sat until dawn slowly began to creep in behind the trees. Holly had no idea what to do next. They couldn't just leave the place like this and not tell anyone. Police wouldn't believe anything she told them unless she went to the locals. Cole said they wouldn't come near the place, but maybe if she told them it was over, they would come retrieve the bodies scattered across the property.

She couldn't take her eyes off Allie. It was hard enough to lose your first-born child, to lose your daughter. But the last words she'd forced out before dying for a *second* time within a few hours were, "*Mom, help me...*" She'd failed to do that and would live the rest of her life knowing she didn't do enough. She not only lost her daughter, but the grandkid she didn't even know she was going to have until a few hours ago.

And then she thought of Spencer. He'd lost his dad, his sister, and any ounce of child-like wonder. He'd seen dead bodies, ghosts, his dad trying to kill them. But he was *alive*. Holly would do whatever she had to do to make sure he got the help he needed to succeed.

Holly looked down at Spencer and realized he'd fallen asleep leaning on her shoulder. The kid would fight a nap if his eyes were forcing themselves shut, but here he was, lying in the center of a mass gravesite, sleeping on her. She laughed at the thought, then continued crying while she rubbed his head. When she got back to the city, she would call the Feds, let them know about the Costello situation and get whatever protection they would offer. She would hire a company to drain this pond and fill it in; better to be safe than sorry. After all that was done? She would be the best mom she could be to a boy who desperately needed it. She would be his rock.

THE END

ACKNOWLEDGMENTS

I want to start, as always, by thanking my wife and kids. I've spent a lot more time dealing with book stuff this past year, writing two novels, a short story collection, and some comic scripts. Without their patience, I wouldn't be able to do that. I also want to thank my editor, Joseph Sale, on working his magic once again to help make this book be the best it can be. James La Chance gave it one final edit to help tighten it up even more before its release. I can't forget Matt Seff Barnes, who again provided me with a cover that alone will help sell me a ton of books. When I sought out a cover artist, I found myself scrolling through Matt's work on his website, loving it so much that I hired him to do the cover for *The Cursed Among Us*. What most don't realize is that while searching his site, I came across the cover you are holding right now. It is the absolute truth when I tell you that I bought this cover on the spot, and THEN came up with the book to fit it because I loved the image so much. Don't get me wrong, I already had an idea floating around in my head, but much of the story was inspired by this one image. Thank you to all the beta/ARC readers that took the time to read this book before its release, providing me their feedback and giving me hope that I had something people would dig reading. Last, but certainly not least, thank you to D&T Publishing for taking a chance on me and my book. Dawn has made my first experience working with a publisher so easy and she's been great to work with. Thank you all for taking a trip, *INSIDE THE DEVIL'S NEST*.

ABOUT THE EDITOR / PUBLISHER

Dawn Shea is an author and half of the publishing team over at D&T Publishing. She lives with her family in Mississippi. Always an avid horror lover, she has moved forward with her dreams of writing and publishing those things she loves so much.

D&T Previously published material:
ABC's of Terror
After the Kool-Aid is Gone

Follow her author page on Amazon for all publications she is featured in.
Follow D&T Publishing at the following locations:
Website
Facebook: Page / Group
Or email us here: dandtpublishing20@gmail.com

JOHN DURGIN

John Durgin is a proud HWA member and lifelong horror fan who decided to chase his childhood dream of becoming a horror author. Growing up in New Hampshire, he discovered Stephen King much younger than most probably should have, reading *IT* before he reached high school—and knew from that moment on he wanted to write horror. He co-founded Livid Comics in late 2020, co-creating and writing his debut comic titled *Jol* (pronounced Yule), a Christmas horror series for all ages. After publishing that, the itch to expand his writing was one he had to scratch. Through Livid, he wrote his second comic which released in the spring of 2022 titled *Dead Ball*. John also co-launched a podcast called The Livid Comics Lair, where they talk with many of today's best horror authors, comic creators, and all things that go bump in the night like UFO and paranormal investigators. His true passion was always to write horror novels, and in 2021 he started submitting short stories in hopes of getting noticed in the horror community and launching a career. He had his first story accepted in the summer of 2021 in the Books of Horror anthology, and an alternate version of the story in the Beach Bodies anthology from DarkLit Press. His debut novel, *The Cursed Among Us* released June 3, 2022, to stellar reviews. Next up, his sophomore novel titled *Inside The Devil's Nest*, will release through D&T Publishing in January of 2023.

Twitter- @jdurgin1084

Website- www.johndurginauthor.com
Instagram- @durginpencildrawings
Youtube channel- Livid Comics

Inside the Devil's Nest by John Durgin

Edited by Joseph Sale and Jamie LaChance

Cover by Matt Seff Barnes and Ash Ericmore

Formatting by J.Z. Foster

Inside the Devil's Nest

Made in United States
Orlando, FL
25 May 2023

33463773R10146